Forever Engaged

Ashtyn Newbold

Copyright © 2025 by Ashtyn Newbold

All rights reserved.

No part of this book may be reproduced in any form or by any electronic or mechanical means, including information storage and retrieval systems, without written permission from the author, except for the use of brief quotations in a book review. Any references to historical events, real people, or real places are used fictitiously. Names, characters, and places are products of the author's imagination.

ISBN: 9798290891125

Cover design by Ashtyn Newbold

Three Leaf Publishing, LLC

www.ashtynnewbold.com

Chapter One

Cornwall, Summer 1813

Standing on the cliff's edge, the ends of Sophia's hair tossed with the wind. They were bleached golden from the many mornings she had spent with Isaac sitting in the pink sea thrift and watching the sunrise.

He paused for a moment to watch her loose curls and the white fabric of her skirts moving in the breeze on the precipice. The sun was setting, casting a warm glow over her skin. Waves crashed on the rocks below, and he felt a similar impact on his heart as he imagined another day soon when Sophia would wear white.

A smile split his face, and he nearly tripped as he made the final few steps up the trail.

Sophia turned at his approach. The fading sunlight caught her blue irises, and her smile formed a set of dimples in her cheeks.

Issac had first met Sophia on a walk near his grandfather's estate six months before. Her family had just arrived in Cornwall, her mother having recently inherited the neighboring estate from a distant relative. Sophia had never seen the sea before that day. At that point, she had still been a London girl with lace gloves and muddy half boots, hair pulled back tightly into her bonnet as she tentatively approached the cliff's edge.

But she had stayed ten feet away.

Isaac had showed her the best place to watch the sunrise later that week, and she had dared to stand closer to the edge. He had shown her the caves, the best beaches, and the ruins of Trelowen Castle. Isaac had only been in Cornwall one year, but showing Sophia all that he had discovered while living with his grandfather had altered him irrevocably. Over the past six months, he had fallen quite madly in love with her.

"I thought I told you not to stand so close to the edge," Isaac said as he met her on a patch of grass. This spot had become their meeting place, but today Sophia had managed to escape without her chaperone. The moment she reached him, he took both her hands. He held them like fragile things—like two birds that might fly away at any moment.

"I thought I told you to stop pestering me about it." Her smile grew wider.

With her first London Season approaching, the trail of freckles across her nose had been a subject of contention with her mother, but Isaac loved them. Sophia liked to say that each one represented one of their days together. Isaac liked to say each one represented one of their stolen kisses. Either way, she wouldn't need the complexion of a London girl. Not anymore.

A nervous look interrupted her smile. "Did you speak with him?"

"Speak with who?" Isaac grinned.

She gave a breathless laugh. "My father, of course." One of her eyebrows twitched upward.

Isaac tugged her closer, catching her by the waist. She settled into his arms, still giving him that curious look.

"I cannot confirm it."

"Isaac!" Her expression collapsed into a relenting smile. "I will die of curiosity."

He kissed the tip of her nose before leaning his forehead to hers. He could have told her the truth but teasing her was far more enjoyable. "I'm afraid it's a secret."

She laughed, but he caught her lips with his before she could ask any more questions. He kissed her until the sun fell below the horizon.

Isaac had spoken with her father that afternoon—and he had given his approval for their marriage. Isaac and Sophia had both been worried about her father's response considering the plans her parents had for her debut Season.

They knew how likely it was that Sophia could make a better match in London.

Her manners and grace were far beyond Isaac's upbringing, but his unexpected inheritance of his grandfather's estate had elevated him just enough to stand a chance. But despite Isaac's shortcomings, Sophia's father knew how in love they were. Surely he only understood a fraction of it, but it was enough.

Isaac held Sophia's face in his hands, her skin soft under his palms. At first their love had felt fragile, like a shell that might wash away or shatter. A passing conversation, a polite nod, a walk along the cliffs. Isaac's heart had changed so slowly, yet so drastically, and he would never be the same. He had lived twenty-two years belonging to the land and sea and the stars of the sky. But now he was Sophia's.

He took her hand and pressed his lips to her palm as he always did before closing her fingers around it.

"A keepsake," he said.

She smiled, holding onto it tight as she walked away. He wished she could stay longer, but her parents would wonder where she had gone.

And Isaac needed to keep their good opinion.

His heart swelled with the secret he held. But he wouldn't—couldn't—propose to Sophia without a ring. It wasn't commonplace, but his grandfather had given his late wife a ring for their engagement and had encouraged Isaac to do the same. He had seen one in a local shop that he knew Sophia would love. It was simple, a thin gold band with a single pearl at the center. He would purchase it tomorrow, and then they could be engaged. Officially.

He stumbled through the dim light until he made it down to the main road and back home. His cheeks ached from smiling by the time he stepped inside the candlelit entryway of Morvoren House. His grandfather, just a few months short of his seventy-fifth birthday, dined early but retired late. Isaac often heard him wandering the corridors at night, leaving a trail of candlelight and creaking floorboards.

But tonight, as the last moments of daylight faded, the house was silent.

"Grandfather?" Isaac was eager to tell him the news—to shed this secret from his shoulders. He was going to marry Sophia. Grandfather would love that news. After twenty years without one, Morvoren house would be sure to have a mistress. Grandmother had died decades before, and since, it had just been Grandfather and his servants within these walls—until the year before when Isaac's mother had died, and he had moved to Cornwall.

Isaac bounded up the stairs two at a time, swinging around the corner with one hand on the banister. His smile fell, and dread sank through his stomach.

Grandfather lay at the base of the second-floor staircase, arms and legs bent awkwardly at his sides.

Isaac's balance faltered as he ran forward. He fell to his knees and gripped Grandfather's shoulder, giving it a slight shake. His heart raced as he examined him. He watched his back rise and fall with a labored breath.

"Grandfather?" His voice shook as panic overtook him.

He must have fallen down the stairs.

Where were the servants? Why was he alone? Isaac screamed for help, keeping his eyes fixed on Grandfather's face, where a dark bruise had already spread across his weathered forehead. His eyelids fluttered, his wrinkles deepening with a flicker of pain. His thick white hair was stained with blood, and a small puddle had begun to form on the floor beneath him. Isaac touched his face, his cold hand having no effect on Grandfather's consciousness.

A footman reached the top of the stairs, and Isaac immediately sent him to call for the doctor. It felt like an eternity before the young physician reached them, emptying his bag of supplies on the floor beside Grandfather's prostrate frame. He worked quickly, washing his wound and wrapping white bandages around his head.

"His leg is broken," the doctor said in a methodical voice, his brow furrowed as he observed each of Grandfather's limbs. "I will have to set the bone."

Isaac sat back on his heels, his head spinning. His throat clenched with emotion. Seeing a man who Isaac had always known to be strong become so fragile didn't seem real. But Grandfather had been aging rapidly over the past few years. That was when he had named Isaac his heir and later invited him to live at Morvoren. Perhaps he had realized how breakable he had become.

All the joy Isaac had felt on those cliffs at sunset was pushed aside, drowned in this nightmare. With Grandfather's broken bones wrapped, the doctor helped carry him to his bedchamber. The doctor assured Isaac he would watch over Grandfather through the night, so hours later, Isaac wandered back to his own room with dried tears on his cheeks and a raw throat. How Grandfather fared through the night was critical, the doctor had said, and morning would bring conditions, good or bad, that would determine his outcome.

Sophia flooded Isaac's heart as he fell asleep—a smile, a reassurance, a whisper, a hug. When he saw her again, she would help him see reason. Grandfather would recover. He was resilient like that. He had to recover. Isaac wasn't ready to be master of a house, to manage the land and finances of Morvoren. He felt untrained and unprepared. At twenty-two, he didn't know much of the world. His parents were gone, but they had taught him duty. Grandfather had taught him friendship. And Sophia had taught him love. But there was still so much he didn't know. He could feel the emptiness, the inexperience, washing up inside him until he could hardly breathe.

Grandfather wasn't awake by morning, nor was he awake by the next evening.

Isaac sat in a chair beside his bed, keeping a cool cloth on his forehead and reading him books he wasn't certain he could even hear. Grandfather's favorite books were about history, daring men and their quests for adventure and discovery. His favorite characters were real people, with secrets and scandals, moments of strength and moments of weakness.

But Isaac was afraid that soon, Grandfather would become a piece of history too. A character. A footprint left in the sand. If only Isaac had known him better. If only he had visited him more often and not just come to Cornwall to retrieve his inheritance.

His troubled thoughts kept him alert despite his lack of sleep, and he hardly had time to think of the ring at the shop in town. His chest felt empty, his heart aching with each passing hour. Isaac hadn't even had the chance to tell Grandfather the news of his upcoming engagement. Now he feared he never would.

By the second morning, Grandfather was still asleep. Isaac

rubbed his weary eyes, staggering down the stairs and out the front door. He mounted his dark horse, leaving Grandfather under the care of the physician. He didn't want to worry Sophia, but she should know what had delayed his proposal. His heart ached, and unshed tears caused a lump to form in his throat. Once he saw her, everything would be better.

All he wanted was to hold her hand.

He rode swiftly to Lanveneth House. The structure was weathered cream stone, with lush, well-tended gardens, and a coveted view of the sea. Sophia had told Isaac she never wished to leave Cornwall, but that she would leave Lanveneth for him. He smiled at the not-so-distant memory as he led his horse up the drive.

He knocked on the door, and it opened at the hands of the Hales's butler. Isaac had knocked on that door countless times, stealing chaperoned conversations with Sophia in the drawing room, or strolls around the property. Her parents had become comfortable with the courtship, happy to see him, even. The butler had always been grim but accommodating.

Today, his wrinkles were a little deeper.

"Is Miss Hale in?" Isaac asked.

The butler's gaze dropped. "The Hales have left Lanveneth, Mr. Ellington."

Isaac's skin grew cold. For a moment, he lacked the ability to grasp the butler's words. "Left?"

"They have vacated the premises, sir."

Isaac's chest tightened, the edges of his vision blurring in confusion as he caught sight of the white sheets covering the furniture behind the butler. "When?" Isaac blurted.

"Yesterday evening."

Isaac took a step back, his muscles stiff. His mind raced. "Where have they gone?"

"I'm afraid I'm not at liberty to say."

Isaac shook his head. "Surely they wouldn't care if I knew their whereabouts. Has an urgent matter called them away? Is Miss Hale well?"

The butler stood still, his grim expression unreadable.

Panic rose in Isaac's throat. His voice burst out. "Tell me something!"

"I'm sorry, Mr. Ellington. I have a letter for you, and nothing more." His gloved hand extended a folded square of foolscap. "From Miss Hale."

Isaac took the letter, his fingers shaking. He walked down the steps, bending his head over the written words. There had never been a need to exchange letters or written notes, since their houses were so close to one another. Sophia's hand was elegant, just as he would have expected. The dark lines and curves blurred under his tears.

Dear Mr. Ellington,

I have enjoyed my time spent with you in Cornwall, but I have awakened to a sense of my place. It is with my family in London as I have always planned. I do not have the words to fully explain why I have left, but that I require more than a life in Cornwall.

I wanted to bid you a proper farewell in person, but I believe Byron's words: 'All farewells should be sudden, when forever, else they make an eternity of moments, and clog the last sad sands of life with tears.'

I pray that you will forget me. Do not try to follow me. Please recognize that I am gone forever, for that is what I wish to be. In time, I hope you will come to forgive and understand my decision.

. . .

Sincerely,
Miss Hale

Isaac lowered the letter, his entire body numb. He turned around, a desperate surge of pain clawing at his heart. The door of Lanveneth was closed now, the butler nowhere in sight. Isaac had no choice but to face the truth of the words in front of him.

Sophia had indeed left Lanveneth, but she hadn't left it for him.

Grandfather died that night, fading from one world to the next in his deepest sleep. Morvoren House was Isaac's, and Isaac's alone.

At twenty-two, Isaac still didn't know much of the world. But he knew grief. He knew that his heart could shatter in an instant.

And he knew that he would never stop loving Sophia Hale.

Chapter Two

FOUR YEARS LATER

Isaac Ellington could think of at least ten places he'd rather be than in a crowded London ballroom dressed as a fox.

"I never should have allowed you to select my costume," Isaac muttered, touching the ties on the back of his half-mask. He would have been content with the attire if not for the ears.

Pointed, orange ears.

"At least *yours* is fitting to your personality," he said.

His cousin, Percy, grinned beneath his red and black mask. His raven black hair swooped above it, with a few strands falling over the front. He was dressed as Mephistopheles, a devil in disguise. He thrived on skirting the edge of scandal and earning as many glances as possible. Ladies would think he looked dangerous and flirtatious in his costume.

And they would think Isaac looked like a household pet.

Isaac's mask would be staying firmly tied to his face that evening, for more reasons than one. He didn't know who else had been invited to the private ball at Lady Bradford's townhouse that evening, but there were a few gentlemen in London he would rather avoid. Percy would have been one of them if he wasn't the only family Isaac had in Town.

"Do you know if Mr. Baker was invited?" Isaac surveyed the room carefully from their place on the outskirts, but the theme of the ball made recognizing anyone quite difficult.

Guests in elaborate masks and costumes moved and prattled in circles. The scent of burning candles, fresh flowers, and something spiced—clove punch, perhaps—perfumed the air. Every chandelier sparkled amid the jewel-toned silk hanging from the ceiling. Gold mirrors reflected the flicker of hundreds of candles, and the soft notes of a string quartet drifted from behind a lattice of white roses.

Percy laughed under his breath. "Is it true Mr. Baker blackballed you from White's *and* Brook's? Even I have evaded such a misfortune. But as you know, I am always discreet."

"It wasn't about indiscretion." Isaac knew that his cousin spent time in the company of many ladies beneath his station. It had earned him the reputation of a rake, but only amongst other participating gentlemen, not the general public. Somehow Percy managed to charm his way through anything.

Isaac on the other hand was always genuine in his romantic pursuits—his pursuit of a wife—though his execution was decidedly lacking. He drew a deep breath through his nose. "I made the mistake of courting Mr. Baker's sister."

Percy snatched a champagne flute from the tray of a passing servant. "Miss Baker has a large dowry."

"Yes." Isaac sniffed and cleared his throat.

"And she is very accomplished." He smirked as he took a sip from his glass. "And attractive."

"Yes, I know." Isaac couldn't hide the vexation from his voice. He ignored Percy's smug grin. He continued surveying the crowd, searching for any sign of Miss Baker's fiery red hair or that of her brother's. It was not easy to miss, even with the costumes.

"Then why, pray tell, did you change your mind?" Percy asked. "If she was such a fine catch, and you are in pursuit of a wife…you must have known how it would enrage her brother—"

"I didn't expect to change my mind. I just…" Isaac paused, his jaw tightening. "I never wanted to hurt Miss Baker. I thought if it ended amicably, then her brother would be forgiving. I didn't expect him to blackball me."

"One enemy is all it takes to be banished from the elite clubs." Percy clicked his tongue. "It seems you have become even more of a heartbreaker than I am." Percy seemed to take pride in the statement, even as it simultaneously crippled Isaac's heart with guilt.

"That was not my intention."

"Yet it is so." Percy's teeth flashed white beneath his mask. "Why commit yourself to only one woman?" His eyes followed a blonde woman in a roman costume with a crown of gold laurels. She cast a demure smile in his direction.

Isaac's shoulders tensed. He wanted to explain himself, but Percy would think him a fool. In this case, it would be best to let him assume Isaac was a disinterested rake rather than a man desperately in love with a woman he hadn't seen for four years. A woman who had, quite brutally, broken his heart and left it useless. Percy would never understand. No matter how hard Isaac tried to fall in love and commit himself to another, he failed. He ran away.

And now he had to face the consequences.

"I *do* wish to marry," Isaac said, his quiet voice becoming lost in the music. "I am simply not very good at it."

"At marrying?" Percy blurted out a laugh. "Nor am I. Although that may change soon."

Isaac's eyebrows shot up, shifting his mask and fox ears higher. "You? Marry?"

Percy's smile turned sly. "I am considering it. I have taken an interest in a certain young lady. Our courtship is new, and her sister has proven to be…problematic, but I don't see any reason why I won't succeed in the venture."

"You have set your cap at her, then?"

Percy took another sip of champagne. "I suppose I have."

"Who is she?"

"The stepdaughter of a new acquaintance of mine. The Viscount Blackstone. Have you met him?"

Isaac shook his head. He had been in London less than two months, and he had spent all his energy on his courtship with Miss Baker. He had already managed to strain a great deal of his connections through that reckless courtship. Making new connections was going to prove difficult.

Percy crossed his arms, tilting his head to one side. "I managed to win Lord Blackstone's favor by pretending I had a great interest in the behavioral patterns of the great horned owl. In truth, I can think of nothing more excessively boring. At any rate, he has regarded me highly ever since, and seems to have a tendency for overlooking the flaws of men he thinks share his peculiar interests. I'm a recent member of his club. Blackstone's—on the edge of Mayfair and St. James's."

Isaac gave him a curious look. "And how does Lord Blackstone feel about you courting his stepdaughter?"

"He is surprisingly accommodating." Percy lowered his voice with a grin. "But I have been treading carefully. It is a delicate subject. Lord Blackstone is rather…protective of his stepdaughters and has high standards for them."

Isaac gave an understanding nod. "As he should."

Percy's upper lip curled. "It's deucedly inconvenient. I have work to do still in procuring his favor before I make my intentions known. Perhaps you should apply at the club. You can vouch for me when the time comes."

Isaac hesitated. That would test his loyalty to his cousin, to be sure. He wasn't certain he could vouch for Percy while keeping his own honor intact. He knew how Percy treated women, and how he spent his spare time gambling, drinking, and keeping questionable company. Isaac was fond of the man, in a detached way—an obligatory, familial way—but he would never recommend him for marriage.

Isaac excused the idea with a wave of his hand. "I'm sure I won't have the opportunity. I'm not likely to be accepted."

"He elects his own members." Percy leaned closer with a whisper. "Lord Blackstone himself was blackballed from White's, Brook's, and Boodles years ago. He sympathizes with outcasts like you."

Isaac narrowed his eyes. He wouldn't have chosen such a harsh word, but he *was* intrigued. If he found a new club at which to socialize, he would certainly feel less hopeless in his marriage endeavors. Perhaps he could start afresh with his connections… *and* avoid courting any of their relatives this time.

"Would you be willing to introduce us?"

Percy nodded. "And I'd be willing to wager my right to

flirt at Almack's that Lord Blackstone is here this evening. There is no possible way that man would miss the opportunity to flaunt a costume." Percy drained his glass before casting his gaze around the room. It only took him a few seconds to locate his target. "There. At the top of the staircase."

Isaac followed his cousin across the floor, only locating the man who must have been Lord Blackstone when they were already on their way up the stairs. He wore white robes, a bejeweled turban on his head, and a mask with large tusks. The lower half of his face exposed a few short grey whiskers and a grin.

Isaac stood back a pace as his cousin approached the viscount. Despite his shortcomings, Percy had a way with people that Isaac would be wise to emulate. He won favor in an instant, and his flaws were overlooked by anyone under the influence of his easy smile.

"Good evening, my lord." Percy stopped on the balcony overlooking the ballroom and gestured at Lord Blackstone's costume. "Will you allow me to venture a guess at your identity this evening?"

Lord Blackstone chuckled, a deep sound that vibrated from his core. "Could this be Mr. Ellington?"

"I am not Mr. Ellington any longer," Percy said in a serious tone. "Tonight, I am Mephistopheles."

Lord Blackstone tipped his mask forward to examine Percy's costume. His perfectly round, dark eyes were surrounded with deep wrinkles and topped with wiry grey brows, the hairs sticking out every which way. "How daring. I would have expected you to dress as the great horned owl."

"That was my second choice. And you must be…" Percy tapped his chin, "an elephant tamer."

FOREVER ENGAGED

Lord Blackstone reared back in surprise before another deep chuckle escaped him. His fingers fluttered over his obviously expensive dressings. "My—how on earth did you know? Others have been incorrect in their assumptions all evening. Some have guessed a Maharaja, others an elephant itself, but my strivings to depict a great and powerful tamer were not in vain, it would seem." His joy was contagious, and Isaac found himself smiling.

Percy leaned forward. "I am glad to hear it. Would it delight you further to learn that there is another Mr. Ellington in our midst tonight?"

Lord Blackstone replaced his mask, but Isaac caught his interested expression. "It would indeed."

On cue, Isaac made the final step to stand beside Percy. He gestured at Isaac with a dramatic sweep of his hand. "Lord Blackstone, meet my cousin, Mr. Isaac Ellington."

"An honor, my lord." Isaac smiled, feeling suddenly less ridiculous about his choice of costume. Perhaps it would be a help, not a hindrance, knowing how Lord Blackstone loved animals.

"A pleasure to meet you, young man!" Lord Blackstone's gaze surveyed him from head to toe. "A feline of sorts? A caracal or bengal, perhaps?"

Isaac laughed. "A fox, my lord."

Lord Blackstone's eyes blinked through his mask. "Ah. Yes, yes, I do see that now. You must keep your wits about you this evening, for my stepdaughter is dressed as a huntress. I should hate for you to find yourself in her line of fire." He laughed heartily to himself.

"I thank you for such a timely warning," Isaac said. "I shall remain alert."

Was he referring to the stepdaughter that Percy was

pursuing? Isaac couldn't help but wonder what Lord Blackstone actually thought of the courtship. He didn't seem inclined to disapprove considering his seemingly high opinion of Percy.

"I have relayed to my cousin the details of your remarkable establishment," Percy said. "He wishes to apply to become a member of Blackstone's."

"Do you, now?" The viscount turned his attention to Isaac. "Well, I would be delighted to receive you at the club to become better acquainted. You may drop in tomorrow at your convenience. I should hope we recognize one another when the time comes." Once again, he made himself chuckle.

Isaac gave a thoughtful nod. "I shall ask for the elephant tamer at the door."

Lord Blackstone seemed amused by that. Good. Isaac might not have been as charming as Percy, but he did have his moments.

The viscount's chuckling was only interrupted by his deep gasp. His eyes rounded in horror at something behind Isaac's shoulder. "Run! Poor fox—I'm afraid your end is nigh. The huntress is ascending the staircase as we speak."

If Isaac wanted to gain Lord Blackstone's favor, he would have to play along. With an amused smile, he turned around. A brunette woman in a flowing white gown and satin gloves was making her way up the stairs, unaware of the charade her stepfather was creating, nor her central role in it. She wore a crescent moon headpiece and a short cape, with a quiver of arrows on her back. A silver mask covered the upper half of her face, and her unsmiling lips gave her a cold appearance.

Isaac stared at her, his temperature dropping as her eyes

met his through the mask. His heart picked up speed, his throat drying out like a winter leaf.

This sort of thing had happened before.

A flash of brown hair, blue eyes, a laugh with the same melodious tone—he was prone to mistaking women for Sophia. He was prone to wishing he had found her again, and conjuring up images that weren't real. He shook himself of his imaginings, resuming a relaxed posture as the young lady reached the top of the staircase.

Her attention breezed past Isaac and went straight to her stepfather. "Prudence wishes to leave," she said in an urgent tone. "She will not stop complaining about how the mask makes her face itch."

Isaac's shoulders stiffened.

Her voice.

Sophia's voice.

It is only your imagination, he assured himself. This was a routine haunting, nothing more than a cruel joke. His mask was itching his face as well. It was making him sweat. He wasn't thinking clearly, but the evidence was difficult to ignore. Not only did this woman look and sound like Sophia, but she also had a sister named Prudence.

"I warned Prudence against using lace in her design." Lord Blackstone sighed. "Our hostess has insisted that masks be worn throughout the entire evening. Unless your sister is otherwise unwell, we are staying a while longer. Where is your aunt?"

The masked woman spoke again in her clear, soft tone. "On a chair with a plate of cheese."

Lord Blackstone's cheerful expression faded. "I look forward to the day your mother joins us in London," he muttered. "I cannot tolerate Mrs. Liddle's neglect. Not only that, but she hardly put a thought into her costume. I shall have to take it upon myself to find new acquaintances for you." His gaze slid in Isaac's direction. "And what opportune timing. I have just become acquainted with this mischievous fox."

Was Isaac to play along with Lord Blackstone's theatrics? His face was already hot. The similarities that the young woman bore to Sophia had flustered him. A wave of nerves pierced him like an arrow.

Her eyes met his, and his heart beat hard against his chest. Isaac had only seen that shade of blue once—the shade that matched the Cornish waters at sunset. The stoic look she had displayed with her stepfather faded at the impact of their gazes.

Her eyes flashed with recognition.

He stood in silence, his throat raw. He forgot the motions of breathing in and out, becoming a statue under her gaze. The mask concealed much of her face, but now that she was in front of him, he couldn't mistake the curve of her chin, the shape of her lips, and the golden-brown tone of her hair.

Was he wrong? Perhaps it wasn't her. The last time he had seen Sophia, she had been a stepdaughter to none. Her father had been very much alive.

But it had been four years.

The woman's throat shifted with a swallow, and her eyes lowered to his cravat. Was his reaction making her uncomfortable? Most likely. He scolded himself, urging his mind and heart to relax. If he was wrong, and this was not Sophia, then he was making a very strange first impression on Lord Blackstone's stepdaughter.

"The hunt is on, is it not, my dear?" Lord Blackstone nudged her with a grin.

"Forgive me, sir, but I only hunt pheasants." Her voice sent a chill over Isaac's spine, like walking into an abandoned house alone at night.

He collected himself enough to reply. "There is nothing to forgive. I would much rather not be hunted."

Her eyes shot up to his again, this time with clear curiosity. And a hint of fear. He had rattled her somehow.

Had she recognized his voice, too?

Her lips parted, as if she wished to say something more, but no words came out. Isaac's heart raced, his instincts growing stronger. If this woman wasn't Sophia, then he wasn't Isaac Ellington—and Lord Blackstone wasn't an elephant tamer.

"A truce?" the viscount interrupted with a wry smile. "Have the huntress and fox formed a rare alliance? Brava!" He clapped.

Percy joined him with rapturous applause.

Isaac drew a deep breath—his first in what felt like minutes. The air was heavy and tense with dread. He counted the seconds that passed in silence. What could he do? Until he knew her name, he couldn't ascertain whether he was right or wrong—sane or mad.

Isaac's voice shook as he tore his gaze from the woman's face and addressed Lord Blackstone. "Since we are allies, may I inquire after your stepdaughter's name?"

"You may indeed," he replied. "Tonight, you may call her Diana—Goddess of the Hunt." Lord Blackstone was clearly still amused, apparently unaware of Isaac's tense emotions. "But on other occasions, you may call her Miss Sophia Hale."

Chapter Three

"And this, my dear, is Mr. Isaac Ellington."

Sophia's ears rang, her stepfather's muffled voice echoing inside her head.

Isaac Ellington.

For a moment, she doubted she had heard him correctly. But then she looked at the man's face again. She had seen his eyes through his mask. No matter how many years had passed—four to be precise—one could never forget the eyes of the person they once loved. They were the windows to his heart, which he had freely given to her on the cliffs of Cornwall.

Just before he had taken it away.

She stood in shocked silence as heat creeped up her neck. Blood rushed past her ears, throbbing, pounding, making her limbs shake. She didn't know whether to freeze or to flee. If only sinking into the floor and disappearing were an option. For the first time that evening, she was grateful for the mask hiding her face.

Her legs shook as she lowered herself into a curtsy. Isaac bowed.

They were both silent.

Isaac's height had been the first indication of his identity. He towered over her stepfather and his companion, the other Mr. Ellington. Besides his stature, she had immediately recognized his dark hair, his golden-brown eyes behind his mask, and his lips. Four years later, he was still the only man she had ever kissed.

He was still the only man she had ever loved.

It was a secret, a piece of her heart that she rarely revealed to anyone. Her history with Isaac Ellington had held her back from countless opportunities, and she despised him for it. He had broken her heart, yet she had still been unable to forget him.

She had hoped to never see him again, but here he was, and she was reacting exactly the opposite of how she would have wished to.

"Mr. Ellington is an excellent candidate for my club, is he not?" Stepfather could always be relied upon to force a cheerful air into a space where it did not exist. "I expect we should all become more acquainted in the near future." His chipper tone made her skin simmer with nerves. No. She did not wish to become further acquainted with Isaac Ellington.

She squared her shoulders and drew a slow breath, correcting her expression despite the turmoil within her. She needed to prove that he did not affect her. She didn't want him to think that he still had any sort of hold on her after so many years. How weak. How pathetic and silly she would look if he knew that he was the reason she had never married. He had broken her beyond repair, and before that, he had set a standard for what her heart was capable of feeling for a man. That standard had never been reached, not once in her mother's efforts to keep her in the marriage mart. But when Lord Blackstone became her stepfather two years before, he had thought himself capable of finding her a match.

And now, he had almost succeeded.

"Ah, there you are, Miss Hale." A jovial voice came from the stairs behind her. "Did you forget that you promised me a dance?" Sophia was rarely eager to see Lord Finchley, but this was an exception.

The tension deflated from her body as she turned away from Isaac, taking Lord Finchley's outstretched arm. "Of course not. I have been looking forward to it."

The earl was dressed in a sapphire blue coat, peacock feathered mask, and polished black boots. His blond curls spilled from behind his mask, coiled and shaped by an attentive valet. His arrogant smile was nothing compared to that of Mr. Percy Ellington, who craned his neck in search of her sister, no doubt. At least Lord Finchley was a respectable gentleman, one who seemed to have a genuine interest in marriage.

Mr. Percy Ellington's interest in her sister had been troubling her for weeks. Sophia could sense a fortune-hunting rake from miles away, but Prudence was still too young to have developed such a talent.

When Sophia had first become acquainted with Mr. Percy Ellington, she had wondered if he was a relative of Isaac's, but tonight it had been confirmed. As a result, she now had even more evidence to suggest that Prudence should stay away from Percy. If he was any relative of Isaac's, then he was not to be trusted with something as fragile as Prudence's young heart.

"Please excuse us," Sophia muttered in no particular direction as Lord Finchley led her down the staircase. Her heart still hammered. She felt as if she had been thrown into the sea, cold and shocked and drowning. Her lungs struggled for air as the image of Isaac's face seared itself behind her eyelids. The candles blurred together in streams of light, the emerald tones of the gowns and capes of the room lumping together.

"Are you unwell?" Lord Finchley's voice was just as muffled as the rest.

Sophia swallowed hard, gathering her composure. "No, I am quite well." She would need to focus in order to remember the steps of the dance. She couldn't risk ruining Lord Finchley's opinion of her. She had already made up her mind to marry him if the opportunity arose, so she couldn't allow a chance meeting with a man from her past to sabotage her. She was three and twenty after all. Much of society considered the failed Seasons of her past a hinderance to her future success. She was halfway on the shelf already, and Lord Finchley might notice if she wasn't careful.

Situated at the center of the room, she and the earl began their dance. Her mind raced with distraction. Her skin burned beneath her mask, and she made the mistake of looking toward the balcony.

Isaac stood at the base of the stairs now. He held his mask in one hand, his face in clear view.

Sophia bumped into Lord Finchley, stepping firmly on the toe of his polished left boot.

"*Oof,*" he grunted in pain, bending over at the waist. He recovered quickly, leading her into the next steps of the dance. She stumbled again as she struggled to catch up to his movements. Her throat was tight. She had never danced so horribly in her life, and she never would have dared to make such a mistake while dancing with an earl.

Aunt Hester, seated against the wall, watched from behind the thick glass of her spectacles. Her hand froze— a cube of cheese an inch from her parted lips.

Sophia's mortification rose at Lord Finchley's pained expression. He was clearly embarrassed to be dancing with her. She gritted her teeth, finally reclaiming her wits enough to finish the final steps without error. Her heart sank as she made her final curtsy. Surely an earl of thirty-six years hadn't waited so long to marry only to select a wife who couldn't perform a simple dance.

"I'm sorry," she whispered. "You were right. I am not well." It was the only excuse she could give.

Lord Finchley's expression transformed to a look of concern. "I knew my intuition was correct. I shall fetch you a cup of water at once." He bowed before striding toward the drink table.

Sophia caught her breath, but the room was still spinning. Her relationship with Lord Finchley had finally caught the attention of the *ton*, and there was enough gossip to suggest that he might offer a proposal soon. Had her inadequacy that night changed his decision at all? Time would tell. Her nerves refused to settle as she felt Isaac's gaze on the side of her face, burning a hole through her mask. It was his fault she had forgotten the steps.

Fear crept into her heart as he took a step toward her. Was he...was he coming to speak with her? She choked on a breath. She couldn't face him yet. She wasn't prepared.

Panic seized her muscles, and she walked in a straight line toward the door.

She was unfamiliar with this particular townhouse, but

stairs to the dining room. Mama, Papa, and her younger sister Prudence were already waiting at the table.

"Good evening." Sophia sat down with a little too much flourish. She softened her smile so as to not appear as giddy as she felt. Her parents had expressed their disapproval at her meeting Isaac alone. If she didn't hide her emotions, they would suspect where she had just been.

Prudence cast a knowing smile in Sophia's direction before taking a bite of potatoes from her plate.

Sophia met Papa's gaze. Perhaps if she looked hard enough, she could read the details of the conversation that had occurred between he and Isaac that day. Papa's eyes were clear and blue, framed with dark eyebrows that sloped downward on the edges. There were times he looked sad when he was not, and times he looked sad when he actually was. She hardly knew how to tell a difference, even after nearly two decades in his company.

He was more silent than usual tonight, his expression stoic and distant.

Perhaps he was sworn to secrecy, because Papa didn't breathe a word about his conversation with Isaac. Not at dinner, not in the drawing room, and not as he bid Sophia goodnight. It was all right. Sophia liked surprises, and Isaac did enjoy surprising her. She had no doubt he would propose to her the next day, perhaps when they met to watch the sunrise.

When she went to bed that night, she dreamed of wild things—happy things she had no business dreaming of or deserving. A life in Cornwall with Isaac—hosting parties and dancing and swimming and raising children. She had never dreamed of London. That was Mama's dream, not hers.

When the first streaks of light split the clouds, she put on her cloak and half boots and sneaked out the front door. The walk to her and Isaac's meeting place was short. The earliest birds made *their music in the sky, swooping down over the choppy sea below the cliffs. Wind snatched at her hair and skirts, biting her nose with cold. Isaac was usually there first, but today, she had beat him. She waited until the sun climbed over the clouds and the sea sparkled with morning light, but Isaac never came.*

Had something delayed him?

She sat beside a patch of pink sea thrift and dangled her feet off the edge of the jagged cliff until Louisa's cap and dark curls appeared above the crest of the path beside her.

The maid breathed heavily as she reached Sophia, resting one hand on her hip. "Yer father wishes to speak with ye, miss. Make haste back to the house."

It was startling that Louisa knew where to find her, but she agreed with a brief nod. Scrambling to her feet, she followed the maid back to Lanveneth House.

"In here, miss." Louisa stepped aside as Sophia approached the polished walnut door to Papa's study. Usually, she found him sitting behind his desk with a pipe and a pile of ledgers. But when she opened the door, his desk had been cleared off, and he was working on filling a nearby box with every last scrap of paper.

He looked up at her entrance, his quick movements slowing down for a brief moment. His downturned eyes looked heavier today, underscored by dark grey circles. There was a strain behind his features that made her pause in the doorway.

"Sophia, sit." He gestured at the chair across from his desk. "Please sit."

She brushed the loose strands of hair behind her ears, a nervous flutter entering her stomach. Something was amiss, to be sure. Papa was never so urgent. His calm demeanor had been a source of steadiness in her life, something that could be relied upon. Her insides swirled with nerves until he finally set down his papers and sat across from her.

"We are leaving Cornwall today. Since you were not in your room this morning, Louisa has packed most of your things already."

"What?" Sophia struggled to speak, her throat too dry. "Papa—what on earth do you mean? We cannot leave so suddenly—"

"I'm afraid you have no choice in the matter, my dear. Your mother and I have already made our decision. We are removing to London without further argument." Papa's words were choppy, broken up by his rapid breathing.

"Papa!" Sophia stood, shaking her head. "What is so urgent about going to London? I thought we were staying here another fortnight."

"That was the plan, yes, but we have decided an early arrival will allow you to better prepare for the Season. You may feel better situated at our London address before the crowds arrive."

"I don't wish to go to London!" Sophia corrected her panicked tone by clearing her throat. "I thought you knew that—I thought you spoke with Mr. Ellington yesterday."

Papa's eyes finally lifted to hers before flickering away. A slow exhale escaped his chest. "My conversation with Mr. Ellington has been heavy on my mind since yesterday. I haven't had the heart to tell you the nature of it."

Sophia swallowed. When she had seen Isaac the day before, he had refused to tell her the details as well. He had been playful and mysterious though—as he always was—taking any excuse to flirt with her and tease her. She hadn't thought anything negative of it. In fact, she had hoped for the best.

Her throat was dry, but she managed to speak a few words. "Tell me now, Papa. Please."

He crossed his arms. Without the rustling of all his papers, the room fell into eerie silence. "He came to me requesting your hand in marriage, and I gave my approval. However, when we came to the subject of your dowry, he found it insufficient. He confessed that he was expecting more." Papa's voice echoed in Sophia's ears. "I do not trust that his motivation for courting you was ever sincere."

Sophia scowled, dread sinking through her stomach. "That cannot be true. Isaac is not motivated by money as other men are."

"Perhaps you do not know him as well as you think." Papa sighed. "It has only been half a year since you met him. It takes much longer than that to know someone's secrets." He lit his pipe and took a deep inhale through it.

Sophia felt as if she had been lit on fire from the inside, and the destruction had already begun. She couldn't escape the pain that spread through every inch of her. "No. I don't believe you."

Papa rifled through a few of the remaining papers on his desk and withdrew a letter. "He wrote you this. I suspect the contents will be similar to what I received from him this morning."

Sophia fought the emotion clawing at her throat, taking the letter cautiously from Papa's hand. Isaac had never written to her. He had always claimed that important words should be spoken face to face, rather than written on paper.

Dear Miss Hale,

After much reflection, I am writing to inform you that my intentions have changed. My feelings for you were genuine, as was my hope to marry you, but there are other things to consider in a marriage besides love. I have been forced to be practical, and in my discussion with your father I have learned that your dowry is much smaller than I anticipated. There are repairs to be made on the house, and considerations to be made for my future. I cannot waver in my determination to find a match who will fulfill my requirements, and nor should you.

I wanted to bid you a proper farewell in person, but I believe Byron's words: 'All farewells should be sudden, when forever, else they make an eternity of moments, and clog the last sad sands of life with tears.'

I hope you will succeed in London. I hope you will learn to love another. I hope you will forget me eventually and forgive the pain I have caused.

Sincerely,
Mr. Ellington

Sophia's hands shook as she lowered the letter, and tears spilled down her face. She wiped at them as she turned around, hiding from Papa's view.

She had to see him. She had to see Isaac and demand that he say these things aloud to her. Only then could she believe that he truly meant them. On the cliffs the day before, he had seemed so happy. How could he have changed his mind so quickly?

She dropped the letter on the floor. "I am going to speak with him." She started for the door, but Papa rushed around his desk to stop her.

"I would strongly discourage such an action, my dear. Your mother would agree. A young lady must never beg for a man's hand, nor declare her feelings so erratically. His decision has been made, and you must learn to live with it. You are better off without him. I do not trust a fortune hunter, nor an indecisive man whose intentions can change on a whim." He held her shoulders between his hands. "I'm sorry, Sophia. I truly am."

Sophia's posture crumbled at her father's touch, and she stepped into his arms. He held her tight, and she melted into his comforting scent of tobacco and old leather. "I promise, you will find happiness with another." His deep voice rumbled through his chest. "There are plenty of men in London who will find you sufficient. There are plenty of men who will love you better than Isaac Ellington ever could."

As Papa held her, Sophia's gaze fell to the letter on the floor. Through her tears, she read those words again. 'All farewells should be sudden, when forever, else they make an eternity of moments, and clog the last sad sands of life with tears.'

A sob shook her body, and she struggled to breathe. How could she not make an eternity of this moment? It was the moment her heart was breaking. And she doubted it would ever be the same again.

Chapter Five

Standing on the corner of Mayfair and St. James's, Isaac took a deep breath. The front door of Blackstone's loomed ahead, flanked by pillars of golden stone. The night of the masquerade, he had humored Percy with the idea of joining the club.

But now, he *had* to be accepted.

If the eccentric Lord Blackstone was to be Isaac's closest connection to Sophia, then he would fight for his opportunity to be a member of the club. Isaac's relationship with Lord Blackstone could very well be his only hope of speaking to her again. His heart still stung when he thought of the night before. She had snubbed him. He never should have followed her into the corridor, but he had thought she would have at least cared to know how he had spent the past four years. Instead, she had acted as if she had never known him—as if they hadn't once been in love.

Perhaps *she* hadn't.

Isaac had told himself countless times that she must have

never loved him, but he had struggled to believe it. Upon seeing her again, he was finally learning to. Yes, he was about to plead his case to join Blackstone's in order to be close to Sophia, but not so he could beg for her heart. It was so he could finally give it back.

If he wanted any hope of falling in love with someone else, he would need to forget Sophia Hale for good. His courtship with Miss Baker had proven that. He needed Sophia to taint the perfect image he still held of her. He needed as many opportunities as possible to see the real Sophia Hale, the one who had written him a brutal letter, who had claimed that farewells should be sudden and forever, and who had pushed him away at the ball the night before.

The girl he had known, bright and beautiful and kind, needed to be destroyed, and Sophia was the only one who could do it.

Isaac took a deep breath before lifting the knocker, which was in the form of a crow's head. Until then, the exterior of the club had looked perfectly ordinary—a Palladian facade, a neat balcony, and a clean black door. Perhaps this crow knocker was his first sign that Lord Blackstone's club would be far from *ordinary*, much like the man himself.

Isaac struck the door with the crow's beak three times. Within seconds, it was opened at the hands of a doorman. He held a small book in one hand, his eyes flickering over Isaac in a swift, yet thorough manner.

Before the man could speak, Isaac cleared his throat. "Good day, I've an appointment with Lord Blackstone."

"Your name, sir?"

"Mr. Isaac Ellington."

The doorman opened the book in his hands, eyes settling somewhere on the page with a nod of approval. "Yes, he is expecting you. Come in, I will direct you to his study."

Isaac lowered his head as he entered the establishment, removing his beaver hat and coat. The entrance hall was dark, decorated in deep red and dark walnut. Various portraits and animal heads of all varieties covered the majority of the walls. Dozens of glass eyes seemed to follow Isaac as the doorman led him toward the staircase.

Isaac was almost distracted enough by his purpose in being there to overlook the peculiar details of the specimens on the walls.

Almost.

On his way up the stairs, he noted an overstuffed owl, glass eyes far too close together, with a cravat around its neck. On the first floor, the doorman led him past a sitting room of sorts, and then through a long gallery flanked by rows of more deceased creatures than Isaac could count. Was Lord Blackstone a hunter? A collector? Either way, the assortment was impressive. And a bit unsettling.

Was Percy shamming him?

Had he recommended the club to Isaac for his own amusement?

It wouldn't surprise him in the slightest.

His eyes traveled the length of the walls, catching sight of a few more peculiar specimens on the open shelves. A rabbit in riding boots, a marten holding a tiny violin, a fox in spectacles, another owl in a cap, and a goose wearing a string of pearls.

Isaac shook his gaze from the goose just in time to see Lord Blackstone stepping out from a door at the end of the gallery. Without his elaborate costume, he looked smaller, frailer, his grey hair sticking out more on one side than the other.

His large brown eyes widened when they settled on Isaac. "Could this be the mischievous fox from the masquerade? Your height betrays you, young man." A chuckle escaped Lord Blackstone's nose, his mouth still closed in a tight, but friendly smile. "I would recognize you from a mile away."

Isaac didn't know what he had done to earn himself the title of *mischievous*, but Lord Blackstone seemed to have already adopted the description. Hopefully it was an endearment. "You have caught me, my lord. As it seems you have caught all these other magnificent creatures." Isaac gestured at the walls. "An impressive collection."

Lord Blackstone's wrinkles deepened. "If you think I have hunted these dear specimens, you are mistaken. Each and every one died of natural causes. I ensure such details before I acquire any of my animals. It is a matter of principle, of course." He clasped his hands in front of him, his eyes darting around the gallery with a gleam of pride. "Not only that, but I have refused to cage them with any manner of glass. As free in death as they were in life, I declare."

Isaac's voice evaded him for a brief moment. He hid his surprise and tried to think of how Percy would reply. "That is very considerate. I must say I experienced a deep sense of contentment from the specimens from the moment I entered the club."

The viscount's face lit up. "Did you, now? How remarkable."

Isaac gave a thoughtful nod, pausing when his gaze collided with what looked like a mummified bat. A small plaque on the shelf in front of it read *'Beatrice.'*

"To have such a sensitivity to the creatures, I would venture to guess that you share my love of exotic animals?"

Isaac didn't want to lie as blatantly as his cousin, but since Lord Blackstone had opened the door for him, he would be a fool not to walk through it. "I do. The more exotic, the better."

Lord Blackstone grinned, raising a heavy-knuckled finger. "Remind me to show you the billiard room after your interview."

Isaac smiled back, nodding with enthusiasm, though his stomach knotted. It would depend on if the interview went in his favor or not. Lord Blackstone was sure to have questions about Isaac's membership in other clubs—or lack thereof. He must have let his nervousness slip through his expression, because Lord Blackstone gave an amused chuckle.

"You have nothing to fear. For how much I enjoy the other Mr. Ellington of my acquaintance, I am already quite determined to acquire both of you."

Isaac's first thought was for the taxidermy gallery, but surely that couldn't be the viscount's meaning. He laughed through his discomfort. "You must allow me to die of natural causes first, my lord."

Lord Blackstone's wiry eyebrows shot up, and for a moment Isaac thought he had gone too far with his joke. But then Lord Blackstone's lips parted, and a thundering laugh burst out. He rested a hand on his middle, tears pooling in his eyes. "A clever one, you are! And fortunate indeed that I share your rather morbid sense of humor." His eyes gleamed with amusement as he caught his breath.

Isaac's shoulders relaxed. Perhaps Lord Blackstone's favor wouldn't be so difficult to obtain. He wasn't intimidating in the slightest, and he seemed eager to see the good in everyone. With a little more confidence, Isaac followed the viscount down the rest of the gallery until they reached his study.

"Please do have a seat," Lord Blackstone said as he settled into his place behind the desk. On the wall behind him was a large portrait of a badger wearing a formal jacket. Isaac didn't flinch. Nothing about the decorating choices could surprise him anymore.

Lord Blackstone lit his pipe, taking a deep breath through it before regarding Isaac seriously. "I do find these interviews rather difficult to conduct, but I ought to maintain at least a small degree of rigidity in the rules of my establishment."

"I understand completely."

"Good. Right then." Lord Blackstone exhaled a puff of smoke. "Tell me more about yourself and your situation. Do you spend most of your time in London?"

"I have grown rather fond of Bath, my lord. I rent a townhouse there most of the time, besides when I visit my uncle's estate in Yorkshire at Christmas. I don't have any siblings, nor living parents, but I did inherit my father's small cottage in Surrey and an estate in Cornwall from my grandfather."

"Cornwall, you say? My dear Lady Blackstone has an estate near the Zennor coast. In fact, she resides there at this very moment, settling business with the steward before she makes her trip to London. I don't expect you have heard of Lanveneth House?"

Isaac had tried very hard to forget that place. He pushed away the image of the cream stone and the highest window where Sophia had often watched for him. "It does sound familiar."

"Unfortunately, it hasn't been well loved. It is quite far

removed from any notable towns, so Lady Blackstone rarely visits anymore. She far prefers town life, you see. She left it to the management of her steward and a small number of servants. Do you spend any time at your Cornish estate?"

"No, none at all." Isaac's voice was faint. He hadn't returned to Cornwall since his grandfather's death. He had feared that Sophia's family still frequented Lanveneth House, perhaps even Sophia with her husband and children. Isaac never would have guessed that she was still unwed, and that their family had as good as abandoned the house, just as he had Morvoren.

"Hmm. Well, Cornwall does seem an undesirable place to settle down." Lord Blackstone frowned. "My stepdaughter, Prudence, and her mother are quite fond of the place."

He didn't mention Sophia.

Isaac remembered Prudence clearly, though he was certain she had been altered even more than Sophia in the past four years. When he had known Prudence, she had been less than fifteen years old, somewhat headstrong, but never lacking in wit. He could still see her thoughtful green eyes and dark brown hair, with her hard-earned smile flashing every once in a while. To think that she was of marriageable age—that Percy was courting her—was enough to send a shock through his entire being. How could little Prudence be the subject of Percy's pursuit? A surge of protectiveness followed the thought, and his stomach became unsettled.

Lord Blackstone arranged a few papers in front of him. "Right then. I have read your letter of introduction from your cousin, which speaks highly of the strengths you possess." He leaned forward. "But it is not your strengths which led you to apply for my club, is it Mr. Ellington?"

Isaac shifted in his seat. Being honest would be his best

course of action. "No, my lord. Difficult er—regrettable circumstances caused me to be blackballed from White's and Brook's."

"Would you care to explain these circumstances? I assure you, I am more understanding than most. I find it quite fulfilling to offer men a chance for redemption." He flashed a smile. "While letters of recommendation often speak of a man's strengths, I am far more interested in his weaknesses."

Isaac took a deep breath but maintained eye contact. Lord Blackstone was perfectly still, blending in with the portraits and animals in the room.

"I was courting the sister of one of the members. The attachment became public more quickly than I anticipated or intended. A proposal was expected by her family, that gentleman included, but I—I couldn't follow through. My ending the courtship led to the deep disappointment of the young lady, and I am ashamed of my behavior. I have vowed not to repeat it."

Lord Blackstone was silent for a long moment. He seemed to be contemplating the weight and consequences of Isaac's confession. "A difficult situation, indeed." His chipper tone was duller than before, and Isaac felt his hope melting away. "How long ago did this incident occur?"

"A month, perhaps less."

Lord Blackstone's smile faded. "What prevented you from offering the expected proposal?"

Isaac looked down at the desk. "I didn't love her. I tried to. I wanted to." He swallowed. "But I couldn't. It has been a great difficulty for me to progress from courtship to marriage. This is unfortunately not the only time I have failed. It is no excuse, really, and I understand how unreliable I must seem."

Lord Blackstone interlocked his hands atop the desk. "I do appreciate your honesty. What I am hearing is that you are an indecisive young man, but that your intentions are not entirely wicked."

Isaac gave a hesitant nod. *Not wicked at all.* He would have liked to correct the statement, but he kept his mouth shut.

Lord Blackstone studied him a moment longer before sitting up straighter. "We all make mistakes, Mr. Ellington, and more mistakes are made in love than in any other business, I daresay." He gave a soft smile, then reached behind him and withdrew a piece of pale pink stationary. "I shall allow you a probationary period of three months. So long as your behavior proves exceptional, you shall be permitted to remain a member of Blackstone's beyond the first quarter."

Isaac tried not to appear as surprised as he felt. "Thank you, my lord."

"I do have a few conditions that are specific to your circumstances." His unblinking eyes put an instant stop to Isaac's celebration. Perhaps Lord Blackstone *was* a little intimidating.

"Of course," Isaac said.

Lord Blackstone slid a quill and inkwell toward a blank sheet of paper and began writing, reading the words aloud as he went. "During this probationary period, you shall not be permitted to court or form attachments with any relations of the gentlemen of Blackstone's. No sisters, cousins, daughters," his eyes lifted from the page, "or stepdaughters. I do like you, Mr. Ellington, but I would never allow you to court one of mine. Any father would do all he could to protect his daughters from such a public rejection. I hope you understand."

"Yes—entirely."

This was a good thing, he assured himself. If courting Sophia was against the rules, then he would not even be tempted to try. He could become acquainted with the harsher side of her character, which would enable him to move on. Yes. It was exactly what he needed.

"It's not likely to be a problem," Lord Blackstone continued, "given the circumstances of my eldest, but I thought I would take the proper precautions."

Isaac's shoulders stiffened. "Circumstances?"

"Miss Hale is expecting a proposal from Lord Finchley. I believe you would have seen him at the ball. The peacock."

Isaac's heart squeezed. He struggled to find his voice. "I thought he was a pheasant."

"He might as well be one, for Sophia has successfully hunted him down." Lord Blackstone gave a deep chuckle. "Please sign to indicate that you understand." He slid two papers toward Isaac, then the quill and ink.

Isaac followed the instruction immediately, if only to further prove his commitment to keeping Lord Blackstone's conditions. His heart stung at the news of Sophia's courtship, but he pushed the feeling away. He would do well not to think of her more than necessary.

He read the other terms on the papers in front of him, which mentioned the payment of his dues, how to purchase event vouchers, and information about the club itself. Lord Blackstone went over each subject individually, until Isaac was fully instructed.

"Do you have any questions for me?" The viscount asked.

Isaac's mind raced. He had been assailed with new information, but he couldn't forget his goal. Becoming close to Lord Blackstone was a vital part of his plan. He remembered Percy's strategy—how he had feigned interest in the great horned owl. Would the same tactic work a second time? With a different animal, perhaps?

Isaac searched the room for his target, which he found within seconds. "Yes, actually. I noticed this remarkable tortoise...does it have a name?"

Lord Blackstone sat up straighter, his features softening. "Oh, yes. That is my new addition Archibald, the rare Seychelles giant tortoise. There are times my feet grow rather swollen, and the height of his shell serves as a remarkably comfortable footstool."

"I admire your resourcefulness." Isaac smiled, struggling to hide his amusement. "Perhaps you might teach me more about the species. I have great interest in...herbivores." He grimaced at his own attempt to sound intelligent. In truth, he knew very little about animals.

Lord Blackstone appeared slightly offended. "Well, the first thing you must know is that this particular species of giant tortoise is not strictly herbivorous. They are rather opportunistic, you see, and will eat just about anything small enough to bite into."

"Including your swollen feet, I daresay, if you don't take care."

Lord Blackstone threw his head back with a hearty laugh. "I suppose you are right. Archibald, were he alive, would surely be a great threat to my extremities."

Isaac smiled, but his heart was still heavy with the news of Sophia's courtship. It was ridiculous how his heart could feel something entirely without his permission. No matter how enthusiastically he told himself to be grateful for the news—that it would benefit his efforts to move on—his heart refused to listen.

He cleared his mind enough to speak again. "I am grateful

to have met you, my lord, for you can easily correct my misinformation about tortoises. I am certain there is more to be set straight."

"And I will gladly do so!" Lord Blackstone stood, ushering Isaac back out into the corridor. "I should hate to have any gentlemen of my club misinformed about their co-inhabitants. If you are not otherwise engaged, I will receive you for dinner tomorrow evening where we may discuss my footstool at greater length."

"I would be honored, my lord."

The old man flashed Isaac a quick smile before eagerly leading him back down the gallery. The tour of the first floor covered a large sitting room, a few private meeting rooms, a library, and billiard room. There, a giraffe neck sprung out from the floor, stretching up until it grazed the ceiling. Isaac met several gentlemen as they moved from room to room, all of whom were agreeable and didn't seem to greet him with any hostility. So long as they weren't friends with Mr. Baker, they would have no reason to distrust him.

On the second floor were guest rooms, and on the ground floor were several card rooms, a dining room, and a spacious drawing room where Isaac made several additional acquaintances. The atmosphere was relaxed and comfortable, the scent of smoke cutting through the unpleasant scent of what Lord Blackstone had called their 'co-inhabitants.'

When the tour ended, Lord Blackstone left Isaac with an official invitation to his townhouse, and the opportunity to stay at the club and socialize for as long as he wished. Already, Isaac was comfortable in his surroundings. He was no longer on-edge. Perhaps Blackstone's could become a home to him, at least while he was in London.

In the far-left corner of the drawing room, Isaac caught

sight of Percy, peering over his glass of brandy with a smile. His black hair and jacket blended him into the dim surroundings.

Isaac couldn't help but wonder how long he had been watching him.

Percy had likely perched himself there in the corner of the room in order to entertain himself with Isaac's reaction to the club.

Percy set down his glass as Isaac approached, his smile growing smugger with each step. "I see you were welcomed with open arms," he said, his voice wavering with suppressed laughter.

"I think I may have proven myself a worthy competitor for the title of Lord Blackstone's favorite *Mr. Ellington.*" Isaac took a seat in the empty chair across from his cousin. "I have spent the morning wondering if you sent me to apply here as a joke."

"I confess that was part of it. However large, I will leave that up to your interpretation." Percy grinned as he drained the last few drops from his glass.

The unsettled feeling returned to Isaac's stomach as he remembered that Percy—more of a mischievous fox than Isaac would ever be—was attempting to court Prudence Hale. The match couldn't possibly be less advisable for the young girl.

Isaac chose his words carefully. "I was given conditions that I must uphold during my probationary period. Blackstone requires that I not court any relatives of other club members…with an emphasis on his stepdaughters."

Percy relaxed into his seat. "Well, I am glad not to have you as my competition for once."

Isaac frowned. "For once?"

Percy shrugged, flaunting a devil-may-care smile. He was silent for a few seconds. "All I mean to say is that you would be a fierce competitor for a lady's affections. You are far more amiable and richer than I am, although significantly less handsome."

A laugh blurted out of Isaac's mouth. "Significantly?"

"The truth stings." Percy tugged on his cravat, leaving a gap between the fabric and his neck.

Isaac glanced around the room again. There were several gentlemen engaged in deep conversations, some laughing, some drinking, and others engaged in quiet study. Despite being full of so many deceased creatures, Blackstone's was also full of life. It was an interesting contrast, but Isaac quite enjoyed it so far.

He addressed his cousin seriously. "I think Blackstone's will be vital for my future connections. Thank you for recommending me."

"You are most welcome." Percy stretched his back and stood. "All I ask is that you return the favor, should the occasion arise."

Isaac's brow twitched, but he nodded anyway. He had been afraid of this. Knowing so much of Percy's past, Isaac wasn't entirely certain he could speak highly of his character and keep his own integrity intact. It was a dangerous favor to owe.

With a firm clap on Isaac's shoulder, Percy strode out of the drawing room, leaving Isaac alone at the table. He settled into his chair, crossing his arms over his chest. He scowled at nothing, working through the events of the day in his mind. Not only had he succeeded at becoming a member of Blackstone's, but he had obtained an invitation to dine with the viscount and his family.

He hadn't fared well seeing Sophia at the ball…even when she had been wearing a mask. What would happen when he saw her face again? He would have to trust himself to keep to his convictions.

His heart, on the other hand, could not be trusted at all.

Chapter Six

"Guests?" Prudence met Sophia's gaze in the mirror as her maid arranged her long dark hair. "How many?"

Sophia approached the back of her sister's chair. "Does it matter? Stepfather will be sure to serve something strange no matter the number." She took a brief glance at the pale green gown draped over her reflection, the overlay adding a shimmer to the otherwise dull fabric.

Prudence grimaced. "Why does he think serving detestable foods is impressive?"

Sophia helped the maid place a few pins with an amused smile. "They are not detestable, they are *exotic*."

Prudence released a huffed breath, one dark eyebrow lifting. "If Mama were here, she would not allow it."

Sophia nodded her agreement. "Stepfather will be sure to take advantage of her lack of protest. I suspect he has been awaiting this opportunity for a long time." Their mother wasn't arriving in London for another month. She had already missed several parties and events, leaving much of her chaperoning duties to their Aunt Hester. While Sophia was glad Aunt Hester had accompanied them to London, she was growing increasingly frustrated with her judgment.

She, much like Prudence—and much like Stepfather—had been fooled by Percy Ellington. Sophia was fairly certain he was one of the guests who would be at dinner that evening. But she didn't dare guess at who else might attend.

Prudence took one last look in the mirror before standing to face Sophia. Her peach gown was the perfect color for her complexion, bringing out warmth from her green eyes. Sometimes Sophia was surprised at how much her sister had grown. In Sophia's mind, Prudence was still a child—still dependent on her, willing to listen to her advice, and eager to please. Age had gifted Prudence with beauty, and though she remained humble, she had gained a great deal of confidence.

And a hint of defiance.

At eighteen, Prudence was still learning the ways of society, who she could trust—and who she could not. Sophia had made it her quest to ensure Prudence learned correctly.

"Do you think Percy will be one of the guests?" Prudence asked with a sly smile.

Sophia adjusted her sister's necklace. "I should hope not."

She scowled. "Why don't you like him? He has only ever been kind and gracious toward you."

"Of course he has." Sophia tried to pinch Prudence's cheeks, but she ducked out of the way. "Prue!"

"No." Prudence crossed her arms. "I shall look pale as a ghost at dinner if you do not explain why you dislike Mr. Ellington."

His name rang through Sophia's head, setting off her defenses. Perhaps it had always been his name that unsettled her. When she had been Prudence's age, a Mr. Ellington had hurt her deeply, after all.

Sophia's distrust of Percy Ellington was not based simply on his name, though, and not simply on her senses. Her maid had given her valuable insight into his character, and his rakish behavior that he brushed into the darkest corners of society. He was good at hiding things and keeping secrets. He was good at presenting himself however he pleased. He was well aware of the masking quality of his charm, and he used it shamelessly.

Explaining all of this to Prudence had never been fruitful, though.

"I have already told you many times, Prue, and you won't listen. I don't trust his intentions."

Prudence's nostrils flared, but she said nothing. Sophia had learned to keep her mouth shut on the matter, since her resistance seemed only to fuel Prudence's desire for Percy even more. If Sophia continued to make him a forbidden prize, then Prudence would become even more attached to the idea of him. It was a delicate balance of warning and watching. But she would do anything to save Prudence from the same fate she had endured from an Ellington.

"You cannot blame Percy for Isaac's mistakes." Prudence touched Sophia's sleeve gently. "They are not the same man."

Sophia held her sister's gaze for a long moment. After the masquerade ball, Prudence had noticed Sophia's mood and had pried the truth out of her. Over the years, Sophia hadn't spoken of Isaac, but Prudence still remembered him and all that had occurred between them.

Sophia nodded, her throat dry. "That is true. But Percy could be even worse."

Prudence groaned. "You, my dear sister, are far too cynical. Why must you assume the worst of everyone?"

Sophia turned toward the mirror again to distract herself, pinching her cheeks as hard as she could. "Because I would rather be pleasantly surprised than devastated by disappointment." She faced her sister again. "Would you not?"

Prudence shrugged. "I would rather be optimistic." A faint smile touched her lips. "Perhaps you should be, too. Isaac Ellington might have been a fool all those years ago, but he could very well come to his senses now. I know you are still pining for him."

"I am not *pining* for anyone," Sophia snapped. She drew a deep breath to steady her nerves.

"Not even Lord Finchley?" Prudence gave her a skeptical look.

"Besides him," Sophia corrected in a quick voice.

Prudence still seemed doubtful, but content to put the subject to rest. It was only fair that Prudence could scrutinize Sophia's courtship if she was going to do the same to hers. Sophia had never forgotten her father's words. *"There are plenty of men in London who will find you sufficient. There are plenty of men who will love you better than Isaac Ellington ever could."*

There hadn't been *plenty*, but there was Lord Finchley.

He had called upon her earlier that day, and she was relieved to find that he hadn't held a grudge over her poor dancing. Hopefully he was one of their dinner guests that evening…though he hadn't mentioned receiving an invitation.

With Prudence at her side, Sophia made her way downstairs to the drawing room. She could hear voices from within, muffled behind the partially closed door. Her stepfather's laugh was difficult to mistake, booming through the walls of the house. There were no barriers that could contain it.

Sophia paused at the door and listened, steeling herself for the worst. If Percy was there, she would have to spend the evening glued to her sister's side, playing chaperone while Aunt Hester squinted at poetry through her spectacles.

Apparently vexed by Sophia's hesitant entry, Prudence brushed past her, pushing the door open with deliberate force. Sophia followed quickly behind, straightening her spine to its full height and surveying the room.

She quickly realized that the sense of dread she had been feeling was not without cause.

Isaac Ellington stood near her stepfather. Her heart fell, and her palms perspired in her gloves. Her lungs felt heavy, and the Persian rug felt like a sheet of ice as she walked deeper into the room.

What on earth was he doing here?

She noticed Percy nearby, and suddenly the invitation made sense. Both men were Stepfather's new friends, and both were equally dangerous.

As expected, Percy's focus was on Prudence as she made her confident entrance. Sophia felt like a dog being dragged by a lead, traipsing into the room on Prudence's heel. She quickly corrected her thoughts, forcing herself to stand straighter. She could not give Isaac the satisfaction of thinking she was intimidated by him.

His eyes met hers. She had no mask, no dim room, no costume. She had never felt a gaze so heavy or tangible as Isaac's as he took her in—every inch of her—every feature. If only she could read his mind. Was he noticing how old she looked—how altered from the girl he had pretended to love? She was not as young and vibrant as Prudence anymore, though she did make an effort to look after her appearance. Despite feeling Isaac's rapt attention, she pretended only to notice him in passing. Her heart in her throat, she stopped in front of both gentlemen and offered a curtsy.

Both men bowed, and Sophia took the opportunity to release the tense breath in her lungs. On the outside, she knew how she appeared—composed and quiet. No one would be any the wiser, not even Isaac. She was well-practiced in concealing her true emotions. Some people would call it deceptive, but she called it wise. No one could make any assumptions about her if they weren't given any clues.

A few words of greeting passed between Percy and Prudence, leaving Isaac and Sophia in silence. Her stepfather was watching with an expectant expression. It would be strange not to speak to Isaac at all. Her stepfather had no knowledge of their history, and surely not an inkling that any history existed at all. With him observing so closely, she had no choice but to look at Isaac.

"Good evening, Mr. Ellington." It was a bleak attempt at conversation, but it was still something.

"Good evening, Miss Hale."

He wore a black jacket and white cravat, hair combed neatly, his jaw freshly shaved. Never had a well-dressed and well-groomed man been so threatening. Did he even realize how harsh he had been? How unfeeling? Panic rose in her throat when her stepfather walked to the door to greet an arriving guest, leaving her alone with Isaac.

"I'm sorry if my presence here upsets you," he said in a low voice. "When your stepfather invited me to dinner, I didn't know how to refuse."

FOREVER ENGAGED

"Why should I be upset?" Sophia interlocked her fingers in front of her. "That was a very long time ago."

She didn't have to specify what *that* was. It encompassed far too many things.

"There is no need to dwell on the past," she continued in a quick voice. "Let us agree not to speak of it and move forward as new acquaintances."

"I agree." Isaac lowered his head in a nod. "Acquaintances would be more suitable than strangers."

"Yes, much more suitable." Her voice was so quiet she wondered if he had even heard her. She studied his face for too long. The silence made her anxious, but not a single word came to her lips. If they agreed not to speak of their past, then what was there to speak of?

Her mind was blank.

"Your stepfather has very unique taste," Isaac remarked, casting his gaze around the room. "But there is a surprising lack of taxidermy here."

Sophia found her voice. "It wasn't always so lacking, but my mother isn't fond of it. She requested that all the specimens be moved to the club. Did you apply there?"

"I did. My cousin encouraged it."

She cast a glance at Percy, who was already deep in conversation with Prudence. Of course he was. Her jaw tightened. At the door, her stepfather was welcoming an older couple into the drawing room. She recognized them as Lord and Lady Strathmore, their neighbors in the square.

She turned her attention back to Isaac. "Was it your cousin who brought you to London?"

Isaac shook his head. "Percy and I have never been close. In truth, I came to London to find a wife."

His blunt words sent a shock through her skull. She hid

the sensation well, as she always did, keeping her face neutral. "It would seem your quest has been unsuccessful thus far."

"Yes, but I am undeterred." His jaw tightened for a moment. "I am not one to give up on something I truly want." His clear brown eyes took her in, and she caught a hint of resentment—or distaste. Only the latter made sense, and it sent a pang through her heart. Was he trying to remind her that he had never wanted her? Did he think he was doing her a service by attempting to stamp down her hopes before they could rise? Anger surged under her skin.

Sophia couldn't help but use her one weapon against him. If Isaac thought she was going to grovel for his attention, he was wrong. "An admirable trait. Lord Finchley shares that quality, as he has demonstrated in his courtship with me."

"I heard about your attachment. My sincere congratulations. He was the peacock, yes?" Isaac's tone was difficult to read. She couldn't tell if he was being sardonic or genuine. Either way, it irked her.

She regarded him seriously. "At least he wasn't wearing orange ears."

A faint smile tugged on his lips. "A fair point. What else does he have to offer besides his excellent choice of costume and, of course, his title?"

"Many things. He's kind, well-connected, and dependable." She lifted her gaze to his. "And he finds my dowry sufficient."

Isaac held her gaze, seemingly unaffected by the hidden meaning in her words. "How romantic."

Sophia narrowed her eyes, a string of protest burning on her tongue. There was more she wanted to say, but Stepfather was headed in their direction again. She lowered her voice. "I assume my stepfather is...unaware that we were previously acquainted?"

Isaac's dark lashes shielded his eyes as he adjusted his sleeves. "I kept that information to myself. He did put me under express orders not to make any attempt to court you, and that's without even knowing our history. So I assure you, I have no intention of repeating it."

Her heart pounded, a wave of heat climbing her cheeks. At least he was honest. He hadn't wanted her then, and he didn't want her now. But why had her stepfather forbidden him from courting her? Why had that even been part of their conversation? So many questions assailed her; she couldn't grasp onto a single one.

Before she could speak again, her stepfather appeared beside her.

"Mr. Ellington is a delight, is he not? A wonderful addition to Blackstone's, if I do say so myself." His cheerful tone fell flat in her ears, overpowered by the anger that made her skin hot. How could Isaac be so harsh and unapologetic? *He* was the one who had rejected her before. He had once been so thoughtful and gentle with her emotions. Now, he seemed to be toying with them. At least her stepfather had her best interests at heart. For whatever reason, he had forbidden Isaac from courting her—not that he had needed to be encouraged not to. He had made that clear.

"Is he not?" Stepfather repeated.

Sophia's face burned as she realized she hadn't agreed with his assessment. *No, Mr. Ellington is not a delight. He is a nuisance.* It was painful to do so, but she nodded. "He is," she grumbled.

She felt Isaac's gaze on her back as she hurried to Prudence's side, interrupting her close conversation with

Percy. Anyone with sense would be able to see that Percy was dangerous. Even the way he looked at Prudence made Sophia's stomach turn.

When it was time to remove to the dining room, Percy extended his arm to Prudence. Sophia was afraid Isaac would offer her his, but her stepfather intervened. "Mr. Ellington, would you please escort Mrs. Liddle to the dining room? She requires a stronger arm and sharper eye than mine."

Isaac nodded, offering his elbow to Sophia's aunt as she bustled a few steps forward. Short and round, Aunt Hester had an inviting, friendly appearance. Her chin touched the top of her chemisette, her face nearly retreating inside like a turtle in its shell. Her eyes gleamed with admiration as she allowed Isaac to escort her forward.

With a grateful smile, Sophia took her stepfather's frail arm. As they made their way to the dining room, he cast her a sneaky smile. "Lady Strathmore asked about your painting of Cornwall. She offered a place for it in her upcoming charity auction. It would be displayed in the gallery at Christie's."

Sophia's brows shot up. She hadn't thought her painting to be anything extraordinary, but Stepfather had insisted on hanging it on his drawing room wall. She never would have expected anyone to stop and admire it. "Oh. Yes, I would like that very much." She had no trouble parting with the painting for a worthy cause. It would only serve her efforts to bury her past. Thinking of Cornwall meant thinking of Isaac—and that was no longer allowed.

"Capital!" Stepfather exclaimed. "She also informed me that she has heard the news of your courtship with Finchley. She gave her utmost approval of the match."

Sophia forced a smile, already dreading the dinner

conversation. "I am glad to hear it." As satisfying as it would be to discuss her courtship in front of Isaac, it would also be awkward.

When they reached the dining room, she was seated beside Percy, with Prudence and Isaac straight across. The first course began with general introductions, polite conversation, and a surprising lack of exotic offerings. But after a few minutes, the conversation died. Aunt Hester chewed silently on a chunk of bread, magnified eyes blinking fast as she observed the others at the table.

Isaac took a sip from his glass before regarding Lord Blackstone with a serious expression. "I wonder, were a Seychelles giant tortoise dining with us this evening, would he prefer the potatoes or the carrots?"

Stepfather chuckled. "I suppose it would depend on the preference of the individual. Not all tortoises are alike. Much like people, each has their unique opinions. Personally, I would always choose potatoes first. And what would you choose, Mr. Ellington?"

"Potatoes, without question."

"And you, Sophia?"

She met Isaac's gaze, wiping her lips with her serviette. "Carrots."

"My point is made." Lord Blackstone grinned. "Differences of opinion are quite natural in all species."

Isaac paused, casting his gaze at the chandelier in thought. "I suppose a better question would be which might the tortoise choose when presented with a plate of beef or a plate of carrots? While not strictly herbivorous, as you said, I wonder if they still prefer vegetation over meat."

Stepfather's eyes widened in thought. "If only we could present this scenario to a tortoise. I would be most curious as well. Would he choose what he is most comfortable with, or would he choose something unfamiliar and unknown? A fascinating question, indeed."

"I think he would choose the meat," Sophia said as she lowered her spoon. "After some time, I suspect he would have grown weary of carrots. He might realize that the meat is more valuable and leave the carrots to rot."

Stepfather blinked. "A valid hypothesis, my dear."

Sophia speared a potato with her fork, keeping her gaze fixed on her plate.

Percy's voice cut through the air. With a flick of his head, he moved his black hair out of his eyes. "I am of the opinion that he would choose both." His voice dripped with arrogance. "He might eat one before the other, but if he is opportunistic, he certainly won't leave any food behind."

"Certainly not," Stepfather said. He seemed to be vastly enjoying this conversation, and blissfully unaware that both men were only pretending to care about his favorite creatures. Sophia could see straight through Isaac's and Percy's ploys to win her stepfather's favor. It infuriated her.

Stepfather smiled broadly and clapped his hands twice, triggering the footmen in the corners of the room to step forward with four new trays. "In the spirit of our discussion about Archibald, let us test how opportunistic you all may be with your dietary choices."

Sophia frowned. Who the devil was *Archibald*?

Stepfather chuckled to himself as the footmen placed a tray on each section of the long table. "I keep the cellars stocked handsomely with my most intriguing goods, which have been imported from around the world. Much like the Hamadryas baboon, I am usually one to hoard my prize resources most aggressively." His smile grew with pride as his guests examined the trays. "However, in company so agreeable, I cannot help but share the abundance."

Sophia exchanged a glance with Prudence.

Mama adored their stepfather, and so did Sophia, but there were times his antics were a bit extreme. If Mama were in London, she would have strongly protested such a display.

Sophia studied the offerings on the tray that rested between Percy and herself. There were a few varieties of nuts, sliced fruits, dried fruits, candied petals, and a few other items that were completely unrecognizable.

"What you see at the center of the tray is one of my favorite delicacies," Stepfather said in a casual voice. "Pickled eel in spiced syrup. To the left, you will find candied tamarind pods."

The smell radiating from the tray made Sophia's stomach lurch.

"I invite you all to taste whatever you'd like, and please do report your findings to the group!"

Sophia pinched a small, dried fruit between her fingers. It was the safest option, to be sure. She popped it into her mouth as the others at the table made their selections. It was overly sweet and chewy, sticking to her teeth as she attempted to swallow. She took a sip from her water cup and accidentally met Isaac's gaze.

When she had known him, he hadn't been afraid to eat anything. She could still see the fish heads poking out of the stargazey pie that he had packed from his grandfather's house. Isaac had teased her about her unwillingness to try a bite. When he had pushed the pie toward her, she accidentally knocked it out of his hands, sending it tumbling down the cliffside and into the sea below. They had vowed to keep the ordeal a secret from his grandfather's cook, who had spent hours making that pie. Her sides had ached from laughing so hard.

She pushed the memory from her mind, focusing on Isaac as he picked up a curved nut from the tray. He popped it in his mouth.

Stepfather's attention was on Percy as he took a daring bite of the pickled eel. Prudence released a giddy laugh, even applauding as he swallowed.

From across the table, Isaac stilled.

His brow furrowed. He coughed once. Then again. Violently.

Sophia straightened in alarm as he reached for his glass. He took a large drink of water, but when he set it down, his face was redder than before.

"Good heavens," Stepfather exclaimed. "Mr. Ellington? Are you all right?"

Isaac didn't answer, a sheen of sweat appearing on his brow. He coughed again, this time continuously for several seconds.

Sophia's heart pounded. Lady Strathmore leaned back in her chair, pressing a hand to her chest in dismay.

"What did he eat?" Stepfather asked in an astonished voice.

"This one." Sophia's hand shook as she pointed at the tray.

"I believe that is what the natives call a cashew." Stepfather's brow furrowed. "The raw shell contains a rather tricky substance known for its potential adverse effects on the body, but I was told they would arrive properly processed. I have tried them once before and the effects were mild." His smile faded as he observed Isaac.

Sophia's heart fell. "Something is wrong. Look at him!"

Isaac leaned over, a hoarse sound coming from his throat as he breathed. His eyes watered.

Stepfather's wiry grey eyebrows furrowed in deep concern, but he seemed frozen in his chair.

Sophia couldn't hold still any longer. She pushed her chair out behind her, nearly stumbling over it as she rushed around to the other side of the table. Her movement triggered the response of Aunt Hester, who set down her spoon and followed Sophia to Isaac's side.

The plates and silver trays rattled as Stepfather finally sprung to his feet.

Sophia froze beside Isaac, her heart in her throat. What could she do? He appeared to be struggling to breathe, his skin growing redder beneath his chin and spreading up his face. Standing there would not be helpful at all, but her arms were pinned to her sides.

She was afraid to touch him.

Don't be a coward, Sophia. She ordered herself to move—to do something. She took his face in her hands, his skin hot under her palms. "Mr. Ellington? Can you hear me?" His eyes fluttered closed. Could he breathe at all?

His cravat appeared to be too tight, so she tugged it loose.

Lady Strathmore gasped.

Sophia couldn't worry about propriety at the moment. Beneath the cravat, his neck was red and swollen. "Call for the doctor!" she directed the order at Aunt Hester, but one of the footmen ran from the room. The others stepped closer to observe Isaac's condition.

Removing the cravat seemed to have helped, but he still breathed in a shallow rhythm. With a firm hold on his face, Sophia tipped his head back. It seemed to help him breathe with less effort.

Stepfather held Isaac's arm, keeping him upright in his chair, while Percy stabilized his other side. Sophia watched Isaac's chest rising and falling quickly, her fingers shaking as they buried into his hair to hold his head back. In the most foolish of her dreams, she had hoped to do that again someday. But not like this. Fear prickled down her spine. She closed her eyes against the tears that burned unexpectedly there.

"What a peculiar idiosyncrasy," Stepfather muttered. "I did not react adversely to the cashew at all. I should have considered that each body is unique in its peculiarities of constitution, I suppose. But what a fascinating discovery."

"This is not a scientific experiment, stepfather!" Sophia's voice was shrill with panic. "He could be dying!"

Stepfather scowled. "Do calm yourself, my dear. He looks quite alert to me."

Chapter Seven

Isaac's throat may have felt like it was on fire, but that didn't stop him from noticing Sophia's face above him, blue eyes flooded with tears. Her cheeks were wet and flushed, her hands buried in his hair as she held his head back.

He gathered as much air as he could with each breath. It was cold as it rushed past his itching throat. He felt ill enough to vomit, but he refused to do that in such a moment, not with Sophia as a witness. The panic he had felt when his throat first began to swell had only hindered his ability to breathe, but now he knew that he still could...at least for now.

He heard Lord Blackstone's voice—something about an idiosyncrasy—and then he noticed all the other faces hovering around him. He had been alert through the entire ordeal, though severely distracted by the panic inducing sensations burning through his body.

That blasted exotic nut had done *this* to him?

He stared up at Sophia's tear-stained cheeks, and the

pressure of each of her fingers suddenly became apparent under his hair. If he wasn't still fighting to breathe, he would have been mortified. She had been the first to run to his aid, and now she was crying over him? It was painfully embarrassing, but it was also telling.

She might not have hated him as much as he thought.

With all the horrified expressions around him, he was desperate to lighten the mood. He blinked up at Lord Blackstone, whose grey hair was even more disheveled than usual. "Are you trying to murder me, my lord?" His voice was barely a hoarse whisper.

"Of course not!" the viscount sputtered. "I am as baffled as you are, Mr. Ellington."

Isaac mustered up a smile. "Would you have called this a death by natural causes?"

Lord Blackstone's eyes widened in a mixture of dismay and amusement. "It would have been purely accidental, if that is what you mean."

Isaac laughed, but it hurt. He sucked in a deep breath of air through the small space that remained in his throat. His condition had made him a little too bold, or even delirious, but he felt well enough to assume he would survive. He hoped so. He had to survive at least long enough to ask Sophia why she was crying.

She blinked fast, but her eyes looked dryer than before. Upon seeing her face for the first time tonight, Isaac had been surprised by how similar she looked to his memory, frozen in time, yet refined by age. He wouldn't have thought it possible that she could grow even more beautiful, but she had. Her curled lashes, wet with tears, framed her thoughtful blue eyes. Her skin was milky white, without the freckles he remembered, and her hair was no longer bleached on the ends from the sun. She was a London girl once again, because that was the life she had chosen over the one he had offered her.

He couldn't afford to forget that.

He shunned his admiration, focusing on keeping his breathing steady and his body calm. He had never reacted so adversely to any food before, but he would have appreciated a warning before being served a potential poison.

"Perhaps more water?" Lord Blackstone offered.

Isaac nodded, gulping down the rest of his glass with the help of his cousin. He might have been mistaken, but Percy's mouth hovered on the edge of laughter. He would never let Isaac forget this embarrassing moment and the newfound delicacy of his constitution. It was humiliating enough to make his face burn. An egg could have been cooked on his cheek for how hot it felt.

Isaac had never been the strongest man in any room, or the most talented at riding or dueling. He had always been the tall, rather ungainly one. Not only that, but he was far more emotional than other men of his acquaintance. He was prone to accidents and blundering, even in his conversations. If this incident were to befall anyone at the table, it wasn't a surprise that it had been him.

His throat itched, but there was nothing he could do to scratch it. His stomach lurched with discomfort.

"Let us help Mr. Ellington to one of the guest rooms," Lord Blackstone instructed. "The physician will be here soon to examine him."

Isaac felt Sophia's hands slip away from his hair, and he leaned into Percy as he and Lord Blackstone helped him to his feet. His legs shook from the shock of the ordeal, but he managed to stand. A footman stepped in for Lord Blackstone, and the two men led Isaac out to the corridor and up the stairs.

The guest room was growing dim, but a few candles were lit at the bedside. Isaac managed to cast up his entire dinner once he was away from the other guests. He felt better instantly, though his throat and lungs still burned with the effort to breathe. The physician, a man near Isaac's own age, had very little knowledge to offer, having never encountered a poisoning by exotic nut before.

Isaac couldn't blame him.

With a wet towel to cool Isaac's skin and reduce the swelling, and instruction to rest and drink water, the man left the house just after dark.

Isaac stared up at the ceiling. He doubted he would sleep. He didn't dare, not while his breathing was still so labored. He glanced at Percy, who sat in a wooden chair beside his bed. "Don't feel obligated to stay here all night," Isaac rasped. Lord Blackstone had already left the room to report the state of Isaac's condition to the others at the house.

Percy laughed. "I can't have Miss Prudence or Blackstone thinking me heartless, now can I? As far as they know, I am here to tend to your every need like the caring cousin I am." He laughed before leaning his head back on his chair and closing his eyes.

Isaac grimaced. It was difficult to make Percy Ellington look like a saint, but that blasted cashew might have just made it possible.

~

Isaac awoke with a sore throat, but most importantly, his soul still inhabited his body. He hadn't died in the night, not even after enduring Percy's constant snoring. Sunlight bled through the edges of the curtains, just enough to indicate that dawn had broken.

Isaac dressed quickly in his clothes from the day before, combing his hair with his fingers. He kept his movements quiet as he crept out of the room and toward the staircase. After the humiliation he had endured the night before, he wanted to sneak out of the house before being seen. He was presentable enough to make the journey home on foot, and the exercise would do him good.

His emotions felt bottled up inside him, the pressure growing more intense by the second. The source was difficult to name, but one thing was certain:

Sophia was not as cruel as he had hoped.

Beneath her nonchalant facade, she must have still cared for him a little. She didn't wish him dead, at least. Isaac didn't know whether to be relieved or disappointed. He needed her to prove herself as harsh as the letter she had written him if he wanted to forget her, but that no longer seemed possible. She had proven that her heart wasn't entirely cold, and Isaac could already feel his own thawing.

That was unacceptable.

It would be best to avoid her from now on. He would make excuses to avoid Lord Blackstone's invitations in the future. Fleeing from his house was the first step, even if he was still a little unsteady on his feet.

At the bottom of the staircase, Isaac turned right, unsure of the direction of the front door. His coat and hat would be there somewhere, but if not, he was certain Blackstone could have them delivered.

His legs moved quickly, his long strides carrying him down the silent corridor. As he approached a corner, he avoided a collision with a young woman by inches. A flash of white fabric and dark hair was all he saw at first, but then the image cleared.

Sophia clutched a leather book to her chest, eyes open wide. "Mr. Ellington!"

"Forgive me," he blurted. "I didn't mean to startle you."

She took two steps back, putting a few feet of distance between them. She examined him with a swift glance. "You're awake. You're…well."

He nodded, the edges of his face on fire. "I was looking for the front door."

A hesitant smile touched her lips. "Are you lost?"

"Am I?"

She nodded. "The entrance hall is that way." Her gaze flickered in the opposite direction that he had been heading.

"Ah." He swallowed, remembering how tender his throat still felt. The events of the night before came pouring back to him, but he really, *really* did not want to acknowledge them. However, he did owe Sophia some expression of gratitude, no matter how painful it would be to remind her how weak he had appeared. He rehearsed the words in his mind.

"I-I'm glad to see you well again," she said before he could speak. Her voice was barely above a whisper. "You frightened me."

Isaac should have exercised more caution, but he couldn't help but look at her. In the morning light from the nearby window, her hair picked up the golden tones he remembered. In the light, he saw a few faint freckles on her nose, and one darker one near the top of her lip.

That one had always been there.

His heart physically ached at the sight of it, so he looked

down at the floor. "You might advise your stepfather to keep his cashews to himself in the future."

"I should hope he has learned his lesson." Sophia's voice wavered with amusement. "I sincerely apologize on his behalf."

Isaac shook his head. "There is no need to do that. I survived."

"Narrowly."

"It seems I have you to thank." He met her gaze. "You were the first to come to my aid."

Sophia's eyes rounded in denial. "I did nothing. I was worried, that was all. It quickly became clear that you were in no serious danger." Her hands tightened around the book she held. She may not have intended it, but the motion drew his gaze to the title on the leather spine.

An Account of Curious Idiosyncrasies and Unnatural Complaints

A slow smile tugged on his mouth. "A bit of light morning reading?"

Sophia's cheeks darkened a shade. "My stepfather sent me to fetch it from his library." The words spilled out so effortlessly, Isaac almost believed them. Almost. He would have rather believed that she had awoken that morning thinking of him—worrying about him. His heart was weak, grasping onto the smallest shreds of hope. He quickly reminded himself of his place.

"Well, that was very thoughtful of him."

"I thought so too."

Isaac concealed his smile as he studied the blush on her cheeks. "What is it like to have Blackstone as your stepfather? Are all his dinner parties so eventful?"

Sophia seemed surprised that Isaac wished to continue

their conversation. In truth, he was too. He should have been marching off in the opposite direction, but now his feet seemed to have embedded themselves in the marble floors. So long as Sophia was still standing there, he couldn't move.

"Not quite." Her laugh sent a spiral through Isaac's stomach. It had been far too long since he had heard that sound, yet it was instantly familiar. "It is no secret that he is eccentric. But despite that, he has one of the most open and kind hearts I have ever known. That is why my mother married him. She is quite happy as his wife."

"Blackstone said your mother is at Lanveneth?"

Sophia nodded. "The 'regal Lady Blackstone' is enjoying the spoils of being a viscountess. She now divides her time between here, her husband's estate in Norwich, and Cornwall. She will return to London in a few weeks."

Isaac considered his reply carefully. If they were to move forward as new acquaintances, then speaking of Cornwall would be a dangerous subject. "Is Lanveneth House still in good repair?"

"The steward manages it well. I haven't seen it in years." Sophia's voice faded, and she hugged the book tighter. "How is Morvoren?"

Isaac cleared his throat, flinching at the pain it caused. "I haven't set foot there since my grandfather's death."

Silence fell between them for a long moment. Sophia brushed a strand of hair behind her ear. "I imagine your grandfather's death was difficult for you."

He felt a deep ache in his chest. Sophia didn't know that his grandfather had died just moments after he had learned of her departure. She didn't know how the two events had aligned so cruelly. "And your father's death must have been difficult for you."

Her clear blue eyes met his. "The loss was most difficult on Prudence. There were days I feared she couldn't bear it. He fell ill so suddenly." Her forehead creased.

"Prudence seems to be enjoying London at least."

"Yes, but she misses her dogs at Lanveneth. She speaks of little else." Sophia offered a smile.

Isaac remembered the two spaniels that had followed Prudence everywhere she went. The memory brought a smile to his face. "Flora and Thistle?"

Sophia gave him a look of surprise. "You remember their names?"

"Of course."

She looked down at the floor. "Well, besides the dogs, she *has* taken an interest in another subject."

Isaac sensed the unease in her voice, and immediately knew what she was referring to. "My cousin?"

Sophia's eyes flew up to his. "So you are aware of their attachment?"

Isaac nodded, that uneasy feeling entering his stomach again.

She hesitated, resting her chin on the top of the book. "I wondered if I might rely on your help with something."

Isaac folded his arms across his chest, feeling the quick beat of his heart against his breastbone. "Anything." He cringed inwardly at how eager he must have sounded. This was the woman who had broken his heart and had flaunted the fact that she was now courting an earl. But she had also come to his aid the night before, without question. He owed her a small favor at the very least.

She walked a pace closer, a nervous twist to her expression. "You mentioned that you and Mr. Ellington don't have a close relationship. Is that true?"

Isaac nodded, his shoulders tense.

"I wondered what honest assessment you might give of his character."

He exhaled slowly through his nose. He had been dreading a question like this.

She seemed to sense his hesitation. "I wouldn't ask if I didn't have reason to doubt the honor of his intentions."

The genuine worry on her face muddied Isaac's conscience. After what Percy had done to recommend him to Blackstone's, how could he speak against him? He bit the inside of his cheek, looking at the floor as he gathered his thoughts. "I do believe Percy's intentions are to marry her. He told me just that the other day. It did...surprise me to learn that he's interested in marriage. In the past, he's spoken quite freely against it."

Sophia scowled, a skeptical tilt to her head. "Why do you think he would be determined to marry Prudence specifically?"

Isaac shrugged. "He might have fallen in love with her."

She shook her head. "I think it's because he learned of Prudence's inheritance. She will receive Lanveneth House."

A wave of shock rolled through Isaac's chest. "Why not you?"

"My mother knows Prudence loves it more, so she named her in her will. I did not want it." She looked away, brushing her hair behind her ear again as it fell out of place. "But it seems that your cousin does."

Devil take it. Isaac sighed, raking a hand over his hair. Percy had always been openly envious of Isaac's inheritance of their grandfather's Cornwall house.

This must have been his way of procuring his own.

After learning that Isaac was orphaned, Grandfather had

taken Isaac under his wing. He had two sons—Isaac's father, and Percy's father. Isaac had been Grandfather's choice for his heir not based on birth order, but on his own preference. Percy was clearly still irked.

"Prudence is far too stubborn to listen to me," Sophia continued. "She is convinced that Percy is honest in his feelings for her. But I fear that he would marry her solely for the house, and then break her heart."

Dread sank through Isaac's stomach. That was exactly what Percy would do.

In the company of men, Percy would be the first to admit that he would never be loyal to one woman. Isaac's jaw tightened.

Sophia's brow twinged with worry. "I have already expressed my concerns to my stepfather, but he thinks too highly of Mr. Ellington. He won't listen. But perhaps he *would* listen to someone who knew Percy better..."

Isaac's stomach twisted. "Are you asking me to give Blackstone a reason to withdraw his support of the match?"

Sophia held his gaze for a long moment. "If you are willing, then yes, I am."

Conflicting emotions surged up in his chest.

"I did help save your life, you know." Her voice was bolder than before. "One might say you owe me a favor."

Isaac stared at her determined expression, his heart in his throat. "Percy may not be the most respectable man, but I have no wish to ruin him," he began in a slow voice. "Exposing his faults to a viscount would damage his connections for good."

Sophia's eyes flickered down. "Very well. I should not have asked."

Isaac's heart lurched. How could he leave her so downtrodden?

He tried to remind himself of how she had left him in Cornwall in a much worse state than this, but his memory was foggy behind the dejection in her features.

She dropped into a quick curtsy, her jaw tight. "Good day, Mr. Ellington." She turned away.

Without thinking, Isaac took one large stride forward, stopping her by the arm. "Sophia—wait."

She whirled around, a clear look of surprise on her brow. It could have been from his abrupt touch, or from his use of her Christian name. Both had been entirely accidental.

He lowered his hand as quickly as possible, brushing it on the side of his trousers awkwardly. His heart raced as he tried to formulate his thoughts. "You must know that I do not support Percy's actions. Prudence deserves to be loved, not hunted for her belongings. I will do all I can to persuade him against the courtship."

She raised an eyebrow. "And if that is unsuccessful?"

Isaac searched his mind for an idea. "Then I will help you sabotage it."

"Sabotage? How is that easier on your conscience than warning my stepfather?"

"It would be pointless…and rather ruthless for me to say something that might have my cousin dismissed from Blackstone's. Perhaps we can help Prudence see Percy's true character for herself. We might be able to drive them apart without any obvious interference."

Sophia wore a business-like scowl on her forehead. "She will be heartbroken. But it is the only way to ensure her future happiness. As you said, she deserves to be loved for more than her belongings." She met his gaze, and there was a hint of fire behind it—a pointed look that seemed as if it were meant to disarm him. Was it...accusation?

Within seconds, her features shifted back to a thoughtful expression. "How do you suggest we begin our sabotage?"

Isaac grimaced. "Perhaps we shouldn't call it that."

"Is there a more delicate word you wish to use?"

He tapped his chin with one finger. "Disruption? Impairment, perhaps?"

A hint of a smile touched her lips. "Very well. How do you suggest we begin *disrupting* the courtship?"

"Keep me informed with the details of their next outing. Perhaps you and I can accompany them to...gather information. Then we can make our plan according to what we observe."

She gave a swift nod. "That sounds reasonable."

Isaac paused to gather his wisdom, because it seemed to have flown straight out the window of Lord Blackstone's townhouse. He had been determined *not* to spend time with Sophia. It was easy to forget that she was just as dangerous as Percy.

She could break Isaac's heart a second time if she tried.

She was here in London, doing what she had always wanted to do—courting a rich and titled man who could give her more than Isaac could. Did he really want to plant himself in a position to witness the progression of her courtship with Lord Finchley? It sounded miserable. But he couldn't leave Prudence helpless. He had to do something.

"I'll speak with Percy first," Isaac said after a long moment. "Perhaps I can change his mind without all this...interference."

He doubted the conversation would be successful, but he had no choice but to try. Being *acquaintances* with Sophia was bad enough.

Being allies could be disastrous.

Chapter Eight

Prudence looped her arm tightly through Sophia's as they walked against the wind in Hyde Park. Sophia brushed at the loose bits of hair escaping the front of her bonnet.

The sun was high, with hardly a cloud in sight. Compared to the rain that had soaked the grass the day before, it was a vast improvement, even if there was a slight breeze. A small inconvenience in the weather couldn't deter the majority of the people in London, though. Hyde Park was the place to be seen, to cross paths with members of the *ton*, to watch for emerging courtships, and search for new gossip. Sophia had delighted in the idea of promenading here when she was younger.

But only then. Now, she dreaded the mandatory outing.

"It's fortunate that Lord Finchley didn't see you clinging to Mr. Isaac Ellington last night," Prudence said abruptly.

Sophia jolted, shooting a scowl at her sister. "Keep your voice down."

A promenade in Hyde Park was not the time to say

anything potentially scandalous aloud. Sophia looked behind her to ensure no one had overheard. The only person who might have heard was Aunt Hester, but from the look on her face she was still oblivious. She was wrestling with her parasol, which seemed intent to blow away.

The upper half of Prudence's face was shadowed by her bonnet, the sun highlighting her mischievous grin. "Or might I say *unfortunate* that he was not there to see it."

"There was nothing to see," Sophia said in a calm voice. "Even Lady Strathmore understood the desperate nature of the situation. My actions were necessary."

"And rather telling." Prudence peeked at Sophia's face. "You still care for him."

Sophia scoffed. "How could I care for the man who deserted me because my dowry was insufficient? I hope you don't think me so insensible. Mr. Ellington and I have made a promise not to concern ourselves with the events of the past. It is over and done with."

Prudence sighed. "Is there no chance that you might love him again?"

Sophia laughed, fighting the discomfort in her chest. "If I loved him, it would be very much against my will."

"That *is* typically how love operates, is it not?"

Sophia kept her chin high as they passed a very wealthy looking couple. "I believe there is some choice involved." Sophia had made the choice *not* to fall in love with Isaac again, and she intended to keep that promise to herself. She would not be governed by her heart as she had been when she was Prudence's age, even if Isaac continued to act as charming as he had that morning. He had been kind. Considerate. He was willing to help her protect her sister.

What if there was a part of him that regretted his decision to end their courtship? What if he had changed?

These were the questions she couldn't afford to ask herself—yet here she was, asking them anyway.

She shushed her thoughts, turning her attention to another task.

"Have you met Mr. Timothy Baker?" Sophia asked, leaning closer to Prudence's ear. She pointed her gaze at a tall man with fiery red hair who stood beside a tree up ahead. "He is a very respectable man, with a great deal to offer. Perhaps Stepfather can arrange an introduction for you."

"Why on earth would I want that?" Prudence cast a dagger at Sophia with her gaze. "I am courting Mr. Ellington."

"You have hardly considered any other options!" Sophia tightened her arm around her sister's. "You cannot make your decision so hastily."

"You may believe that love is a decision, but I do not. I am in love with Mr. Ellington, very much against my will, in fact, and there is nothing to be done to change that." She lifted her chin. "At any rate, I already know Mr. Baker's sister. See the young lady beside him? Miss Baker was introduced to me just last week, if you must know. If you wish, I shall meet her brother this very moment if only to prove that no other man can claim my heart."

Sophia resisted the urge to groan. Prudence's dramatics were exhausting at times. There was no cure for her stubbornness. Meeting Mr. Baker would be fruitless now. Just when Sophia was prepared to abandon the idea, she caught sight of two familiar men in the distance. Her heart leaped.

Isaac—alongside his nefarious cousin—was walking in their direction. He wore a navy-blue jacket with tan breeches, a pale blue waistcoat and white cravat. His polished boots and dark hair shone in the afternoon sunlight. No one should be allowed to look so handsome.

His expression was serious as he spoke with Percy, who wore his usual flippant smile. Were they discussing his courtship with Prudence? The two men didn't seem to have noticed them yet. If Sophia acted quickly, Prudence wouldn't notice them either.

She began tugging against her sister's arm, striding with purpose toward Mr. Baker and his sister.

"At least slow your pace," Prudence hissed through her teeth. "You look prepared to attack him."

Sophia obeyed, but the moment she slowed down, Prudence gasped. "Is that Mr. Ellington?" Her feet froze, planting them both just a few yards short of Sophia's target.

Blast it. Prudence tugged Sophia toward the two men and away from Mr. Baker. Their sudden movements would likely be disorienting to poor Aunt Hester. She had already fallen a great distance behind. Sophia tried her best to make it look like she wasn't being dragged, but Prudence's strength was alarming.

Isaac noticed their approach, slowing his steps.

Percy's gaze settled on Prudence. She offered a subtle wave with her gloved fingers. Her cheeks had already turned a deep shade of pink. How was it that Mr. Ellington always knew exactly where to find her sister?

A ridiculous grin pulled on Prudence's mouth. "He looks handsome today, does he not?" she whispered, her lips barely moving.

Sophia's heart fluttered deep inside her chest as her eyes connected with Isaac's. Both Ellington men were handsome, there was no question. Even after nearly dying over a tiny exotic nut, Isaac looked well. More than well. And he didn't even have to try. With enough effort, he could steal almost any heart he wanted. Except Sophia's, of course.

Percy reached them first. "Good afternoon, Miss Hale, Miss Prudence. Never have I seen such lovely young women at Hyde Park." He cast a flirtatious smile at Prudence.

How could she not see how ridiculous he was?

Sophia pinched her shoulder blades together, keeping her posture straight as she greeted both men. If Isaac had spoken to Percy about stopping his pursuit, then it obviously hadn't worked. Percy's attention was locked on Prudence, and she was clearly besotted.

"May I beg you to accompany me for a turn?" Percy extended his elbow toward her.

"We were just about to return home," Sophia interrupted. "Perhaps another day."

Prudence shot her a scowl. "He did not ask *you*." Her face softened, and she instantly took his arm. And then they took off in a sedate pace across the grass. Aunt Hester followed, which only gave Sophia a small sense of peace. Every moment Prudence spent with Percy, she became more attached. The more attached she became, the more she would overlook. Sophia felt entirely helpless to stop it. A surge of frustration gripped her shoulders.

The sleeve of Isaac's navy-blue jacket came into view. "Well? We can't leave them unattended, can we?"

Sophia looked up slowly, a sense of dread in her stomach. She wasn't certain she wanted to be left unattended with *him*. Prudence and Percy grew smaller up ahead, but Sophia could still hear her sister's flirtatious giggling. She didn't have a choice.

She took Isaac's arm, keeping her grip loose—barely there.

"I tried to reason with him," Isaac said in a low voice as they set off behind Aunt Hester. "I accused him of courting her only for Lanveneth...and he didn't deny it."

Sophia glanced up at the tightened edge of his jaw. "Did he say he would cease his pursuit? It doesn't appear that way."

Isaac gave a humorless laugh. "No, it does not."

Sophia's legs had to work twice as fast to keep up with his long strides. They slowed their pace when they were within a few yards of Aunt Hester's heels. They couldn't risk being overheard.

"I worry that the more I try to dissuade him, the harder he'll try," Isaac said.

"That sounds like Prudence."

Up ahead, Percy adjusted her shawl, his hand lingering on her lower back. Sophia glared at the back of his head. "There must be a way to forge a divide between them." Her heart ached. "Unless it's too late."

Two women with a small pug on a lead walked by. The dog's tongue hung out of its mouth, dribbling a trail of drool onto the grass. It gave her an idea.

"Does Mr. Ellington like dogs?"

Isaac shook his head. "He dislikes all animals. He has only pretended to like them so as to gain your stepfather's favor."

Sophia raised an eyebrow at him. "Much like how you pretended to be interested in the Seychelles giant tortoise?"

"I was interested! Deeply." His eyes gleamed with amusement.

She hid her smile. "At least *you* were punished for your lies at dinner. Mr. Ellington has yet to be caught."

She looked up in time to see Isaac's jaw slacken. "Are you implying that I deserved to be killed by that exotic nut?"

"Killed, no. *Nearly* killed, yes." She tipped her head up to look at him. "The question is, have you learned your lesson?"

"I have learned not to eat from a tray of unfamiliar delicacies, if that's what you mean." He grinned, and his smile sent a warm spiral through her chest.

Her skirts tossed with the breeze. She watched the toes of her boots as she walked. "I hope you have also learned not to pretend to be interested in something when you're not." She dared to look at his face. She wanted him to feel guilty for what he had done to her in the past. She wanted him to take responsibility for it, but he continued to act oblivious.

His brown eyes reflected the sunlight, a curious look behind them. "If it will prevent another near poisoning, then I shall never feign interest in anything ever again. I assure you, I have learned my lesson."

Sophia hid her disappointment at his reply. He didn't seem to have caught her meaning. "Well. Now it is time that your cousin learns his."

Isaac peered down at her with misgiving. "Do you have a plan?"

"Prudence adores dogs. At least once weekly she bursts into tears over her longing for Flora and Thistle." Sophia pressed her lips together in thought. "Perhaps the four of us might have a picnic this week. It will be your duty to ensure Percy's dislike of animals is exposed through our conversation. To emphasize the point, I will invite Lord Finchley."

Isaac's brow furrowed, and he walked in silence for several seconds. "Because he's a...peacock?"

Sophia burst into laughter. "No—I mean, he has two very

large dogs. I will ask him if we might have access to his gardens for our picnic. He keeps his dogs in the stables."

Isaac looked down at the grass, a faint smirk on his lips. He didn't seem quite as amused as before. "Very well. We shall plan a picnic with Lord Finchley." His tone was edged with distaste, and against her better judgment, it caused a flutter of satisfaction to erupt in her chest.

The thought struck her again: Did Isaac regret the day he had written her that letter? She banished the thought at once. It didn't matter whether he regretted it or not. He had done it, and if watching her court Lord Finchley was to be his punishment, then he might finally learn his lesson. The moment Percy was out of Prudence's life, Isaac could be out of hers. Their alliance was temporary.

She reassured herself with that thought as she and Isaac concocted the rest of their plan.

Chapter Nine

In the polished marble floor of Lord Finchley's townhouse, Isaac saw Sophia's reflection.

He looked up in time to see her walking down the staircase on Lord Finchley's arm. She wore white, a bouquet in one hand, a sheer veil over her face.

"My dear Lady Finchley, please welcome our guests," the earl said. His voice echoed off the lofty walls. The ceiling was higher than any townhouse Isaac had ever seen, stretching up and up toward a painting of angels in a beam of light, as if to indicate the heavens above them.

Sophia floated down the staircase, stopping a few paces in front of Isaac. Her veil lifted magically from her face, revealing her blue eyes, brown hair, and freckles from the Cornish sun. She stared up at him softly at first, gently—but then her mouth twisted in a smirk.

Her eyes grew dark.

"I have everything I have always wanted. Are you not happy for me?" Her gaze pierced through him. "Are you not happy for me, Mr. Ellington?"

Lord Finchley joined her at the base of the staircase, brushing his lips against the side of her neck. Isaac tried to speak, but no words came out. His chest was compressed, and he couldn't breathe.

Sophia smiled. "Well, almost everything." Her eyes shifted to the stairwell, where a row of animal heads were mounted on the wall, each with a wooden crest bearing its name. A tortoise named Archibald, a badger named Gilbert, a giraffe named Arabella, a bear named Cornelius...and one empty space in the middle.

"Lord Finchley and I are in search of a new specimen for our home." Sophia's voice swam in his ears. "My stepfather made a suggestion that we could not refuse."

Isaac's vision blurred, then focused on the wooden crest that had just appeared in the empty space on the wall.

Isaac

~

He jolted awake, sitting upright in his bed. His skin was hot, his sheets sticking to his bare chest. He pushed his blankets to the floor, rubbing both hands over his face as he caught his breath. He could scarcely remember ever having such a vivid nightmare in his entire life.

"Blast Lord Blackstone," he mumbled, collapsing on his back. His body buzzed with energy, as if he had truly been moments away from running out the door of Lord Finchley's townhouse.

Of *Lady* Finchley's townhouse.

His heart raced, so he rubbed a circle over his chest. It did little to soothe him. He glanced at the window. Streams of faint daylight escaped the edges of the curtains. He wouldn't dare sleep again now, not at the risk of finishing the nightmare. Although, at the moment, his reality was not much better. Sophia was indeed courting Lord Finchley, and Isaac would be spending time with both of them that day.

Aside from the threat of becoming taxidermy, his nightmare could soon become very real.

He stumbled out of bed before calling a servant to fetch him a pot of tea. And something stronger. Leaning both hands against his desk, he calmed his racing thoughts. He had been determined not to care who Sophia married, but he did care. Too much. He hadn't seen her for three days, but he had spent many of his afternoons at Blackstone's, mingling with the other gentlemen there and drinking a little too heavily. Sophia's presence in London, their interactions, her determination to protect her sister—it had all upended him, leaving his heart in turmoil.

She was still the same woman he had fallen in love with those years ago.

He shook himself of his ridiculous thoughts. If she *was* the same woman, then he ought to be careful. She would draw him in, and then break his heart. She had a different man in sight, and her feelings for Isaac were never enough for her to sacrifice her ambitions. *She is colder than she seems,* he reminded himself repeatedly as he went about his morning.

When it was time to gather at Lord Finchley's address, Isaac collected his beaver hat and his coat and took a coach to Berkeley Square. It was still a little early in the season for an outdoor picnic, and today the air was particularly chilled. He was grateful, for perhaps it would remind him of what he had been telling himself about Sophia.

She is colder than she seems.

Isaac knocked on the front door of Lord Finchley's townhouse. His heart hammered in his chest, his stomach in knots. He was prepared to run out the door the moment he stepped inside if he found any taxidermy on the walls—even the smallest squirrel or rat. Lord Blackstone's club had obviously altered Isaac's subconscious in some way, planting a new aversion inside of him.

The butler opened the door and ushered Isaac inside. The ceiling was not nearly as high as it had been in his nightmare, but the staircase was similar. He swallowed hard as he followed the butler's directions to the back door. Thankfully, the floor wasn't the same dark marble, and there wasn't an animal in sight.

Not a stuffed one, at least.

Out the back window, two excessively large dogs bounded across the grass. Danish mastiffs, by the looks of them. One picked up a stick before dropping it in front of Lord Finchley's polished black boots.

Sophia was already outside, standing beside Prudence and their aunt as they observed the earl's interaction with the dogs. Isaac's chest tightened at the sight of Sophia, eyes fixed on Lord Finchley and his fine attire. She had been waiting four years for the chance to be a countess or something of similar rank. If she was this close to succeeding, nothing could stop her now.

Isaac took a deep breath as he opened the door. The moment he stepped outside, both dogs looked in his direction. Fortunately, he was fond of dogs, otherwise he would be intimidated by the size of them. The darker of the two dropped the stick that had been in his mouth, a stream of drool following it to the ground.

Then they both bolted in Isaac's direction.

He braced himself for their enthusiastic greeting, but Lord Finchley called them away just in time. They seemed to be well-trained and obedient, at least.

"My apologies, sir, I hope they didn't startle you." Lord Finchley strode toward Isaac. His pale hair was formed in stiff, uniform curls, like that of a statue. The knots of his cravat were elaborate, the fabric just as stiff as his hair. In Isaac's nightmare, Lord Finchley had been much more imposing, with a large stature and dark eyes. In reality, his frame was rather slight, his eyes a pale, icy blue.

"Not in the slightest," Isaac said. He forced himself to smile as he walked farther onto the grass.

Lord Finchley chuckled. "I am glad to hear it. In truth, I never trust a man who is intimidated by dogs, especially such gentle creatures as these."

"Nor do I," Prudence said with a laugh. "How could anyone dislike James and Ronald?" She stared lovingly at the dogs, so Isaac could only assume those were their names.

Sophia exchanged a glance with Isaac, her lace gloves interlocked in front of her. No one would ever know that she was hiding a devious plan behind her polite expression. "I wholeheartedly agree. If a man does not appreciate dogs, I instantly assume other unforgivable flaws must exist within him as well."

Lord Finchley smiled, seemingly pleased by her assessment. It put a bitter taste in Isaac's mouth.

Mrs. Liddle, Sophia's aunt, piped in. "My late husband disliked dogs, but he was still a very agreeable man." A few wisps of dark hair stuck to her forehead. Despite the chill in the air, her face was flushed.

Prudence covered her mouth with a laugh. "I'm sorry, aunt. We did not mean to discredit Uncle Liddle. He was very agreeable, indeed. *I simply could never marry a man who wouldn't adore my dogs as much as I do. It is my own preference, I suppose.*"

Mrs. Liddle withdrew her fan, batting away a fly as it buzzed near her face. She kept her eyes fixed on the dogs as they chased one another in circles across the lawn. "We are each entitled to our own opinions, I suppose."

Isaac could hardly believe the luck of their conversation. It was the perfect prelude to Sophia's plan. "Does Mr. Percy Ellington like dogs?" she asked her sister in a casual voice.

Prudence gave a firm nod. "I believe so. He didn't show any signs of objection when I told him about Flora and Thistle."

Isaac figured this was the best time to provide his contribution. He cleared his throat. "It is my understanding that my cousin despises dogs. Almost as much as he despises all other animals."

Prudence's forehead creased with a deep scowl. "That cannot be so. Stepfather has told me how intrigued Mr. Ellington is by his collection at Blackstone's."

"Perhaps we should put him to the test," Sophia said with a shrug. "We shall see how he responds to James and Ronald when he arrives."

Lord Finchley laughed loudly, and the sound grated on Isaac's nerves. "How could anyone not love them? It would be impossible not to." He walked closer to Sophia and extended his arm, which she took with a grateful smile. A set of dimples appeared in her cheeks.

Isaac looked away, and the knots in his stomach tightened. He could easily envision Sophia being a countess. Her mother's marriage to Lord Blackstone had given her valuable connections, and now her dream was within reach. His heart sank like a rock to the bottom of a lake, stirring up his buried emotions like silt. If he had the power to interfere, he would. But he felt helpless. He was there to help drive Percy and Prudence apart, yet now he lacked enthusiasm for the task.

There was a different courtship that he would much rather sabotage.

"I do not see a picnic," Mrs. Liddle muttered. She had meant it only for Prudence's ears, but Isaac overheard. "I was told there would be an array of cheese and crackers."

"Not to worry, aunt. I expect Lord Finchley is waiting until the dogs are put away."

Isaac was intent to ignore Sophia's proximity to the earl, so he followed Prudence's gaze toward the dogs instead, who had taken a moment to rest beneath the shade of a tree. Both dogs panted, massive ribcages expanding. Suddenly, they both froze, jaws closing around their bobbing tongues.

Their ears lifted, and they jumped to their feet.

Isaac turned just in time to see Percy stepping out the back door of the house. The gold buttons on his waistcoat gleamed in the sunlight, pulling tight around his figure. He didn't seem to notice the dogs as he stepped out onto the lawn. He held a gilded black walking stick in one hand, digging it into the grass without a care for Lord Finchley's landscaping.

A deep bark came from one of the dogs.

Percy's smile fell, and he retreated a step. The dogs closed the distance between them in seconds, and Isaac had only a brief second to wonder why Lord Finchley hadn't called off their approach like he had with Isaac.

He glanced to where the earl and Sophia had been standing but found that they were no longer there. Had Sophia led Lord Finchley away for that very purpose—to leave Percy at the mercy of the dogs? Isaac knew they were harmless, so he had no intention of intervening either. He held his breath as he watched the scene unfold.

Percy released an outraged gasp as the first dog reached him. "Back! Back!" He swung his walking stick forward, narrowing missing the first dog's front leg. He swung again, this time striking the thick muscle of the second dog's hindquarters. The dog yelped, bounding a few paces away. His companion retreated as well, tail and ears dropping.

"Mr. Ellington!" Prudence nearly tripped on her skirts as she rushed toward the dogs. She gasped, stopping in front of the one Percy had struck. Her dark curls whipped across her forehead, her gaze hot with anger. "How dare you hurt this poor innocent creature? He meant no harm to you!"

"Of course he did." Percy straightened his waistcoat, brushing his hair out of his eyes. He was clearly flustered. "What the *devil* are they doing out of the stables? They should be restrained at all times with behavior so wild."

"They were only greeting you!" Prudence's face was flushed, her eyes gleaming with moisture.

Percy finally seemed to process her reaction, his features softening. "You're right, Miss Prudence." He set his walking stick down, raising both hands in front of him. "You are entirely right. I acted impulsively."

She kept one hand on the dog's head, her shoulders still tense.

Isaac walked forward, joining Prudence beside the startled dog. He crouched down, softly touching the place he had been struck. The dog flinched, one dark brown eye darting in Isaac's direction.

"You hurt him." Prudence scowled at Percy, her lower lip quivering. She looked equal parts betrayed and angry. A pang of guilt struck Isaac's chest. He hadn't expected Percy to react so aggressively.

But Percy didn't seem to feel guilty at all. He sighed. "The creature will recover in no time at all. He looks like a resilient thing, does he not?"

Prudence was silent. She continued coaxing the dog back into good spirits, scratching behind its ears. Her forehead was still creased, and Isaac could feel the weight of her disappointment.

Percy sputtered out a laugh, drawing one step closer to Prudence and the dog. "You mustn't be angry with me, Miss Prudence. Surely you understand that my actions were purely instinctual and not malicious."

She glanced up, leveling him with her gaze. "I would have hoped your instincts would be kinder."

Percy's jaw tightened, and he approached the dog tentatively. As if to prove that he could be gentle with it, he reached out his hand. A deep, quiet growl came from the back of the dog's throat.

Percy snapped his hand back with a grimace.

"Well, he certainly doesn't have any reason to trust you now," Prudence said in a sharp tone.

Percy drew a deep breath through his nose, turning his attention to Isaac. "Surely my cousin can attest that I am usually much more patient with animals. I am fond of all living creatures, in fact."

Prudence stood up straight, opening her mouth before Isaac could reply. "No. Your cousin told us that you *despised* all animals. I didn't believe him until now."

Isaac froze. Percy's gaze might as well have been an arrow for how swiftly it punctured him. Awkwardness thickened the air.

"I can't imagine why my cousin would say such a thing." Percy's voice was cold, his eyes just as bitter as he stared at Isaac. "It is entirely untrue."

Sophia and Lord Finchley came into view from the rose garden, seemingly unaware of all that had just occurred. Sophia held a red rose—an apparent gift from the earl. She laughed at something he said, but then her eyes took in the scene in front of them.

Isaac felt ill. Percy still glared at him, and Prudence was nearly in tears. Sophia seemed to sense the tension, letting go of Lord Finchley's arm and rushing toward her sister. The earl jogged across the grass behind her. His curls should have moved with the motion, but they remained rigid on his head.

"What has happened?"

Percy cleared his throat, lowering his head in a bow. "Please do excuse me, my lord. My deepest apologies, but I must take my leave at once." He spun around, fetching his walking stick from the grass before departing through the back door of the house without another word.

Isaac had never seen him so uncollected.

He would have to find a way to explain—to apologize for not defending him. But all Isaac had done was tell the truth. Percy had condemned *himself* for being cruel to the dog. Perhaps it had even been enough to help Prudence see sense.

Lord Finchley paced forward in confusion before turning back toward Sophia and her sister. "What on earth did I miss?"

Prudence wiped her nose, her face emerging from behind Mrs. Liddle's shoulder. "Mr. Ellington does not like dogs."

Isaac withdrew his handkerchief, extending it to Prudence. She was silent as she took it, smothering her face with the fabric.

Sophia met Isaac's gaze. If her sister wasn't so distraught, she would have been celebrating; he was sure of it. They had made a deep crack in Percy's plan to secure Lanveneth House.

And he would not be pleased.

"Well, upon my word." Lord Finchley sighed. "He certainly didn't have to leave on account of my dogs. It is no great ordeal to send them back to the stables." He squinted against the sun in Isaac's direction. "Did they frighten him?"

Isaac would not go so far as to tell the earl that Percy had struck his dog with a walking stick. He had to remain neutral on some grounds. "I'm afraid they did."

"Hmm." Lord Finchley planted his hands on his hips in clear disapproval. "I suppose Miss Prudence has her answer, then."

"Indeed."

Isaac didn't like conversing with Lord Finchley, mostly because he couldn't find any obvious flaws in him. Besides the manner in which he arranged his hair, he had no reason to dislike the man. Well, besides for the fact that he was planning to marry Sophia.

That was a very good reason.

"I regret that we have lost a guest, but we shan't allow that to ruin our afternoon." Lord Finchley clapped his hands together. "Shall we proceed with the picnic?"

Chapter Ten

"Perhaps I am being too hard on him." Prudence crumpled Isaac's soiled handkerchief in her palm with a sigh. "Percy might have only used his walking stick in an attempt to defend himself."

Sophia hadn't thought it possible, but her sister already seemed to be justifying his behavior. "No." She shook her head fast. "Think of how he would treat Flora and Thistle. You cannot put them in harm's way for a man."

Prudence sniffed, staring blankly into the distance. How powerful were the charms of Mr. Ellington? Could she really be on the brink of forgiving him? Sophia couldn't judge her sister too harshly. She had been catching herself doing the same thing when it came to his cousin.

Her gaze shifted to Isaac. He stood near Aunt Hester, arms crossed over his chest. She could hardly read his expression, but she could assume that he was wishing for an opportunity to flee as Percy had.

The picnic group was peculiar, to be sure.

Sophia could already sense that Isaac was not fond of

Lord Finchley. As emotional as Prudence was, Sophia had half a mind to call the picnic off, but she didn't want to risk offending the earl. He had been very attentive that day and had even cut a rose from his garden for her.

She stared down at the perfect red petals. She urged her heart to swell, to skip, to feel something besides a small flicker of gratitude, but it didn't work. Isaac's efforts to help her protect Prudence were at the front of her mind, taunting her with the vexing urge to forgive even his greatest follies.

With the dogs returned to the stables and the picnic arranged, Sophia joined the others on the gingham blanket near the rose garden. A small stone fountain trickled behind them, and birds chirped as they hopped through the trees. It was peaceful...until Lord Finchley settled down beside her. Sophia stiffened with surprise. She hadn't expected him to sit so close.

Prudence was on her other side, with Isaac and Aunt Hester across the way. In the middle of the blanket was a large straw basket with leather straps. When Sophia had suggested the idea of a picnic to Lord Finchley, she had explained that Isaac was a dear family friend. She wondered what he would think if he knew the truth.

Lord Finchley leaned forward to open the basket, withdrawing two trays of sandwiches, a plate of scones, and several miniature desserts. A servant brought a pitcher of lemonade on a tray, as well as a set of dishes for each guest.

Before Sophia could add anything to her plate, Lord Finchley touched her arm. "Allow me." His mouth curved in a smile as he lifted her plate, filling it with one of each item.

Her face was hot. She sat politely as she waited but couldn't help but notice Isaac's reaction. He leaned back casually on his hands, his eyes fixed on Lord Finchley. His jaw was tight.

Was he jealous of Lord Finchley?

She wanted him to be. After being cast aside by Isaac all those years ago, she had dreamed of the day that he might want her again. She had dreamed of him rushing back to her—begging for forgiveness.

But over time, her heart grew bitter, and her dream changed.

For a long time now, the fondest part of her dream was the moment that she could refuse him. She had dreamed of how satisfying it would be to tell him that he had lost his chance with that letter he wrote her.

Then why did she feel so uneasy about Isaac's jealousy? Shouldn't she be pleased? She took a bite of a sandwich, the pillowy bread giving way to a slice of crisp, refreshing cucumber. A nervous sensation puddled in her stomach as she realized why her dream made her so uneasy.

Refusing him was no longer the fondest detail.

The possibility of Isaac wanting her again made her heart hammer.

She took a sip of her lemonade. It was too tart, but she hid her grimace.

"What do you think?" Lord Finchley asked, tugging her abruptly from her thoughts.

"I love it," she lied, offering a smile.

"Miss Hale looks lovely in pink, does she not?" He leaned toward her, but the question had been directed at the rest of the group.

Sophia laughed, but it sounded forced. She had never been very good at flirting, and she would surely become even worse at it with Isaac watching her every move—her every breath. She felt his gaze burning on her face.

"She does," Isaac said.

Though Lord Finchley had asked the question, he didn't seem to have expected such a sincere answer from Isaac. He had yet to fill his plate with sandwiches. All he had was a cup of lemonade, which rested on a saucer near his leg. Untouched.

Silence fell, and Sophia could feel a tangible tension in the air. She tried to appear unaffected, but her heart raced.

Lord Finchley's shoulders straightened—just a subtle movement. "Mr. Ellington, Miss Hale told me that you are a close friend to her family. How did you become acquainted?" He took a sip of lemonade, his lips puckering as he swallowed. He scowled into the cup. "Hmm. Not enough sugar."

Sophia held her breath. Would Isaac play along? She felt embarrassed that she had called him her friend. Friends did not go four years without speaking.

"It was eighteen-thirteen," Isaac's deep voice answered without hesitation. "Sophia's family had just moved to Lanveneth House, which is a short walk from my grandfather's estate in Cornwall. I had been living with him since my mother's death."

Sophia tried to appear as casual as possible as she listened, sipping on her sour lemonade. She remembered how her heart had ached for Isaac when she had learned that he was an orphan. His father had died shortly after he was born, and his mother had raised him alone on a small jointure. She had fallen ill and died the year before Sophia met Isaac. Sophia had been amazed by his strength and devotion to his grandfather, to his estate, and to the duties that awaited him. It had shocked her to learn that he hadn't been back to Cornwall in years.

Isaac's voice brought her back to the present. "Our proximity as neighbors made it impossible not to become friends." His gaze settled on Sophia with a weight that trapped her breath in her lungs. "We spent a great deal of time together."

A wave of yearning washed over her, but as it crashed, it melted into grief. Those had been the happiest days of her life. If she could, she would live them again a thousand times over. Her heart had been so open—like a rose in full bloom—but now it was tight and coiled like the bud Lord Finchley had given her.

There were no words to describe the freedom she had felt in Cornwall. The hope. Neither were there words to describe the madness, the wild abandon, and the bravery that had led her to fall in love for the first and only time. Back then, she had laughed more. She had explored coves and caves. She had undone her hair, throwing her bare face up to the sun, even dipping her feet in the sea. She had loved without holding back, without any conditions—and she had kissed Isaac without the fear of being caught.

She held his gaze for a long moment. She could see their history in his eyes like a living, breathing thing. It had survived for four years, and it would survive forever. That was the cruelest thing about the past. It never died. She could escape it with passing days and years, but she could never truly forget it.

Isaac didn't seem to have forgotten it either. It was written all over his face.

Lord Finchley cleared his throat.

Sophia looked away from Isaac, her heart pounding.

"Well, *I* have never been to Cornwall myself," Lord Finchley said. "But surely I will make a visit there in the near future." His gaze shifted to Sophia.

Was he...hinting at their marriage?

Her throat was dry, so she drank more lemonade. She grimaced at the flavor.

"Perhaps you can meet Flora and Thistle," Prudence said. She seemed to be slowly emerging from her dismal mood. "They are smaller than James and Ronald, but they are just as endearing."

Lord Finchley grinned. "I would like that very much."

Sophia shifted uncomfortably. She was running out of distractions. She had eaten half her plate, and her cup of lemonade was almost empty. She tried not to notice as Isaac poured Aunt Hester another cup, filling her plate with each item she requested.

"I thought we might play a game." Lord Finchley crossed his legs tightly in front of him, tucking them close to his body. He leaned forward until his back was rounded, and he looked like a ball.

Stepfather would say he looked like a woodlouse bug.

There was something about the position that gave Sophia a strong sense of aversion. She ignored it, as she had with the other aversions she had developed toward him during their courtship. *Heavens*, she couldn't judge the man by the way he crossed his legs when he sat! But this had been her downfall for years now—finding the smallest flaws in men and allowing them to take root in her mind until they were impossible to ignore. Isaac had ruined her. He was still ruining her, because there was absolutely nothing wrong with the way he was sitting on the blanket, long legs stretched out in front of him.

"I do enjoy games," Aunt Hester said, popping a raspberry tartlet into her mouth.

"Well, Mrs. Liddle, do you have any suggestions?" Lord Finchley asked.

Her eyes rounded. "Oh! It is to be my choice?" Her cheeks flushed, and she set her plate down on the blanket. Her lips settled into a firm line, her eyes reflecting deep thought behind her spectacles. She seemed to be taking the honor quite seriously. "I prefer friendly competitions over the more raucous sort."

"I do agree."

"Perhaps we might compete to see how well we know Miss Prudence," she suggested, nodding toward her niece. "It is her birthday soon, after all. We might all make her feel rather special."

Prudence's eyebrows shot up with delight. This seemed to be Aunt Hester's attempt at improving her mood. Prudence did enjoy being the center of attention.

Lord Finchley chuckled. "An excellent idea! I am still becoming acquainted with Miss Prudence, but I will try my best. What about you, Mr. Ellington? Are you equal to the task?"

Isaac cast a smile in Prudence's direction. "I knew Prudence several years ago. She was still a child. I assume she has altered greatly since then."

"She is not as altered as you might think," Sophia said with a teasing smile.

Prudence shot her a scowl, but it was half-hearted.

"Then let us begin!" Aunt Hester dusted the crumbs off her fingers and tapped her chin. "I will pose a question, then we shall all present our answers. Prudence will confirm which is most correct, and then someone else will pose a question. The first person to reach three correct answers wins." She took a deep breath, the ruffles of her chemisette brushing against her chin. "If Prudence were to become lost in the woods for a week, how would she spend her time?"

Sophia could easily guess, but she wanted to hear what the others thought first. Prudence was grinning now, as if she had already forgotten her disappointment with Mr. Ellington.

Lord Finchley spoke first. "Miss Prudence strikes me as a resourceful young woman. I suspect she would first locate a source of water, and then gather as many food sources from the vegetation as possible. Considering her love of animals, she would avoid hunting at all costs."

Isaac's voice cut in. "On her way to find water, she might become distracted by a family of toads beside the stream. She would scoop them up, take them with her, and build a shelter for the lot of them."

Prudence laughed, her lips twisting into a thoughtful smile.

"I know exactly what Prudence would do." Sophia eyed her sister. "She would spend her first night wallowing beneath a tree." She laughed at the dismay on her sister's face. It quickly melted into surrender.

Prudence knew full well that she would.

"After wallowing for a night," Sophia continued, "she would collect as many wildflowers as possible, and make a bouquet to improve her spirits. Then, she would go to the stream to drink water, but she would also swim in it, for Prudence cannot resist an opportunity to swim."

"Oh, very well. You win." Prudence sighed, then her lips curved into a smirk. "Why do I now wish to be lost in the woods?"

Sophia laughed, and so did the rest of the group. Lord Finchley appeared to be thoroughly entertained by Aunt Hester's choice of game. It continued for three more rounds. Aunt Hester took one point, and Sophia took the other two, earning her place as the winner. Isaac and Lord Finchley played along, though their answers were more a display of wit than accuracy.

"It would seem that it is your turn, Sophia." Aunt Hester blinked innocently behind her spectacles. "Since you've won, we shall now compete to see who knows *you* best."

Sophia let out a nervous laugh. "I didn't know that was a rule."

"Nor did I." Aunt Hester pressed a hand to her chest as she chuckled. "I am inventing this as we go along."

Drat. Sophia would have tried to lose if she had known this was the consequence of winning. Unlike her sister, she didn't like being the center of attention at all…especially not in this particular company.

Isaac sat up straighter.

Lord Finchley refilled Sophia's cup of lemonade.

Sophia would have preferred to sink straight down into the grass and disappear rather than play another round of the game. Her palms perspired inside her lace gloves.

"I will pose the first question," Aunt Hester said in a cheerful voice. "If Sophia had to choose one season to spend the rest of her life in, which would she choose and why?"

Lord Finchley peered at her face, eyes narrowed. "It would be summer, to be sure. Miss Hale has commented on many occasions how she loves the increased warmth and sunshine the season brings."

"That *is* the obvious choice," Prudence said with a frown. "What happens if we all answer correctly?"

Aunt Hester contemplated for a moment. "Then I suppose we all secure a point, and the game continues."

"Well, I also think she would choose summer." Prudence studied Sophia's face. "I think she enjoys summer fashions the most—the pastel colors, the light shawls, and the fresh flowers for her bonnets."

Aunt Hester pursed her lips. "I will say spring. The same reasons could apply, but spring brings the most rainstorms, and I know Sophia loves watching the rain. What say you, Mr. Ellington?"

Sophia clasped her hands together so hard they hurt. In all the hours she and Isaac had spent together, they had covered countless subjects. They had shared all their preferences, dislikes, dreams, and stories. But it had been so long ago. She doubted Isaac would remember something so specific as her favorite season.

He held her gaze as he spoke in a confident voice. "I think Miss Hale would choose to spend the rest of her days in autumn. She does love rain, but she also loves a warm fire and a hot cup of chocolate. She cannot reasonably sit by a fire indoors during the summer, and she thinks people who use their fans excessively in public are seeking attention, so she would want the outside air to be cold. Her favorite color is orange, like the leaves when they change, but she chooses not to wear it because she doesn't think it favors her. Personally, I disagree. I don't think there is any color that wouldn't favor her."

Sophia's gaze dropped to her hands. Her heart pounded. Two of her fingers had lost feeling completely from how tightly she was squeezing them. How on earth had he remembered all of that?

She felt Lord Finchley watching her, waiting for her to

declare the winner. "Mr. Ellington is right." Sophia swallowed. "I would choose autumn."

Aunt Hester gasped, applauding with rapture. "What a thorough explanation, Mr. Ellington. I am quite impressed."

Lord Finchley's jaw clenched for a moment, and he took a large gulp from his cup. "Thorough, indeed." He smiled—a little too broadly—and motioned toward Mrs. Liddle. "Someone pose the next question."

The abrupt demand made Sophia's skin crawl with discomfort. It was obvious that Isaac had awoken Lord Finchley's competitive nature.

Isaac popped an entire cucumber sandwich in his mouth, casually inhibiting his ability to speak. He leaned back on his hands, and for the first time all afternoon, he seemed to be enjoying himself.

Sophia snapped the tension in two. "There is no need to continue the game."

"We must." Lord Finchley's brow furrowed. "I have a question. If Miss Hale had to give up tea, playing the pianoforte, or dancing for a month, which would she choose?"

Aunt Hester answered first. "Of the three, I think she would choose to give up dancing. As I understand it, she views it as more of a social obligation than a form of recreation."

Sophia looked down at the blanket in dismay. All her faults would be exposed to Lord Finchley before the day was out. She had given him the impression that she *liked* dancing. There were few people in the world who knew how she truly felt about the activity.

Prudence stifled a laugh. "Yes. She would be quite glad not to dance for an entire month."

Lord Finchley's legs sprung out from their tight position. His chest rose and fell with a deep breath. "Well, then. I didn't know my question would be so easy to answer."

"I only dislike dancing because it doesn't come easily to me," Sophia blurted. She took another sip of lemonade from her cup to hide her face from view.

"I think she would give up the pianoforte." Isaac's voice drifted through the air. "Practicing her music consumes several hours of her day, but I suspect she would rather spend that time painting. I do agree that she would readily give up dancing. She has never been particularly fond of tea either, so giving that up wouldn't cause her great distress." He paused, casting his gaze at the pitcher at the center of the blanket. "Although she doesn't dislike it as heartily as she does lemonade. She hates anything flavored with lemons, in fact."

Sophia's eyes widened. Her cup was just a few inches from her lips. She had been forcing the lemonade down her throat out of politeness, but the bitter, sour flavor had been slowly making her ill.

Isaac's mouth flickered with a smile, but his eyes were serious. Anger surged in her chest. What was he trying to prove? He seemed to be trying to outperform Lord Finchley by any means necessary, even at Sophia's expense.

Now Lord Finchley would know that she had only pretended to like dancing and pretended to like his lemonade. She felt like a fool for accusing Isaac of pretending to like things he didn't. She was just as guilty.

Silence lingered for several seconds, until Lord Finchley finally broke it. "You may only choose one of the three." His gaze was firm as he looked across the blanket at Isaac. "What is your final answer?"

Isaac didn't blink. "The pianoforte."

Lord Finchley's nostrils flared, but he said nothing in reply. "I must go with the general consensus...that she would give up dancing."

Sophia refused to grant another point to Isaac, though she knew in her heart that his answer was correct. She had been dutifully practicing her music for hours every day for as long as she could remember. Her mother had taught her to be prepared if she were ever called upon to perform. But she didn't love it. If she had those hours back, she would have created dozens of paintings instead, just as Isaac had guessed.

Her anger simmered steadily inside her. It was vexing that he knew her so well. The only purpose it served was to make Lord Finchley feel inferior.

She composed herself with a breath. "Three of you are correct." She lifted her chin. "I would choose to give up dancing."

"Hah!" Lord Finchley clapped his hands together in one swift motion. "I knew it!" He tucked his legs close to his body again. "Who would like to ask the next question?"

Prudence raised a hand. "If Sophia could choose one person to be trapped in a carriage with during a rainstorm, who would it be?" The sly smile that followed gave the question a scandalous edge. Even Aunt Hester wasn't oblivious to it. Her lips parted, eyes round.

"What is the matter?" Prudence brushed a small bug off the edge of the blanket before lifting her sharp green eyes to Sophia's face. "I should like to think you would choose me. We never have any shortage of entertaining conversation." She gave an innocent smile, as if that would erase the sly one she had presented before. "That is my guess."

Aunt Hester lifted her forefinger. "She would surely choose her stepfather, for he could keep her thoroughly entertained with facts about every species that has ever set foot on the earth."

Sophia laughed, relieved that the tone of the question had changed.

Her heart pounded as she awaited the next two responses. She prayed that neither of the two men would be bold enough to claim themselves as her chosen companion.

Isaac and Lord Finchley seemed to be locked in a stalemate, neither one saying a word. Perhaps they were both considering being just as bold as she feared. In the silence, she listened to her pulse rushing past her ears. Her bonnet trapped heat against her head, making her cheeks flush hotter.

After what felt like an eternity, Lord Finchley leaned forward, gazing into her eyes for just long enough to make her uncomfortable. She gave a shaky smile.

"I think you would choose to be trapped in a carriage with me." He gave his most charming smile. "I could entertain you easily enough."

Prudence's eyes rounded with delight, and she nearly spit out her lemonade.

"With conversation," Lord Finchley added.

Prudence cast her gaze around the circle, drinking up every reaction.

"Also with song." Lord Finchley flashed another grin. "My voice could put her nerves at ease, I am certain of it." He seemed to be joking, but Sophia could never truly know. He was unpredictable in that way. Perhaps she simply didn't understand his humor well enough yet.

Aunt Hester was so enraptured in the game that she

hadn't touched her plate for several minutes. Lord Finchley straightened his cravat, apparently very proud of his answer. Sophia would never be able to confirm it without feeling wildly improper. Surely he knew that. Was he forfeiting his point only to vex Isaac?

It seemed to be working. Isaac's expression lacked the amusement of all the others. His brows were level, his mouth straight.

"It is your turn, Mr. Ellington," Lord Finchley said, his voice more chipper than before. "Who do you think Miss Hale would choose?"

Sophia drew in a breath, but the air felt thick. Her nerves were on edge, and she was fairly certain that Lord Finchley's singing voice would only make them worse.

"I think she would choose to be trapped in a carriage with her husband," Isaac said. "Once he is in existence, of course." He brushed casually at the knee of his trousers, but Sophia didn't see anything there. His lashes cast a shadow over his cheek, hiding his eyes from her view. "After all, he will be the one she trusts most to deliver her to safety after the storm. He is the one she's least likely to grow bored conversing with. Who better to be trapped with than the man she loves most?" He lifted his gaze, and Sophia's heart tumbled like a boulder down the side of a cliff.

Aunt Hester applauded. "A clever answer, Mr. Ellington. If it were my own decision, I would most certainly choose my dear late husband. Who answered correctly, Sophia?"

"Prudence." She was proud of how calm her voice sounded. "Though I would not object to any of your answers." It seemed to be the safest way to reply without injuring Lord Finchley's pride too severely.

"Fair enough." Lord Finchley bowed his head in mock

disappointment before lifting it again with a grin. Thankfully he didn't seem offended at all. He seemed only pleased that Isaac's answer hadn't been chosen.

"That leaves me with two points," Prudence said. "I need only one more!"

"Would you like to pose a question, Mr. Ellington?" Aunt Hester asked.

Sophia's shoulders stiffened. Isaac's eyes met hers, and he finally seemed to recognize her discomfort. It had taken him long enough.

He paused in contemplation for a long moment. "What is one food Sophia would never taste, even if she were offered a sum of five hundred pounds?"

A relieved laugh escaped her throat.

"Jellied eels," Lord Finchley said. "Even the scent is enough to make my stomach turn."

Prudence grinned wickedly. "A cashew."

Isaac's face broke into a smile. "Stargazey pie."

Sophia laughed. She could still see the pie rolling down the cliffside like a wheel of cheese.

Aunt Hester gave a triumphant smile before giving her answer. "Flora and Thistle stew."

Prudence gasped. She looked like she might throw her plate at their aunt. Sophia burst into laughter. She struggled to catch her breath. "I'm sorry Prudence, but I'm afraid I cannot spare your poor dogs. I would rather avoid a cashew. You've won."

The look of pure outrage on Prudence's face faded at the announcement of her victory. She joined Sophia's laughter, all evidence of her sour mood gone. "I suppose I'll forgive you."

Sophia would have chosen the stargazey pie, but she was

desperate for the game to be over. If she could help it, she would do all she could to ensure Isaac and Lord Finchley never met again, in fact.

"I've heard of cashews," Lord Finchley said, throwing Sophia a curious look. "What about them repulses you?"

"They are rather dangerous. Mr. Ellington was poisoned by one. It made him quite ill."

Lord Finchley's mouth lifted on one side. "That is unfortunate. A matter of a weak constitution, perhaps?"

Isaac's smile looked forced. "I invite you to try one sometime, my lord."

Lord Finchley's eyes flashed with a challenge. "Where might I find one?"

"I believe Lord Blackstone has more in his cellars." Isaac stood, towering over them all. He seemed eager to escape, and Sophia couldn't blame him. He bowed in Lord Finchley's direction. "Thank you for the invitation, but I must take my leave. I wish you all a good day."

To his credit, Lord Finchley stood, returning the gesture. Sophia barely caught a glimpse at Isaac's expression before he turned, making his way back to the house.

"I should have to speak with your stepfather about obtaining a cashew." Lord Finchley's voice tore Sophia's gaze away from Isaac's back.

"No—my lord, I-I would not advise that."

His pale eyebrows drew together. He held perfectly still and statuesque, the edge of his jaw tightening with determination. "I have been told I have a robust constitution. Surely I would not be put out of sorts as Mr. Ellington was."

"It isn't worth the risk." Sophia exchanged a glance with Prudence. This sudden competition between the two men was unsettling. Lord Finchley seemed determined to prove his superiority in every way possible.

When Isaac was out of sight, Sophia's shoulders relaxed, and her heart resumed its normal rhythm. The picnic would be over soon, and she could return home to sort out her emotions. The food was gone, and so were two of the guests. Surely Lord Finchley would put an end to the event soon enough.

But the moment the thought crossed her mind, he leaned forward with an eager smile. "So. Shall we see which one of you knows *me* best?"

Chapter Eleven

Isaac sank into a deep leather chair in the library, a stack of books on the table beside him. He had plucked a few from the shelves that seemed interesting, but he doubted he would be able to relax for long enough to read them. What he needed was a book about how forget a woman, but unfortunately there weren't any such volumes on the shelves at Blackstone's.

Isaac had been avoiding the club for the past several days. Percy would still be furious about Isaac's involvement in the dog scheme at the picnic, so Isaac wasn't eager to face him. Hiding in the library might have been the coward's way, but it was better than making a scene in front of all the other club members. Isaac had been avoiding any social invitations ever since the picnic, but the walls of his own home had started to feel like a cage. The more time he spent alone, the more he thought about Sophia.

His thoughts had grown dangerous, and his feelings even more so. He longed to see her. He had stopped himself from calling upon her multiple times. When they had played Mrs. Liddle's game at the picnic, Isaac had revealed the depth of his connection to Sophia to everyone, and it had clearly made her uncomfortable. All he had wanted was to outperform Lord Finchley, who seemed to hardly know her at all.

It infuriated Isaac, yet he felt helpless to interfere.

He had sensed that Sophia still cared for him, but what if he tried to pursue her again and she rejected him? The thought made his heart sting. He couldn't allow the same woman to destroy him a second time. The moment he tried to win her over, he would be handing her the power to break him.

Was it his pride that was holding him back? Or his fear?

Isaac looked up when the library door opened. He was always startled to see the stuffed bear tucked behind it, teeth still bared in a snarl.

A man stepped through the open doorway with a book in hand, perhaps one he had borrowed from the shelves. Isaac reached for one of his own books, opening it swiftly on the table. Up until that moment, he had been lost in thought, staring into open space like one of the glassy-eyed creatures in the room.

With his book situated, Isaac glanced at the man again, immediately recognizing his dark blond hair and tall stature. It was Mr. Henry Branok. The week before, Isaac had joined him and two other gentlemen for a game in one of the card rooms. Mr. Branok smiled when he noticed Isaac, changing his course in the direction of the table. "Mr. Ellington."

"Mr. Branok." Isaac smiled in return. "I trust you've recovered from our game last week?"

He laughed. "You know I'll never recover from losing to Mr. Jenkinson."

"Nor will I," Isaac said with a chuckle.

Mr. Branok eyed Isaac's stack of books. "What has provoked this deep study?" He didn't bother to hide his amusement.

Isaac knew how strange he must have looked sitting alone with his pile of books, but he was glad it was Mr. Branok of all people who had caught him. The man couldn't judge him too harshly. As an esteemed naturalist, Mr. Branok had traveled the world to gather information for books of his own. Surely he had found himself with similar piles of literature in front of him—but not for the same reasons Isaac had.

He didn't know how else to distract himself from his constant worries about Sophia and Lord Finchley, Prudence and Percy, and his Blackstone's membership that still seemed to be hanging by a thread. Lord Blackstone liked him and felt indebted to him after nearly killing him with the cashew, but that didn't mean he wouldn't cut him out of the club if he ever noticed Isaac's feelings for Sophia. And Isaac liked Blackstone's. He liked being interrupted by a gentleman like Mr. Branok and not being left alone in his own library to think himself into madness.

"It's not a deep study at all," Isaac said. He pushed the books aside with a sigh. "I can't seem to focus on reading today. My mind has been overrun with other matters."

Mr. Branok set his own book down on the table. "Anything you'd like to sort out? The quality of my advice may be lacking, but I have no shortage of it." He smiled.

Isaac wouldn't know where to begin, and he certainly didn't want to overburden a near stranger with his emotions. He conjured up a smile, shaking his head. "Thank you, but I'm afraid there isn't a way to sort this out."

Mr. Branok's face twisted into a scowl. "That sounds like surrender."

"Perhaps it is." Isaac shrugged.

"You don't seem like the sort of man to do that. At least not by the way you played against Mr. Jenkinson." Mr. Branok grinned. "Think of how much worse you would have felt losing to him if you had simply given up."

Isaac couldn't help but laugh. Mr. Jenkinson was a worthy adversary at cards, though Isaac had misjudged him because of his age. At nineteen, he had proven himself to be more strategic and quick-witted than any of the older men at the table.

Isaac stared into the distance in thought, nearly forgetting that he had company. He had battled Lord Finchley at the picnic, but then he had retreated, attempting to bury his feelings for Sophia rather than face them. What if there was a chance that she regretted not marrying him four years before? What if he had a chance to win her back? By staying away, was he handing Lord Finchley the victory?

He would never know if he didn't try.

Isaac had spent the last few days strapping on his armor, hunkering down in a shelter, and waiting for the blows to come. He had dropped his weapons because he was afraid of being hurt. His options were to fight for Sophia, and end up wounded, or to lay down on the ground and be wounded anyway. He might be stabbed either way, but he would much rather be stabbed with a sword in his hand.

Isaac shook himself of his thoughts. "Forgive me, Mr. Branok. I'm a bit distracted today."

The man picked up his book from the table. "No matter at all. I'll leave you to it." He gave Isaac an encouraging smile before taking his book to one of the library shelves.

"Good day, Mr. Branok." Isaac barely managed to blurt the words out as the man left the room. His head was still spinning.

He leaned back in his chair, stretching his legs out in front of him. The longer he waited to do something, the more likely he was to lose. Mr. Branok was right—he couldn't surrender. He wasn't certain how to approach his new challenge, but he was certain of one thing: Sophia didn't love Lord Finchley. She tolerated him, at best. If Isaac played his cards right, he might be able to convince her that he could make her happier than any earl ever could.

Lord Blackstone's stipulations were an obstacle, to be sure, but Isaac would give up his membership at Blackstone's for the woman he had always loved. He would give up everything—even his pride. The realization lit a fire inside his chest. He let it consume him, until he felt strangely empowered.

Leaving his stack of books for another day, Isaac made his way out of the library, through the open foyer, and down the stairs. His mood had lightened, though he still wasn't entirely certain what his next move was. He couldn't knock down Sophia's door—which was also *Lord Blackstone's* door—and propose to her. He would need to tread carefully. If he was observant enough, he might be able to read the odds of his success through his interactions with her. He might be able to gather a little bit of hope.

When he reached the entrance hall, he retrieved his hat and coat. And then the voice he had least wanted to hear grated past his ears.

"Leaving so soon, cousin?"

Isaac turned, one arm already in his sleeve. Percy stood near the exit of the drawing room, dark eyes flashing with anger. He masked the expression with a smile, but it was as fake as the stark white teeth of the stuffed bear in the library.

"I've been here most of the afternoon." Isaac kept his voice polite. "I have business to attend to." He put his other arm in his coat, tugging it over his body.

"Not so quickly." Percy strode forward. His smile fell, and his brows lowered. "I wondered if you would care to explain why you attempted to poison Miss Prudence against me."

Isaac frowned. "Are you referring to me telling her the truth about your dislike of dogs?"

"It was an unnecessary truth to tell."

Isaac turned to face his cousin with a serious look. "All truth should be necessary, Percy. Especially if you hope to marry her. Miss Hale was concerned about your motivations for courting her sister, and it was warranted. You admitted to me that you would only marry Prudence for Lanveneth House. As such, I feel it my duty to protect her from your dishonorable intentions. She thinks you love her."

"And she will continue to think that." Percy's features relaxed to an unsettling state of calm. "I am going to pour out my heart to her when I propose, and she will be unable to refuse. I already have Lord Blackstone's permission. I spoke with him today in his study."

Isaac's stomach wrenched with dread. "I doubt she'll accept you after you displayed such violence toward those dogs."

"Prudence Hale is a foolish young girl. A few complimentary words, and she will be smitten again." Percy's mouth formed a sardonic smile. "If you hadn't left Grandfather's estate to ruin, we might have been neighbors."

"It isn't in ruin." Isaac's vexation rose. "I have a capable steward who manages it well. The land is still profitable."

"Profitable, indeed."

Isaac detected the mockery in his voice, and it stoked a fresh surge of anger. "Prudence will not accept your proposal. Sophia and I will make sure of it."

"Time will tell." Percy doffed his hat with a gloating smile, and then strode out the front door without another word.

Isaac exhaled his frustration. Guilt gnawed at his heart, making his old wounds raw again. Losing Grandfather had been one of the most painful times of his life, and after what had happened with Sophia, Isaac had decided that it was best to leave Cornwall in the past. He couldn't think of Morvoren, or Cornwall, or the sea thrift and sunrises without thinking of all that he had lost. How could Percy hold that against him? Was it his jealousy that had driven him to pursue Prudence in the first place? If Percy had been the one to inherit Morvoren, then this rivalry would never have begun. Prudence would be safe, and Isaac wouldn't feel guilty for leaving the estate behind.

When Isaac closed his eyes, he could still see Grandfather at the base of the stairs, breathing but no longer there. He had vanished in an instant, just like Sophia. Isaac could never live within the walls of Morvoren without hearing Grandfather's rambunctious laughter and creaking footfalls as he fetched his midnight cup of tea. He could never take the cliffside walk he had taken so many times with Sophia without deepening the cracks in his heart. That was why he had left it all behind. Surely Grandfather would understand.

Isaac shook the dismal thoughts from his mind. He couldn't allow Percy to unsettle him, not at such a crucial time. If Percy was telling the truth, he planned to propose to Prudence soon. Time was running out.

He glanced at the door, gathering up his courage. He had

to warn Sophia about Percy's plans to propose. If Lord Blackstone was here at the club, then there was no better time to call upon her.

Chapter Twelve

Sophia's fingers moved swiftly over the keys of the pianoforte, racing through what was supposed to be a thoughtful, slow melody. She had told herself she would play it five times before ending her practice for the day. Her chest felt hollow, her mind numb. She no longer had to focus on the notes in front of her. She had memorized where her hands should go, and they moved precisely as they were trained to. The performance was flawless, if not a little dull. She had always been able to hear a pianist's heart in their music, but hers was not here today. It was far away.

She pounded the keys harder as she finished the song. At least her performance wasn't lacking enthusiasm. She had forced her frustrations out onto the keys, and when the song ended, the drawing room was heavy with silence. The monotony of London, of attending balls and theaters and galleries, of walking each day in Hyde Park, of being on her best behavior—it was all exhausting.

Stepfather asked her each evening if Lord Finchley had

called upon her that day, and how their interactions had gone. She knew that he was writing to Mama to inform her that her eldest daughter might soon be saved from potential spinsterhood by an earl. But despite how hard Sophia had worked to reach this point, she felt nothing but dread in her chest. Isaac would ruin everything for her, just as he had the first time. He had already made Lord Finchley look like a pickled eel. How could she spend the rest of her life with a pickled eel?

She leaned her head forward until it rested on the keys. If Lord Finchley would finally propose, she could be done with all of this. If she was engaged, and her wedding was planned, then her heart might finally stop whispering nonsense in her ears.

"Miss Hale?" A footman stood in the open doorway, making her jump. "Mr. Ellington is here. Shall I send him in?"

She scrambled out from behind the pianoforte, smoothing the wrinkles from her lavender skirts. Her heart raced. "Which Mr. Ellington?"

"Mr. Isaac Ellington."

"Oh." Her stomach twisted with nerves, and her body reacted by sending a burst of heat to the back of her neck. Why did she allow him to make her so blasted nervous? She examined the room, quickly adjusting a tasseled pillow. She straightened her posture with a quick nod. "Yes, do send him in."

The footman disappeared but was quickly replaced with Isaac in the doorway. She hadn't seen him since the day of the picnic. In her mind, she had expected all of their interactions to be in public, at gatherings that they both happened to attend. But now he was here, at her house...and they were certainly not in public.

Aunt Hester and Prudence had taken a trip to the modiste, and Stepfather was somewhere else in Town. Sophia had been looking forward to a quiet afternoon of painting before dinner, but now Isaac had delayed her. He smiled as he met her gaze. Her disobedient heart leaped.

"Mr. Ellington." She lowered her gaze as she declined her head.

His long strides carried him into the room, and he stopped a few feet away with a bow. "Sophia."

She looked up, her heart leaping at the sound of her name. He had always been *Isaac* in her mind, but never aloud. Never. The last time she had lowered her guard enough to call him that, she had grown far too close to him. She chose to ignore his choice of address. "What brings you here?"

He was silent for a moment, his coffee-brown eyes studying her. She felt completely vulnerable, her heart in her throat. He had no idea that she had spent the better part of the past few days thinking of him and wishing to see him again.

And despising herself for it.

"We never had the chance to discuss the progress of our sabotage." His lips curved in a genuine smile, and the sight sent a flutter through her stomach.

She cast him a curious look. "I thought you didn't want to call it that."

"After speaking with my cousin today, I'm no longer opposed."

"What happened?"

Isaac glanced around the room, walking toward a portrait

of the previous Lord and Lady Blackstone, Stepfather's parents. He studied the portrait as he spoke, hands interlocked behind his back. "First, Percy confronted me for my part in revealing his hatred of dogs, and then he seemed certain that Prudence would forgive him. Do you think that's true?"

Sophia took a few tentative steps forward, joining him in front of the portrait. "She was distraught for a day, but then she began justifying his behavior. She is always so determined to see the good in everyone and forget the bad." She sighed. "I don't think what we've done is enough. I think she would still readily accept his proposal."

Isaac's features turned grim. "He already obtained permission from Blackstone."

Sophia's brows shot up. "When does he plan to propose?"

"I don't know. Soon."

A heavy sense of dread accompanied his words. As of that morning, Prudence had already seemed bewitched by Mr. Ellington again, claiming that Flora and Thistle were charming enough to win his affection and change his mind about animals. Sophia had tried to convince her not to overlook his folly, but she, of course, hadn't listened.

"Are you attending Lady Strathmore's ball tomorrow evening?" Sophia asked.

Isaac hesitated. "I did receive an invitation."

"Will you attend? Percy might be planning his proposal for the ball."

A crease appeared in Isaac's brow. "I didn't consider that. Can you think of anything that might ensure Prudence rejects his proposal?"

"No." Sophia shook her head in frustration. "Nothing I say can convince her."

"What if she were to overhear Percy confessing his intentions." Isaac drew a step closer, lowering his voice. "If she heard him say that he doesn't love her…"

"Then she would have no choice but to believe it." Sophia's heart pounded. It was a cruel fate for Prudence, but much better than being trapped in a marriage with Mr. Ellington. If they were to become engaged, breaking them apart would be even more difficult. Tomorrow could be their final opportunity.

"That may be what it takes to convince her," Isaac said in a quiet voice. "To be told in certain terms that she is not loved may be the only way to close her heart to him forever."

"Yes. In most cases, that will be enough." Sophia dropped her gaze to his cravat. His eyes were too intent as they looked into hers. The drawing room was too quiet, and the house was too empty.

Isaac moved down the line of paintings. He stopped in front of the one she had hoped he would miss. His gaze flickered over the landscape. She crept up beside him, feeling suddenly self-conscious.

"I remember this." He turned to look at her. "I was there when you painted it."

Sophia followed his gaze back to the landscape she had painted of the cove by Lanveneth. She could practically see the movement of the wind in the sea thrift and in the white tips of the waves below. Stepfather had found the painting amongst her belongings they had moved to his estate in Norwich. Sophia hadn't looked at the painting in years, so she didn't mind when he insisted that it be displayed at his London house.

The painting had taken her weeks to complete, but Isaac

had joined her for each session, waiting patiently as she worked.

"It's even more remarkable than I remembered." His sincere gaze met hers before he went back to admiring the painting. "It's breathtaking, truly."

"That's enough," she said with a quiet laugh.

His mouth twitched into a smile as he shook his head. "I could stare at it all day."

"Well, it won't be here for long. I've offered it up to Lady Strathmore's charity auction next week."

Isaac paused for a few seconds. "Hmm. I shall purchase it, then."

"No." Sophia jumped in front of him, shaking her head with a laugh. "There shall be no need for that." Her heart thudded when she realized how close he stood. She had trapped herself between Isaac and the wall, and she wasn't even tall enough to block the painting from his view. But that didn't matter. He was no longer looking at it.

"I think you misunderstand." Isaac's gaze moved over her face, dragging slowly across each of her features. "I need that painting."

Sophia laughed, but her heart was in her throat. "Why?" her voice cracked.

"It reminds me of that summer." A melancholy smile touched his lips, and his eyes grew softer. "Of what once was."

Her breathing stalled, and a wave of heat assailed her cheeks. It wasn't so much the words, but the longing in his eyes that unnerved her. "I thought we agreed not to speak of that."

"But we never agreed not to think of it." His features were serious as he placed one hand on the wall to the left of

Sophia's shoulder. She could easily remember the last time he stood this close to her.

It had been their last kiss.

They had stood on the cliffs, his mouth on hers, his hands on her waist and in her hair, his arms wrapping around her until there was no space left. How had they once been so close? Being near to him felt forbidden now, like an ancient rule she was breaking. Her heart had enforced that rule to keep her safe, yet she could hardly recall a moment that she had felt safer than in Isaac's arms. Her heart thudded as she held his gaze.

"Do you think of it often?" The question spilled out of her mouth. She was too curious.

"Much more often than I should." His low voice sent a shiver across her neck and spine. A burst of butterflies swarmed through her stomach. She couldn't move. She was tethered to the wall, somehow trapped by his hand against it, and completely immobilized by his gaze. The rules her heart had given her were growing fainter, dragged down by the raw emotion thrumming under her skin. If she had known that being alone with Isaac would be so dangerous, she would have told the footman to lock the door before he could come inside. Until today, Isaac had been keeping his distance. But that no longer seemed to be his intention.

In fact, he seemed intent to do the opposite.

His gaze settled on her lips, and she felt tugged toward him, despite neither of them moving an inch. He smelled of fresh paper and leather, like an old library, but with a hint of sweetness that made her head spin.

The drawing room door unlatched without warning. Isaac lowered his hand from the wall just as Stepfather walked into the room. Isaac's body partially blocked him from Sophia's view, but she caught the surprise that flashed over his features.

His wiry grey brows lifted. "Mr. Ellington?"

Isaac took a step away from Sophia. Her back still grazed the wall, and she had no doubt that her cheeks were as red as a raspberry.

Stepfather blinked a few times in silence, the wrinkles of his forehead deepening one at a time. "What on earth are you doing here?" His voice was sodden with suspicion as his gaze darted between Isaac and Sophia.

Isaac cleared his throat. "I came to inquire after Miss Hale's health." He stiffened after the words escaped him, as if he realized how ridiculous the excuse was.

"Her health?" Stepfather's large eyes narrowed slightly. "And what was the cause of this sudden concern?"

"Her demeanor." Isaac pressed his lips together. "The last time I saw her…her demeanor was rather grim. I thought she might be out of sorts."

Sophia stepped forward, offering a bright smile in an attempt to diffuse the tension. "It was very kind of Mr. Ellington to be concerned. My demeanor today is much improved, is it not?"

Isaac turned to face her, and she nearly burst into laughter at the look of panic on his face. "Yes. I was pleased to find that her demeanor is entirely ordinary today." His lips twitched, but he corrected the expression before facing her stepfather again.

Lord Blackstone's demeanor, however, was not ordinary at all. It was rarely anything but cheerful, so Sophia was surprised to find him so unamused. "Well, then, if you are content with your findings, Mr. Ellington, then you may be on your way." His expression was stiff.

"Thank you, my lord." Isaac bowed before starting for the door. It closed behind him, and not a moment later, Stepfather's brow collapsed into an unreserved scowl. He stared at the door for several seconds.

"I trust you had a good day, Stepfather?" Sophia asked in a cheerful tone. If she could change the subject quickly enough, then he might stop fretting about Isaac. She might stop fretting as well. Her pulse was still elevated, her mind racing. "Will you be attending Lady Strathmore's ball with us tomorrow evening?"

Stepfather finally turned his attention to Sophia, but his scowl remained. "Where is Mrs. Liddle? And your sister?"

Sophia exhaled sharply. Her efforts to distract him never worked unless she brought up one of his animals. "At the modiste having alterations made to Prudence's gown. For the ball. Tomorrow evening. Will you be attending?"

Stepfather frowned. "How long were you alone with Mr. Ellington?"

Sophia sighed. "Not long. It is no cause for concern."

"He was standing quite close to you." Stepfather's gaze shifted to the wall where she had just been standing moments before. "I am quite observant enough to recognize a romantic endeavor when I see one."

"A *what?*" Sophia never wished to hear those words from her stepfather ever again.

"You mustn't allow Mr. Ellington to woo you, my dear. Finchley would be quite discomposed if he were to hear that you were dividing your attention between him and another gentleman."

"My attention is not divided, Stepfather." Sophia walked closer. "I fully intend to marry Lord Finchley…if he were ever to ask."

He examined her face for a long moment before exhaling slowly. "Well, I don't know what is taking him so long. Perhaps he does need a bit of competition to force him into action. In the wild, males must compete with multiple adversaries for the opportunity to..." he paused "...become further acquainted with their chosen female."

Sophia grimaced. "Lord Finchley does not have competition. There is no cause for concern."

He didn't look entirely convinced, but he relented for now. "Very well."

"Did Mr. Percy Ellington speak with you this afternoon?" Sophia blurted.

"He did, indeed." A grin of endearment overtook his face. "Now *that* is a man who is quite irreversibly in love. He has made up his mind to marry your sister, but you mustn't tell her. She would much rather be surprised, I should think."

"Why did you approve the match?" Sophia couldn't hide the frustration from her voice. "I told you that I was suspicious of his intentions. Mr. Isaac Ellington has even confirmed that Percy is only interested in Prudence for her inheritance."

"For Lanveneth?" Lord Blackstone planted his hands on his hips. "There are much wealthier heiresses in Town whom Mr. Ellington could have pursued. It seems a great deal of effort to waste on an old house like Lanveneth."

"I don't know why he is so determined, but you must believe me. If Prudence knew the truth, she would be heartbroken. He is not to be trusted. He doesn't even like animals!"

Stepfather's mouth turned downward. "Of course he does. He has undertaken extensive research on the great horned owl, in fact, and has displayed the deepest respect for all living creatures on multiple occasions."

Sophia sat down heavily on the sofa, covering her face with her hands. "He is *pretending*, Stepfather! He is fooling you, and he is fooling Prudence." She peeked at him through her fingers. Stepfather was a wise man, but he was optimistic to a fault. He had a club filled with men who had been banished from other clubs for a reason, yet he treated them all like specimens in his collection, prized and carefully curated for his enjoyment. Having been widowed for many years before meeting Sophia's mother, and with no children of his own, it seemed to have been his way of coping with his loneliness. Even as he stared at Sophia now, his dismayed eyes were innocent—filled with hope that she was wrong about his precious Percy Ellington.

She was reminded of her late father, and how rarely he would listen to her. He had hardly spared her a moment of his time, and when he did, it was only to offer some form of instruction or advice about her manners or conduct. Sophia had always felt that he favored Prudence, but she had never understood the reason. Perhaps he had more hope for her success at marriage, or perhaps Sophia simply hadn't tried hard enough to know him. He had grown distant from her in the years before his death, and when he was gone, Sophia had been surprised by the lack of empty space he left behind in her heart.

With a sigh, Stepfather sank into the cushion beside Sophia. His wrinkled hand covered her forearm. "If it will put you at ease, I shall speak with Percy Ellington about his intentions at the ball. I am an excellent judge of character, you know."

Sophia gave him a grateful smile, though his words hadn't

given her a great deal of comfort. Her gaze drifted to her painting of Cornwall, and she was reminded of Isaac's visit.

What would have happened if Stepfather hadn't burst into the room?

She didn't dare think of it. She had been seconds away from doing something foolish and irreversible. She couldn't make the same mistake again.

Chapter Thirteen

The air smelled of rose perfume and beeswax candles. Violins carried most of the tune that drifted from the ballroom of Lord and Lady Strathmore's London townhouse, which was bathed in warm light and filled to the brim with guests. Isaac stepped through the ballroom doors. With Percy at odds with him, he no longer had anyone to lean on at events like this. There was no one more socially apt or charming to hide behind. Isaac was on his own.

He searched the crowd for Sophia. His height allowed him a clear view above most of the heads in the room, so it didn't take long for him to find Sophia's golden-brown curls. Her hair was piled atop her head in an elegant arrangement, a few pearl pins mixed amongst the strands. Her ivory evening gown wrapped snugly around her figure, draping down to an embroidered hem that barely kissed the floor as she walked. Her skin glowed in the candlelight, and he couldn't look away.

When he had called upon her the day before, he hadn't

expected Lord Blackstone to return home from the club so soon. The viscount's disapproval had been obvious, but his suspicions had certainly been valid. Isaac had been deeply considering kissing Sophia, right there in Lord Blackstone's drawing room. It might have been in his imagination, but she hadn't seemed likely to object.

He scanned the crowd for Finchley, relieved to find no sign of those rigid blond curls. Tonight, Isaac had two objectives. First, he was going to keep Percy away from Prudence and coax a confession out of him, and second, he was going to dance with Sophia. Both tasks were daunting, but he had to start somewhere.

Weaving his way through the crowd, he made his way to Sophia's side. Her lips lifted in a smile as he approached. His heart lurched within him. She was far too beautiful tonight. Mrs. Liddle stood beside her, with Prudence just a few feet away. Lord Blackstone was surely somewhere in the ballroom, so Isaac would have to be quick.

"Miss Hale." He bowed, meeting Sophia's gaze. She looked nervous, her gloved fingers clinging to the sides of her gown.

"Mr. Ellington." She curtsied.

He had planned his words carefully, but now they lodged in his throat. He took a deep breath. "I wondered if I might claim your first dance."

Sophia's eyes rounded, her lashes quickly hiding them from view. "You may." The reply was hesitant—cautious.

"I am determined to change your mind about dancing."

She looked up at him with a grin. Her dimples left two deep impressions in her cheeks. "I don't hate it quite as much as everyone seems to think."

"After dancing with me, you might not hate it at all." Isaac had been careful about his attempts at flirting the day before, but if this was his only chance to see her without Lord Finchley lurking about, he would have to make the most of it.

Her throat shifted with a swallow. "I warned you that it doesn't come easily to me. It is more likely that dancing with me will make *you* hate it."

Isaac laughed and shook his head. His heart hammered, and he almost didn't say what was on his mind. He gathered his courage, meeting her clear blue eyes with all the sincerity he felt. "I have wanted to dance with you for the past four years. There is nothing you could do to ruin it."

Her cheeks flushed a soft shade of pink. Did dancing with Lord Finchley make her blush? *Unlikely.* Isaac clung to that drop of hope as tightly as he could.

Sophia's eyes shifted at everything but him, as if she were searching for a new subject. "Has Percy arrived yet?"

"He is usually late. But I haven't forgotten our plan."

Sophia nodded, tucking a curl behind her ear. "I have been nervous all day."

"I did notice a change in your demeanor."

A laugh escaped her. Isaac's smile spread wider. Why did it suddenly feel like they could converse normally again—the way they used to? He had never dared to dream of speaking so freely with her again. His guard was lowered, and it seemed that hers was, too. "My demeanor does have a way of causing me trouble," she said in a thoughtful voice.

"I may need to call upon you tomorrow to inquire after its improvement."

Sophia laughed, but quickly shook her head. "I would not advise that." She glanced behind her at the same moment

Lord Blackstone sprung up beside them. Isaac had never seen him move with such swift agility.

"Mr. Ellington, good evening." The viscount seemed in better spirits than he had been the day before after stumbling upon Isaac with Sophia in the drawing room. The man did seem more reserved than usual though—and more than a little suspicious.

"Good evening, my lord." Isaac offered his friendliest smile.

"Where is your cousin?" Lord Blackstone asked. "I have yet to see him arrive."

"I haven't seen him either, but I will be sure to inform you of his whereabouts as soon as I'm aware."

Lord Blackstone grunted in approval, but Isaac could feel his glassy eyes examining him. All the man needed was a magnifying glass and Isaac would feel like an insect pinned to a board. The viscount positioned himself directly between Isaac and Sophia, and he seemed to be completely unaffected by the awkwardness he had created. His lips were spread thin over a frozen smile, but a warning flashed behind his eyes.

Across the ballroom, couples had begun moving into formation for the first dance. Isaac took one large step to the right until he could see Sophia's face again. "Shall we?" He extended his arm, half expecting Lord Blackstone to intercept him.

Sophia's hand brushed lightly over his sleeve, but then her fingers tightened, anchoring them together as they slipped past the viscount. As soon as they were a safe distance from him, Sophia laughed under her breath. "Please forgive my stepfather."

Isaac stood across from her as they waited for the music

to begin. "At first I thought he liked me, but now I'm not so certain."

"Perhaps he was put off by your weak constitution." Sophia's eyes danced with amusement. Isaac would have been offended, but he was too pleased with the fact that she was teasing him.

The first notes of the song began, and they stepped together. Her hand settled into his, and he felt the impression of each of her fingers on his palm. Even through her gloves, her touch sent a shock through his body.

"My weak constitution has a way of causing me trouble," he whispered with a smile.

Sophia's laughter settled deep inside his chest, burrowing into his heart. She didn't seem nearly as nervous to be dancing as she had when he had first asked her. They turned in a slow circle, her forearm draping over his, their palms pressed together. It was funny that Sophia thought she was a poor dancer. She moved with more grace than any other lady in the room. But perhaps he was a little blinded.

"He was spooked by your visit to our drawing room yesterday," Sophia explained. "He knows that I'm courting Lord Finchley, but now he has it in his mind that you're trying to interfere."

The steps of the dance took Sophia down the line, so Isaac had to wait to reply. He was grateful, because he needed time to think about how bold he was going to be.

They reunited after several long measures. Isaac's pulse thrummed against his cravat. Sophia's lips pressed together in concentration as she stepped toward him, took his hand, and turned in time with all the other ladies. As her ear passed by his lips, Isaac asked, "do you want me to interfere?"

Sophia turned too quickly, her eyes flying up to his.

Isaac's stomach twisted with dread. He had been too bold. However, he found that he didn't care. He had nothing to lose by making his intentions clear. If she rejected him again, it couldn't possibly hurt more than it had the first time.

Her eyes fell away from his, and she missed the last step of the dance. The music faded. Sophia searched his face as they offered their obligatory bows. Time was running out for her reply, but she seemed frozen by his words. Her lips parted, but no sound came out. A crease formed in her brow.

Isaac took a step back as the couples dispersed. This was not the time or place to demand any answers from her. He had clearly made her uncomfortable. The confidence he had been feeling was swiftly fading.

Suddenly, Sophia's face fell. She reached for Isaac's arm, lowering her voice to a whisper. "You must ask Prudence for her next dance. Percy is at the door."

Isaac turned, catching sight of his cousin's black hair and matching jacket, a snowy white cravat climbing toward the base of his jaw. Isaac had completely forgotten his other objective. Percy sauntered a few paces into the room, nose lifted as he surveyed the crowd. Isaac had only few seconds to act before Percy spotted his target.

Sophia started toward the perimeter of the room. She seemed eager to escape Isaac's side. The realization drove a thorn through his heart, the dull ache radiating through his entire chest. *Devil take it*, he shouldn't have revealed his intentions so soon. Not only had he spooked Lord Blackstone, but now he had spooked Sophia too.

He pushed aside his worries and started toward Prudence and Mrs. Liddle. Percy was already on the move, weaving through the crowd in their direction. Isaac cleared his throat as he stepped up beside them. "Miss Prudence, may I have the honor of your next two dances?" He hadn't meant to sound so abrupt, but he had panicked.

Prudence had never been skilled at hiding her surprise. She cast Mrs. Liddle a sidelong glance. "Y-yes, you may?"

Isaac smiled and bowed, which only seemed to confuse her further. Sophia watched from a few feet away.

And so did her stepfather.

"Did he say *two* dances?" Isaac heard Lord Blackstone mutter.

"I believe he did," Sophia replied.

The viscount's face twitched into a frown, and he trained his eyes on Isaac with obvious dismay. There was no telling what the man was thinking, but it likely had something to do with Isaac's immediate dismissal from Blackstone's. Dancing with his stepdaughters hadn't been against the rules, but Isaac's actions could easily be interpreted a certain way. Many courtships began in ballrooms, especially when more than one dance was shared between partners.

Isaac sensed Percy behind him, but he continued to block his path. Now Isaac was the one standing awkwardly between two people—and it was not as effortless as Lord Blackstone had made it appear.

Prudence flicked a dark curl out of her eyes, biting her lower lip as she tried to crane her neck around Isaac's shoulder to catch a glimpse of Percy. He managed to step around Isaac, coming to an abrupt halt in front of Prudence and Mrs. Liddle.

"May I request the privilege of your next dance?"

Prudence gave him a rueful look. "Your cousin has already claimed it."

His smile faltered. "The next one, then."

Prudence shook her head subtly. Her gaze shifted to Isaac. "That one is also spoken for."

Isaac could practically feel Percy's eyes raking over him, sharp and accusatory.

"Ah, there you are, Mr. Ellington." Lord Blackstone strode forward. "I have been searching for you for some time now. May I have a word with you in the corridor?"

Percy's nostrils flared in vexation, but he hid it behind a smile. "Yes, of course, my lord."

Lord Blackstone beckoned him forward with a wave, and the two men started toward the door. Isaac exhaled the tension in his shoulders. He had no idea why Lord Blackstone had pulled Percy aside, but their conversation had come at the perfect time.

Isaac tried to catch Sophia's gaze. They had left too much of their plan unorganized. He was supposed to orchestrate a moment for Prudence to overhear Percy's confession, but he wasn't certain when or if the opportune moment would come. At the moment, Isaac was expected to remain in the ballroom to dance the next two sets with Prudence.

With her stepfather gone, Sophia moved toward Isaac and the two women. She didn't seem quite as uncertain as he was. When he caught her mischievous gaze, he felt an instant sense of relief.

She most certainly had a plan.

"My stepfather agreed to confront Percy about his intentions." Her voice barely carried over the sound of the violins. "You might go to the corridor to find them. When the next set is about to begin, I'll lead Prudence out to fetch you for the dance. We will stay out of sight as we listen. He might not confess, but it's worth a try."

Isaac glanced at the door. He didn't like the fact that

Blackstone was involved, but there was no way around it. Isaac had only meant to keep Percy away from Prudence—not to ruin his relationship with the viscount in the process. But hadn't the friendship only been formed because of Percy's dishonesty? He had been using the viscount to grow close to Prudence. His end goal had always been to obtain Lanveneth. It all seemed so elaborate for a man who already had a country house of his own. What would Percy even do with an old Cornish estate?

Isaac put his questions aside as he followed Sophia's instructions, weaving his way through the ballroom and out the door.

Chapter Fourteen

The corridor was dim, but Isaac could hear Lord Blackstone's voice from around the corner.

"I must confess I am relieved to hear it, Mr. Ellington. I didn't want to believe the speculation, but I do trust my dear Sophia's intuition. I had to make an inquiry of my own. I hope you will forgive me for entertaining the idea even for the briefest moment."

Percy's voice came next, confident and unwavering. "I fully understand your duty to protect your stepdaughters. I would do the same."

"And I trust you will protect and love Miss Prudence for the rest of your lives together?"

"With all my heart."

"Excellent. I shall hold you to it." Lord Blackstone's voice grew louder. A shadow of his lopsided hair flickered across the wall as he rounded the corner. Isaac stepped behind a tall table with a bust and vase. In the shadows, it managed to conceal him for long enough for Lord Blackstone to pass.

Percy followed closely behind him on their way to the ballroom.

Isaac gritted his teeth. How was he going to catch Percy alone? He would never confess in front of Blackstone. The man had already believed each and every one of his lies.

Isaac fell into pace behind Percy, his feet soundless on the dense marble floors. As Lord Blackstone stepped into the noise of the ballroom, Isaac lunged forward, gripping Percy by the back of the shoulder.

He whirled around, stopping just outside the threshold. Lord Blackstone plunged into the crowd, shuffling back to where he had left Mrs. Liddle and his stepdaughters on the other side of the room.

"May I have a word?" Isaac asked.

In the shadows, Percy's features were smug, laced with unmasked animosity. He seemed to think he had won already. He jerked his shoulder from Isaac's grasp and straightened his jacket. "I should hate to keep you from your next two dances."

"It will be brief." Isaac caught Sophia's gaze in the space between two ladies as they crossed the room. He was fairly certain she saw him lead Percy back into the corridor.

Isaac drew a deep breath as he stepped around the corner where Lord Blackstone had been conversing with Percy a few minutes before. "I gave you a chance to withdraw your advances on Prudence," he said.

Percy held perfectly still, his mouth curled in distaste. And then he laughed, his eyes flashing with amusement in the dimness. "Do you realize how many marriages come about for reasons other than love? You must stop acting like I'm some great villain for taking advantage of an opportunity."

Isaac held his breath. He needed to keep the conversation on the right course. He didn't know when Sophia would lead her sister out to the corridor, but these were the details she needed to overhear.

"You already have an estate," Isaac said. "I don't understand why you are so determined to obtain Lanveneth. You might at least help me understand."

Percy groaned. "At what point did you begin making my business your own? It is none of your concern."

"You would marry a woman you don't love in order to obtain an old, rotting house on the very edge of England? It seems like madness."

"And that is the beauty of it. Everyone, including Prudence and her stepfather, believe that I am madly in love with her. Because who would want an old house in Cornwall?" His eyes darkened. "You wouldn't."

"Is this about Morvoren?" Isaac took a step toward him.

"Well, you did take it from me." Percy's harsh voice echoed in the corridor. "And now you are trying to take away my chance at obtaining Lanveneth."

"I didn't *take* the house from anyone. Grandfather chose me as his heir."

"Grandfather was a fool."

Isaac wanted to grab Percy by the collar and throw him backwards into the wall, but he managed to keep his arms crossed. "I won't listen to a word you speak against him. He was like a father to me. He was a good man."

Percy laughed. "There's a great deal you don't know about Grandfather. You may have lived with him for the last year of his life, but you never knew him as I did."

The accusation sent a pang of grief through Isaac's chest. "I knew him."

"Not enough." Percy tugged on his cravat, loosening it slightly. "And you obviously didn't love him enough to look after his estate. But that's quite all right. At least your steward is capable."

Isaac hadn't known Percy harbored so much bitterness. It was alarming. "Perhaps Grandfather could see that you were only pretending to love him in order to win his favor and inheritance," Isaac said. "That does seem to be your way of navigating life."

Percy laughed. "Pretending to love Miss Prudence was much easier, I will confess. At least she's an attractive young woman."

"Do you feel any attachment to her at all?"

Percy hesitated for a brief moment. "No. And the moment we move to Lanveneth, those dogs of hers will mysteriously disappear." He laughed under his breath. "Fortunately, she seems to love me more, so I doubt she'll mourn them for long." He lifted his gaze with a triumphant smile. "I hope you don't think that claiming two of her dances will keep me from proposing to her tonight. It was a valiant effort though; I do applaud you." He stepped forward, clapping one hand over Isaac's shoulder. "You ought to return to the ballroom for that dance."

A faint shadow flickered across the wall, and Prudence's tear-streaked face came into view from behind Percy. Sophia held her hand with both of hers, attempting to hold her back.

Percy turned, immediately falling back a step.

Prudence's nostrils flared, her jaw tightening. Her eyes were wild with anger, a steady flow of tears cascading down her cheeks.

Percy's shoulders stiffened, and for what might have been

the first time in his life, he looked overwhelmed. "Prudence—what is the matter, my dear?"

"I never should have trusted you." Her words shook with anger.

"Prudence, my love, you misunderstand."

Her eyes flooded with tears, but her glare cut through them. "No. I understand you perfectly."

Sophia wrapped her hands around Prudence's arm, pulling her back down the corridor. She collapsed into tears as they retreated. Isaac followed them, but Percy was tight on his heels, apparently determined to catch them. When they neared the ballroom, his pace finally slowed. There was nothing Percy could do to explain away all the things he had just said.

He had been caught, and he knew it.

Outside the ballroom doors, Sophia stopped, tugging her sister into a tight hug as she sniffled. Isaac lingered nearby, digging into his jacket for his handkerchief. His heart ached for Prudence. He knew how it felt to have his heart left in pieces without any warning.

Well, Prudence *had* been warned.

Many times.

She ignored Isaac's handkerchief, wiping at her cheeks with her gloved fingers instead.

"Shall I fetch your aunt?" Isaac asked. "The three of you might return home early."

"Yes, thank you." Sophia's eyes connected with his. They had succeeded. It was a difficult matter to celebrate considering how distraught Prudence was, but Isaac caught the gratitude in Sophia's gaze. Prudence was safe. Sophia's arms tightened around her, and she closed her eyes.

In the ballroom, Isaac had only taken a few steps before

Lord Blackstone intercepted him. His exuberance faded into a stern look. "Ah, Mr. Ellington. What opportune timing. I should like a word with you."

"Er—yes, of course." He glanced behind him. "I was actually in search of Mrs. Liddle. Miss Prudence is…out of sorts and wishes to leave. She is waiting in the corridor."

Lord Blackstone's brows drew together. "Why, pray tell, were you in the corridor with Prudence?"

"Her sister is there as well," Isaac blurted.

Lord Blackstone looked perplexed. "Mr. Ellington, if I did not make myself clear enough the first time, allow me to repeat: You are to keep your distance from my stepdaughters. You are not to call upon Sophia as you did yesterday, especially without her chaperone present. You are not to sneak around the corridors with them, and you are not to claim more than one of their dances." With a huffed breath, he started toward the corridor.

Isaac followed him. "Yes, my lord, I understand. But—you misinterpret my intentions."

"I should hope that is true." Lord Blackstone hardly spared him a glance as he made his way out of the ballroom. The moment he saw Prudence, he rushed forward. "What is the matter, my dear?" He peeked around Sophia, bobbing his head like a bird to catch a look at Prudence's face.

Isaac glanced down the dim corridor. Percy was nowhere in sight. Had he left already? He would be wise to avoid making even more of a scene.

When Prudence looked up at her stepfather, her skin was splotched in red, her eyes liquid. "It's Mr. Ellington," she sobbed.

Lord Blackstone froze, his spine straightening like a board. Ever so slowly, he turned, his sharp eyes fixating on

Isaac. He marched a few steps closer. "What have you done to my dear Prudence?"

"The other Mr. Ellington!" Sophia exclaimed.

Lord Blackstone stopped. Isaac towered over him, yet he had seemed prepared to walk straight into him. The viscount's brows twitched upward. "*Percy* Ellington?"

"What other Mr. Ellington is there?" Sophia asked in exasperation.

Lord Blackstone's gaze flickered up to Isaac's face before he darted back to Prudence's side.

Isaac took it upon himself to find Mrs. Liddle, eager as he was to escape Lord Blackstone's accusations. His stomach writhed with discomfort. He hadn't meant to tear Percy away from all his connections at Blackstone's, but once the viscount knew the truth, he would likely revoke his membership. Isaac himself would have to withdraw. It didn't feel right to stay when he was only there because Percy had recommended him.

He could only imagine how much Percy hated him now. Isaac had done what was needed to protect Prudence, but at what cost?

Isaac found Mrs. Liddle on a chair against the wall, a plate of fruit on her lap, squinting at all the dancers behind her spectacles. She quickly abandoned her post to come to Prudence's rescue, and the three women started directly for their carriage.

Isaac was eager to speak with Sophia—to discuss what had happened that evening—but he would have to wait.

With the three of them out the door, the entrance hall was empty, leaving Isaac alone with Lord Blackstone. Music drifted from the ballroom, a slow melody that did little to fill the awkward silence.

"What an eventful evening, indeed," the viscount said finally. His mouth spread into a somber smile. "I must own that I acted quite like a squirrel this evening. I was certain you were after my acorns." He chuckled.

Isaac puzzled over the comparison for a moment. "I'm sorry to have raised your suspicions."

"Yes, well, my senses must not be as sharp as they once were. I thought Mr. Ellington was sincere." His gaze fell. The poor man seemed genuinely betrayed by Percy. He was not the only one.

"Miss Hale was determined to protect her sister from my cousin," Isaac said. "I called upon her yesterday because she asked for my assistance. I meant no harm to your...acorns."

Lord Blackstone smiled. "I trust that you have no intention of courting either of my stepdaughters?"

Isaac thought of his dance with Sophia, when he had asked if she wanted him to interfere with her courtship. She hadn't answered. But her hesitation gave him more hope than if she had answered with a swift *no*.

Lord Blackstone's question still lingered in the air, awaiting an answer.

Isaac gave a resolute nod. "You have my word." It wasn't a lie. Isaac had courted Sophia before, but he had no intention of doing that again.

This time, he intended to marry her.

Chapter Fifteen

The window of Sophia's bedchamber faced the street, so when she was bored—like today—she watched the horses, carriages, and people down below. She had grown accustomed to a view like this, though she much preferred something more beautiful to look at. She had only lived in Cornwall a short time, but the view from her window at Lanveneth had faced the sea. There wasn't a better view in the world than that.

Prudence played the pianoforte downstairs. For the past two days, she had been flooding the house with constant somber tunes. When she wasn't playing music, she was crying, so Sophia was grateful to hear the notes drifting through the house—even if they were a little too melancholy. The music fit Sophia's mood as well, much like the grey sky with its sodden clouds that looked ready to ring out rain all over the crowded square.

Sophia was dreading the events of the day. She had yet to call her maid to arrange her hair. She would be attending Lady Strathmore's art auction with Lord Finchley that day at

Christie's on King's Street. Sophia could hardly believe that her painting of Cornwall hung on the walls of the gallery. She doubted it would attract many bidders, but she was invited to attend. Lord Finchley had arranged to convey her there in his carriage. She couldn't help but think of Prudence's question at the picnic about who she would most like to be trapped in a carriage with in a rainstorm.

Had Lord Finchley somehow predicted the weather?

The sky did look likely to rain, but thankfully Aunt Hester would be in the carriage with them. Sophia should have been happy to see that Lord Finchley was making their courtship public. Instead, it flooded her stomach with nerves.

She had only attended one public event with him before, and it had caused a significant stir of gossip amongst the *ton*. Before becoming Lord Blackstone's stepdaughter, Sophia and her family had been practically unheard of. But now, she was connected to a viscount (one who was known for his oddities) and courting an earl. She was not accustomed to attracting so much attention. It made her vastly uncomfortable.

"Don't be a fool." She looked at her reflection in the window. She had been schooling her heart to obey her, but it was headstrong in its determination to trust Isaac again.

He had helped her save Prudence.

That was no small thing.

He had hinted that he still had feelings for her—that he might have regretted his choice. She thought of their dance, of his hand on her waist, his teasing smile. She was weak, and she hated herself for it. How daft would she feel if she trusted Isaac again, only to be hurt a second time?

She had a perfectly stable courtship underway with Lord

Finchley. It had been progressing perfectly. Giving that up for a wild, nonsensical romance from her youth would be a grave error, indeed. She would end up like Prudence, alternating her hours between crying and playing dreadful tunes on the pianoforte. She had certainly been there before.

So at the auction, she would give Lord Finchley her full attention. She would behave with as much elegance as would be expected of a future countess. She would give society nothing to gossip about besides how lovely a match she would make for the earl.

Her maid helped her into her blue gown trimmed with white lace, taking great care with her hair. Sophia inspected her reflection as her maid pinched her cheeks. She didn't feel fit to be a countess. When she looked at herself in the mirror in recent days, she hadn't been able to envision that future. Despite her neat hair, clear complexion, and well-fitted gown, she felt like an imposter. Her mind had been on the sea, on Isaac, and the freckles that had long since faded from her cheekbones.

~

Lord Finchley rested one hand on the front of his plaid waistcoat as he helped Sophia out of the carriage. "What do you think of the yellow? Do I look like a dandy?"

"Not in the slightest." Sophia gave him a reassuring smile. Her performance was underway already. Even as she set foot on the cobblestones, a group of passing ladies glanced in her direction. One whispered to her companion behind her gloved fingers.

Sophia gulped. Her heart thrummed fast in her chest. Her stays felt tight beneath her gown—tighter than usual. Rain sprinkled lightly from the sky, marking Lord Finchley's tan jacket with dark dots.

"Oh, blast it." He looked toward the sky, hurrying Sophia toward the front door of Christie's. She held his arm, keeping her head held high as they followed the other attendees into the gallery. The contributors to the auction were given reserved seating at the front of the room. Aunt Hester struggled to keep up, but she managed to remain at Sophia's other side as Lord Finchley rushed them toward an empty space on one of the front rows.

Sophia glanced to her left, noting a few familiar faces from the *ton*. An auction like this provided the wealthy an opportunity to be seen as they donated a fraction of their money in exchange for a painting that might adorn their already crowded walls.

Sophia was simply glad to have her painting displayed somewhere besides her own home.

If she hadn't been connected to Lord Blackstone, her art might have never been seen so publicly. Lady Strathmore's interest in the painting was what had led Sophia here. A swirl of nerves entered her stomach. What if no one liked her work? She could already imagine the silence following the auctioneer's voice. It might fetch a few guineas if she was lucky. She straightened her spine, forcing a pleasant smile to her face as she observed the crowd.

Lord Blackstone arrived a few minutes later, taking the seat beside Sophia. "A pleasant day, is it not, Finchley?" He leaned forward with a grin.

"Pleasant, indeed."

Stepfather glanced up at the display of art on the walls in front of them. Sophia's painting was near the bottom, small in comparison to some of the others. It certainly didn't stand out. The auctioneer took his place behind the wooden podium, arranging a few documents in front of him.

"Do you have your eye on anything in particular?" Stepfather asked Lord Finchley.

"I do." His gaze slid in Sophia's direction.

Stepfather looked far too pleased with that answer. He straightened his jacket, crossing his legs in front of him. "Capital."

Did Lord Finchley plan to bid on her painting? It was an obvious way he could publicize his attachment to her. Sitting near the front of the room, with so many onlookers, his display would be sure to draw gossip. If there was any speculation about whether or not he intended to marry her, it would be swiftly silenced. Sophia's throat was dry. Was she prepared for that? She had to be.

The auctioneer lifted one hand, silencing the prattle of the crowd. Sophia stared up at the pastel-green walls, roughly counting at least thirty frames.

Her back ached as she sat for several minutes, politely applauding each time a painting was sold. The average sale was around twenty guineas. Most of the artists were relatively unheard of, though the work was lovely. Sophia's palms began to sweat as the auctioneer read the details of her painting.

"A landscape of Zennor, by Miss Sophia Hale. Shall we open at eight guineas?" The man looked up from his paper, eyes peering into the crowd expectantly.

Sophia held her breath.

Without wasting a moment, Lord Finchley raised his hand. "Ten." He gave a pale smile as his gaze surveyed the rows of people around them.

The murmurs of the crowd were impossible to miss. Sophia felt them from behind, washing over her in waves.

"Fifteen." A deep voice from the back of the room made her freeze. Her heart picked up speed. She didn't dare turn around.

What was Isaac doing here?

She had withheld the details of the auction from him on purpose. She recalled his words in the drawing room. *I need that painting.*

Lord Finchley rotated in his seat. She watched his brows perch lower over his eyes when he noticed who had bid against him. His mouth settled into a firm line. "Twenty," he called out.

"Thirty."

Sophia's face burned. She kept her gaze fixed ahead, but she could sense Lord Finchley's frustration.

Stepfather craned his neck as he turned around. "Is that Mr. Ellington?" His whisper cracked with disbelief.

"Thirty-five," Lord Finchley declared.

"Forty."

There had only been a few paintings to surpass forty so far.

Lord Finchley exhaled sharply, dropping his hands in his lap. He shook his head, muttering something under his breath. "Forty-five."

"Fifty."

The auctioneer's eyebrows lifted, but he was silent as he took the bids. Gasps rippled across every row. Sophia knew that the reaction was less about the price, and more about the war that was waging in front of them. Why would Isaac not stand down?

A bead of perspiration trickled down Lord Finchley's temple. "Fifty-five."

"Sixty." Isaac's voice was calm, as if he would carry on all day. Sophia didn't doubt he would, no matter the attention he was drawing.

"This is absurd," Lord Finchley muttered. He straightened his shoulders, giving a subtle shake of his head.

"Going once, going twice, sold!" The auctioneer made the declaration, but it was barely heard over the murmurs of the crowd. Their whispers clawed over Sophia's skin, making her lightheaded. Polite applause followed, and Lord Finchley leaned toward her.

"If I hadn't given it to him, he never would have stopped. Ridiculous." The air from his harsh whispers brushed past her ear. He glanced behind him, offering a bow in Isaac's direction, though she could tell it pained him to do so.

Sophia's heart raced as she turned. She was the painter, after all. She would be expected to acknowledge the one who had purchased it.

As she had suspected, Isaac was seated near the back, on the very end of a row. His intense eyes connected with hers. She bowed quickly, then turned around. Considering how public her courtship with Lord Finchley had become, Isaac should not have outbid him. There were far too many ways the action could be perceived. There had been an obvious air of competition between the two men, and all the people in the room had witnessed it.

The whispers were fading, but they continued to beat through the air like tiny wings. Stepfather's bewildered look shifted to a disgruntled frown. "What do you make of that, Sophia?" he asked in a quiet voice.

She had no idea.

The auction continued with the final six paintings. Sophia tapped the toe of her boot softly against the floor. Her emotions boiled beneath her skin, such a diverse mixture that she hardly knew what to feel. How dare Isaac steal Lord Finchley's opportunity like that! He had embarrassed him in front of a large crowd of people. He had refused to bow out, even when the crowd had displayed their shock. Her heart beat loudly in her ears as the auction drew to a close and the guests began rising from their seats. She couldn't speak to Isaac here. She couldn't trust herself to act the part she was meant to play.

Lord Finchley shot up from his chair. He turned around, eyes flitting over the crowd like a bird over a field of mice. "Where has Mr. Ellington gone? I'd like to wish him my congratulations." His voice was laced with bitterness.

Sophia surveyed the crowd, but Isaac wasn't in the place she had seen him before. A wave of relief crashed over her. If Lord Finchley were to 'offer his congratulations', there would be far too many people watching the interaction.

Lady Strathmore, who had been sitting on the row in front of Sophia, stepped around the benches. Her husband engaged Lord Finchley in conversation, giving Sophia a moment to breathe. Lady Strathmore's bright turquoise gown was a perfect match for her eyes, which were round with shock. "Miss Hale! Your painting fetched quite a price. I knew it was extraordinary from the moment I first saw it." She gave a coy smile. "Mr. Ellington clearly felt the same."

Sophia's heart sank. There was no mistaking the look on Lady Strathmore's face. She was already making assumptions about a possible attachment. But unlike the others in attendance, she had further evidence. Lady Strathmore had witnessed the cashew incident and how Sophia had rushed to Isaac's aid.

The audience mingled, but many gazes shifted in Sophia's direction. She pretended not to notice the whispers, but her chest was tight with panic. She didn't know whether Lord Finchley's surrender would be viewed as well-mannered or cowardly. People might begin to question the sincerity of his intentions toward her or speculate about Isaac's noble efforts to steal her attention from the earl.

"Cornwall is close to Mr. Ellington's heart," Sophia explained. "I imagine the painting reminded him of his old home."

"I see." Lady Strathmore nodded, but her lips were still pursed in that knowing smile. She would devour any drama she could find, adding ingredients of her own, mixing it into an elaborate delicacy to share with her friends.

Lady Strathmore moved on to a new conversation with Stepfather and Aunt Hester, leaving Sophia on the fringes. She wandered to the front of the gallery for a closer look at all the paintings that had been purchased that day. Her nerves were on edge, and the study of brushstrokes on a canvas was a calm, quiet exercise that usually served to calm her. Her mind refused to stop racing, replaying the events of the auction over and over. She paced down the row, keeping her back turned to the rest of the room.

Rain pattered on the rooftop, adding to the chorus of loud chatter from all the attendees behind her. She had strayed a little too far from Aunt Hester and the others, but it was what she needed to calm her emotions.

A gentleman stepped up to study the painting beside her. Sophia's heart thudded, a prickle of awareness spreading over her skin. It was Isaac. She knew it. His presence beside her had always been different from any other; her senses recognized him without sight or sound. Her body reacted to his nearness with a mixture of alarm and intrigue. She wanted to be angry. *Furious* even, that he had rivaled Lord Finchley so publicly. But the rage she had prepared herself to feel was quickly bottled up by his eyes as they landed on hers.

"What were you thinking?" she whispered. "Lord Finchley accompanied me here. He had plans to purchase the painting."

Isaac looked handsome in his brown jacket, his hair holding a slight wave, falling softly over his forehead. She should not have been noticing such details, but she couldn't help it. Her heart leaped at the intensity of his gaze. "He could have bid higher if he wanted to."

Sophia scowled. "You were making a scene. He bowed out gracefully."

"I knew he would."

A surge of anger made her breath hitch. "You don't know anything about him. You have met him twice."

"I know that you don't love him."

Sophia's mouth snapped closed. Her face flamed. "You may try all you'd like to sabotage our courtship, but it won't work."

He gave a subtle shake of his head. "I'm not trying to sabotage it."

"Is there a more delicate word you'd like to use, then? Disruption? Impairment?" She could feel the heat from her anger spreading up her neck. She kept her gaze forward, hoping that her face was hidden from anyone who might be observing their interaction.

"What I did today could be seen as a disruption, I

FOREVER ENGAGED

suppose." Isaac turned to face her more fully, obviously not caring about the onlookers. "But sabotage...that would involve a more extensive strategy."

She swallowed, her throat suddenly dry. "Well, I would ask that you not engage in such strategies in the future. Especially not in public," she hissed.

"Of course not." His voice was low, barely above a whisper. "I wouldn't dare use this particular strategy in public." His gaze was on her lips, and impossibly, her face burned hotter. She would have expected to see a teasing smile, but he was entirely serious.

Is that all he thought it would take? One kiss and she would be at his disposal, even after he had cast her aside so effortlessly before? He hadn't even apologized or acknowledged what he had done. They had agreed not to speak of the past, but the past was speaking for them. It was thriving, pulsating in the air like a living heart. But Sophia was not as weak as she once was. If Isaac didn't realize that yet, then she would make certain he no longer had any doubt.

She opened her mouth to speak, but her words were stopped by a hand on her arm. She turned, her anger simmering down at the sight of Lord Finchley. He seemed to notice the tension between them, a deep furrow in his brow as his gaze flickered from Isaac to Sophia. "Mr. Ellington, my congratulations." His voice lacked any expression. "I'm afraid I must steal Miss Hale. The carriage is waiting."

A muscle jumped in Isaac's jaw, and he lowered his gaze to the floor. Sophia held tight to Lord Finchley's arm as they walked away. The street was drenched with rain when they stepped outside. Large droplets still fell from the sky, soaking through her hair and leaving her curls limp.

In the carriage, Aunt Hester removed her spectacles,

wiping the raindrops on her skirts. "That Mr. Ellington is quite persistent."

Lord Finchley slid into his seat across from Sophia. The carriage door rattled closed. He hardly said a word the entire drive home, staring out the window with a heated scowl.

When the carriage finally came to a halt, Lord Finchley stepped down from the edge and helped Aunt Hester out first. Sophia made to climb out after her, but Lord Finchley blocked the way. "Please excuse us for a moment, Mrs. Liddle."

Sophia dropped into her seat in surprise as Lord Finchley stepped back into the carriage and closed the door behind him. He breathed deeply through his nose, a sheen of moisture on his forehead as he stared across the seat at Sophia. He blinked rapidly, shifting his gaze to the floor. She had seen him anxious before, but never this discomposed.

"My lord—" Sophia's heart pounded fast.

"Miss Hale." His icy blue eyes snapped up to her face. "I have been awaiting the perfect opportunity to speak with you alone. I think this moment is as good as any." He leaned forward, snatching her hand with both of his. "I have been putting off this question, primarily because of my own resistance to the idea of marriage. However, as you know, I have been considering the possibility of making you my wife. I'm not certain what has compelled me to ask you at this very moment. Perhaps it is the rain, or being alone together in this carriage, but it has awakened a sense of urgency within me that I can no longer ignore."

He pressed a kiss to the back of her hand before regarding her seriously. "Dear Miss Hale, will you marry me?"

Chapter Sixteen

The question hung heavy in the air, coiling around Sophia until she struggled to breathe. Lord Finchley's eyes were wild with anticipation, and his grip on her fingers was starting to hurt.

Panic gripped her muscles, and her voice refused to give him an answer. She hadn't expected him to ask so soon, and certainly not so abruptly. The nature of his proposal was cold, unromantic, and it made her stomach ill. Isaac's display at the auction must have cut Lord Finchley deeply enough to lead him to this rash decision. This seemed to be his way of retaliating.

"You seem to be acting in haste, my lord," Sophia choked out.

He shook his head fast. "No—I assure you, I have been thinking to do this for quite some time. I have been hesitant over a few minor details, but those are truly unimportant when compared to the many strengths of character that you possess."

Sophia frowned. What minor details about her had

caused his hesitation? Knowing how long Lord Finchley had waited to select a wife, he must have been quite particular. But his choice of words made her feel like he had chosen to settle for her. "Minor details?"

He waved a hand through the air. "It is no matter. I have chosen you to be my wife, if you will have me."

The urgent tone of his voice gave her a similar feeling of aversion to when she had seen him cross his legs and curl into a ball on the picnic blanket. Her head swam, and the humidity in the carriage was making her feel faint.

"I do not feel well, my lord. I-I think I should give you my answer when I am less…indisposed." She wriggled her fingers away, reaching for the carriage door. Her breath came quickly, her heart racing with panic within her chest. No man had ever proposed to her before. She hadn't expected to feel so terrified.

"That is understandable." Lord Finchley wiped at his brow, but he made no move to help her out of the carriage. He seemed to have forgotten where he was, his eyes still blinking fast, a twinge of frustration taking over his expression.

He stood too late, hunching under the carriage ceiling as Sophia jumped down from the step on her own. "Good day, my lord," she heard herself mutter. The rain was cold against the heat of her skin, jolting her back to her senses.

Aunt Hester stood nearby, drenched now from head to toe. The poor woman must have felt it her duty to stay and observe, but now she was shivering. Sophia picked up her skirts, rushing toward the front steps of the townhouse, catching her aunt's arm on the way.

Prudence was playing the pianoforte when Sophia and Aunt Hester came crashing through the front door. Sophia peeled away her gloves and bonnet, only then noticing how violently her hands were shaking.

"Heavens, my dear, what is the matter?" Aunt Hester took Sophia by the shoulders.

"He proposed to me."

Her aunt gasped. "You are engaged?"

"No." Sophia bit her lip. "I didn't give him my answer."

Her eyes flew open wide. "Why not?"

"I don't know."

But she did know. It was all Isaac's fault. He had sauntered into that art gallery with one purpose, and that had been to compete with Lord Finchley—to put him on edge—and to show Sophia that he had meant what he said. Isaac had told her that he needed that painting because it reminded him of that summer in Cornwall—of what once was.

Perhaps even because it reminded him of her.

Her heart was on fire, her skin boiling with hot anger. Tears seared her eyes, but she refused to let them fall. Isaac was tormenting her, and as a result, she was now tormenting a respectable man. Lord Finchley was on his way home in the rain, and she had just brutally run away from his proposal. She had spent weeks leading him to believe she would accept it. How could she reverse the damage she had done?

Was it too late?

Sophia turned away from her aunt to blink away her tears. Through the front window, she saw Stepfather's carriage approaching the house. "Please don't tell my stepfather about the proposal. I need only a little time to think."

"I won't breathe a word of it," Aunt Hester promised.

Before Stepfather could reach the house, Sophia rushed

up the stairs, nearly tripping over her wet skirts. She paced the perimeter of her room and shivered, folding her arms tightly across her chest. Perhaps by enlisting Isaac to help her break Percy and Prudence apart, she had taught him the art of sabotage.

And he was far too good at it.

A knock sounded on her door, making her jump. She crossed the room with hesitant steps, opening the door to reveal Stepfather standing in the corridor.

Blast it all.

Aunt Hester stood behind him, pressing a hand to her chest as she struggled to catch her breath. Her sopping wet hair was still clinging to her forehead. She cast Sophia an apologetic look. She appeared to have chased Stepfather up the stairs.

Unfortunately, Lord Blackstone was quick for his age.

He greeted Sophia with a look of concern. Had he already found out about Lord Finchley's proposal? Surely Aunt Hester could keep a secret for more than five minutes. Or could she?

Sophia's heart fell.

"There you are." Stepfather observed her with a growing frown. "I should like to know what you make of Mr. Ellington's behavior at the auction today. That young man seems to raise trouble wherever he walks. Especially pertaining to you." His sharp eyes took her in. "I perceive that there is something more between you than friendship."

"I assure you, there is not." The denial came a little too quickly.

Stepfather still wore a quizzical look. "How did Lord Finchley endure the embarrassment?"

Not well. Not well at all.

"He is confident enough to overlook the ordeal," Sophia said in a dismissive tone.

"Hmm. Very well. But I shall still have another word with Mr. Ellington."

She jolted. "I don't think that should be necessary."

"From what I witnessed today, I do find it necessary. If I am not mistaken, he seems to have set his cap at you. I have tried to discourage him, even threatened his membership at Blackstone's, but he seems quite undeterred."

Sophia scolded herself for the thrill that raced across her skin.

"I found his reputation rather unsettling when it comes to courtship. An indecisive one, he is, frolicking from one muse to another, his heart leaping from place to place like a toad on a pond full of lily pads." Stepfather smacked his lips in dismay. "I am fond of Mr. Ellington as a friend, but I told him he shall never be permitted to court you or your sister."

Sophia's heart dropped. "What makes you certain of this...reputation?"

"He told me himself. I do respect that." Stepfather paused. "But I shall keep my eye on him. If Mr. Percy Ellington could deceive your sister and me, I have no doubt that his cousin is capable of the same." He crossed his arms, his expression marked with an alarming look of determination. He seemed to snap out of it suddenly, patting Sophia on the shoulder with a warm smile. "Let us hope Lord Finchley calls upon you soon. I expect he will make an offer any day now." He winked.

Sooner than you might think. Sophia placed one hand on the door, eager to close it over Stepfather's sneaky smile. What did he mean about Isaac being a...*toad on a pond full of lily pads?* Her brow furrowed, and her skin grew colder. She had given herself the liberty to think that Isaac might have changed in the past four years. But if what Stepfather said was true, then he was still fully capable of altering his decisions on a whim…of capturing hearts he didn't intend to keep.

Her heart had become bare and vulnerable, exposed to the dangers that only Isaac could cause. She couldn't trust him. Not again.

After some effort, Sophia managed to shoo Stepfather and Aunt Hester kindly back downstairs. She called her maid to draw a warm bath, using her favorite lavender soap in an attempt to calm her nerves. She couldn't leave Lord Finchley waiting more than a day or two for her answer. His pride might have already been bruised enough to ruin her chances of marrying him altogether. The realization brought about a pesky sense of relief, as if she *wanted* to be released from her obligation.

But if she rejected Lord Finchley, what did she expect would happen? Did she think Isaac would swoop in and save her from the repercussions? He could have been toying with her for all she knew. She needed something reliable and safe.

Love was never safe. Not in her experience.

Not in Prudence's.

The somber sounds of the pianoforte still drifted through the house, and Sophia had had quite enough of it. Dressed in a clean gown, with her hair halfway dry, Sophia marched down the stairs and into the drawing room. There would be no more sulking from either one of them.

"Stand up, Prue." Sophia planted her hands on her hips, staring at the head of dark curls in front of her. Prudence's hands lifted from the keys, one eyebrow arched as she turned around.

Her eyes were rimmed in red, her nose and cheeks swollen. "I was almost finished."

Sophia's heart ached at the sight of her poor sister. She looked so small and fragile—far too young to have such a broken heart. If Sophia didn't work hard to mend it, then Prudence could end up much like her elder sister in a few years, still pining over a man with dishonorable intentions. "We are going on a walk," Sophia said in a firm voice.

Prudence narrowed her eyes. "Your hair is still wet."

"I shall hide it under my bonnet. At any rate, it was raining earlier today. No one should bat an eye at it."

Prudence stood with a sigh. "What if Percy is out today? I cannot bear to see him."

"He is the one who should be afraid of seeing *you*. He ought to be ashamed of himself. He is a hateful man."

"But I did love him." Prudence's eyes welled with tears. "I miss Mama. I miss Flora and Thistle. I cannot wait an entire month for Mama to arrive in London. How shall I bear it?"

Sophia wrapped her arms around her sister's small frame, squeezing tight. Sophia wished she could tell Prudence everything—Isaac's sudden flirting, Lord Finchley's proposal, and the hesitation she felt to accept it. But the words remained lodged in her throat. Surely she could bear all of it on her own. She was capable of making the right decisions, if only her heart weren't so involved.

"A bit of exercise will raise your spirits, I'm sure of it."

After a bit more coaxing, Prudence finally agreed to a walk in Kensington Gardens, where she was less likely to see Percy Ellington, and Sophia was less likely to see any of the gossipmongers who had attended the auction that day. The promenade at Hyde Park would draw the largest crowd at this hour of the day, so Kensington was a safer choice for both of them. By the time Prudence and Aunt Hester were ready to leave, Sophia's hair was completely dry.

As expected, Kensington Gardens were serene and quiet. Shaded benches and flowering bushes dotted the edges of the path, and children played on the grass under the watchful eye of their governesses and mothers. The air carried the soft scent of spring blossoms, ringing with the occasional trill of a bird.

Sophia held her parasol at a slight angle to shade her face, though the sun was on its way down for the evening. She walked with her arm looped through Prudence's, keeping their conversation as light as possible. Her sister's mood already seemed to be improving, and she even stopped to smell a bed of primroses.

As they rounded a bend, Sophia expected to find yet another quiet, unoccupied path. Instead, she was greeted by the sight of a familiar gentleman. "Is that Mr. Baker?" Sophia whispered.

Prudence sighed. "Yes, and I already said I was not interested in him."

Sophia gave a mischievous smile. "An introduction wouldn't be harmful. You did say you are already acquainted with his sister."

As soon as the words escaped her mouth, a young woman beside Mr. Baker turned in their direction. She was tall, with fiery red curls that spilled out the front of her straw bonnet. When she saw Prudence, her eyes flashed with recognition. She strode forward to meet them on the path, abandoning her brother and their other companions.

"Miss Hale, is it?" she asked with a smile.

Prudence nodded, coming to a halt in front of her new friend. "Miss Baker, a pleasure to see you again."

"Likewise." The young woman gave a polite nod, her brown eyes shifting in Sophia's direction.

"My elder sister, Miss Sophia Hale," Prudence said. "And this is Miss Marianne Baker."

Sophia greeted her with a smile, listening quietly as the two women discussed the origins of their gowns and ribbons. Sophia's mind wandered again to Lord Finchley's proposal, and her stomach twisted with dread. She had been trying to put it out of her mind, but the urgency of the matter couldn't be ignored.

"You look far too somber to be wearing such a cheerful color," Miss Baker said with a laugh.

It took Sophia a moment to realize Miss Baker was addressing her. She looked down at her pastel yellow gown, forcing a smile to her face. "Forgive me, I was lost in thought. I thank you for the reminder to smile. My sister says I don't do it nearly enough."

"She doesn't," Prudence said with a thoughtful nod.

"Did I hear that you accompanied Lord Finchley to the theatre a few weeks past?" Miss Baker asked.

"I did." Sophia twisted her fingers together.

"I have heard rumors that he is finally ready to marry. Do you think he will propose soon?"

Sophia's face grew hotter. The gossip must have been spreading faster than she realized. "I don't know. One can never rely on such a thing with certainty."

Miss Baker's nose twitched, and she rubbed it with the back of her finger. Her eyes glistened. "No. One cannot."

"No, indeed." Prudence stared down at the grass, the smile wiped clean off her face.

Sophia wanted to groan. All of her efforts to improve her sister's mood had been undone in an instant.

"What distresses you?" Miss Baker asked, touching Prudence's sleeve.

"I will not trouble you with the tale. My sister has dragged me out of the house in order to avoid the subject."

"You may confide in me if you wish." Miss Baker gave a soft smile. "I have been nursing a broken heart of my own."

Prudence scowled, taking Miss Baker's hand as if they had been lifelong friends. "Who broke your heart? I should like to see him sent to Newgate for his crimes."

Miss Baker's eyes lit up with delight. "I should like to see that too." But then her smile faded. "If I may spare any lady the heartache this man has caused me, then I will feel much more content." She leaned forward with a whisper that barely cut through the breeze. "His name is Mr. Isaac Ellington."

Sophia's stomach dropped. Prudence didn't even attempt to conceal her shock as she shot a glance in Sophia's direction. She corrected her expression quickly, but not before Miss Baker noticed. "Are you acquainted with him?" she asked, eyes wide.

Prudence adjusted the pendant at her neck with a nervous laugh. "Yes. He—" she shot a glance in Sophia's direction.

"We knew him when we lived in Cornwall," Sophia finished in a quick voice. "It was years ago." Her throat was dry as she swallowed.

"How I wish I could have met the two of you first!" Miss Baker sighed. "Perhaps you might have warned me. Has he always been so quick to wound unsuspecting women?" Her light brows drew together. "Perhaps not. Perhaps I was the only one he cast aside so easily."

Sophia's heart stung, the pain spreading throughout her

entire chest. Her legs were heavy, her knees threatening to buckle beneath her. Miss Baker was another of Isaac's victims—proof that he hadn't changed his ways. This was the evidence she needed. Blood rushed past her ears, blending the sound of Miss Baker's voice with the distant birdsong. She felt like she was drowning, despair dragging her down to the very floor of the sea. She had almost believed that Isaac was genuine.

And now, she felt like a complete and utter fool.

Surely Stepfather would have a metaphor for how Isaac toyed with his prey, relating him to some sort of animal. But at the moment, all she could think of was her deep disappointment. She had spent years hoping that he had made a mistake by deserting her, but it seemed that the behavior was actually just part of his character.

"I'm certain you are not the only one," Prudence said. Her voice was calm, but she cast a worried glance in Sophia's direction. "When did this happen?"

Miss Baker looked down at the grass. "Just last month. I was led to believe that Mr. Ellington would propose to me. He even asked my brother for his consent…and then…well, he must have changed his mind."

Prudence's sharp inhale reflected what Sophia felt. Only a month had passed since Isaac had demonstrated his cruel ways to another poor young woman. Sophia hadn't been special at all. She may have been the first to wrongfully trust him, but she hadn't been the last.

"Do you know why he changed his mind?" Sophia asked. Her voice sounded strange to her own ears. A distant echo.

"He didn't say," Miss Baker answered faintly.

The array of emotions inside her collided into distinct,

potent anger. Sophia would wager that Miss Baker's dowry was small—smaller than he had expected.

"I—I'm sorry you were so mistreated," Sophia said in a quiet voice. "I hope your reputation hasn't suffered."

"Thankfully no. The people of London have much more exciting things to gossip about than my disappointed hopes." She leaned in and beckoned Prudence and Sophia closer. Her voice dropped to a whisper. "My brother blackballed him from White's and Brook's. His reputation took a greater hit than mine, I daresay." Her lips curved. "I do relish the revenge a little more than I should."

Sophia's mouth grew slack.

That must have been why Isaac had applied to Stepfather's club—and why he had been forbidden to court his stepdaughters.

She straightened her spine as the realization washed over her. Isaac Ellington could not be trusted with something so fragile as a heart. She *knew* that, but now she had been thoroughly reminded. It hurt. It hurt so badly she couldn't breathe.

Like a toad on a pond full of lily pads.

She refused to be a landing place for him. She would much rather see him sink and disappear from her life forever. Hot tears sprung to her eyes, but she blinked them away in a flash. Isaac was not worth her tears. He was a pest that she had carried with her for four years. And there was only one way to cut him free.

While Prudence relayed every detail of Percy's deceit to Miss Baker, Sophia waited nearby. Numb. Shattered.

But determined.

The moment they returned home, she picked up her quill and wrote a letter to Lord Finchley.

Chapter Seventeen

The Right Honorable the Earl of Finchley requests the honor of Mr. Ellington's company at dinner this Thursday, at seven o'clock in the evening at his residence, No. 14 Berkeley Square.

Isaac dropped the invitation on the tea table with a grimace. He had received it two days prior, which was not a great deal of notice at all. It seemed to be an afterthought, as if Isaac hadn't been on the original list of guests. Which wasn't surprising in the slightest.

But why had Lord Finchley invited him at all? The question had been rankling him since the moment he received the invitation. After Isaac had outbid him for the painting, this invitation couldn't be anything but an opportunity for retaliation.

What did the earl have up his sleeve?

Isaac eyed the clock with misgiving. Whatever it was, he would soon find out.

He was only going because Sophia would be there. He hadn't seen her since the auction, and she hadn't been as receptive as he would have hoped to his romantic gesture. Perhaps his efforts were futile. Sophia might have had feelings for him, but her feelings had never been able to triumph over her ambitions.

Perhaps Lord Finchley had sent the invitation in order to prove to his peers that he didn't harbor animosity for Isaac's actions at the auction. He might have wanted to prove that the two men weren't actually battling for Sophia's affections. Without any evidence besides Isaac's behavior at the auction, Lord Finchley might be able to discredit any rumors.

Unless Isaac provided more evidence tonight.

However impossible it seemed, he needed to speak with Sophia alone. He needed to break the rules they had set for themselves and speak of the day she had left Cornwall. If he had the courage, he needed to obtain an answer to the question he had asked her during their dance at Lady Strathmore's ball. Did he have any chance against Lord Finchley?

When he had seen her at the auction, she had seemed angry and flustered—but also overwhelmed. Should he have taken a different approach? He had the sense, deep in his chest, that he was running out of time.

His heart ached, his limbs tense with dread as he set off in his carriage toward Berkeley Square. He leaned back into his seat and closed his eyes, but he couldn't seem to banish his sense of dread. Why did he feel like he was walking into a trap? Lord Finchley was not his friend—therefore his intentions for inviting Isaac to his house could not have been of a friendly nature.

Isaac opened his eyes as the carriage began to slow. The cream stone of Lord Finchley's Palladian townhouse came into view, candlelight spilling from every window that faced the tree-lined street. The sun had nearly retired for the day, glowing faintly enough to light Isaac's way to the wide double doors. His chest tightened at the memory of his nightmare, when Sophia had walked down the staircase on Lord Finchley's arm.

He calmed his nerves, putting on the bold facade he had worn at the auction. If he could display the same confidence he had felt that day, then nothing could rattle him. Lord Finchley's attempts to showcase his wealth and status—his superiority—would not keep Isaac from trying one last time to tell Sophia how he felt. How he had never stopped loving her.

The butler ushered Isaac inside and directed him to the drawing room. Voices drifted through the corridor. The walnut-paneled walls were lined with ancestral portraits of all the previous Lord and Lady Finchleys. Once again, Isaac was relieved to find no sign of taxidermy, though his stomach was still unsettled as he walked into the drawing room.

The party was larger than Isaac had expected, confirming his suspicion that his own invitation must have been sent much later than the others. A gathering of this size would not have been thrown together two days in advance. Lord Finchley's dining table must have been sizeable, equipped to seat at least sixteen guests.

Isaac surveyed the room until he found Sophia, standing near a heavily draped window. She was dressed in white, just like his nightmare. She wasn't wearing a veil, or holding a bouquet of flowers, but the sight was still eerie enough to make him freeze in the doorway.

Amongst the other guests was Lord Blackstone, who

thankfully hadn't noticed Isaac yet either. He had been avoiding his club since the auction, knowing full well that the viscount would have a stern look and several questions for him.

With an inexplicable knot in his stomach, Isaac walked into the room.

When Sophia noticed his approach, her face melted into a look of dismay.

Her cheeks paled.

Isaac slowed his steps, keeping several feet between them. Had she not expected him to attend? She looked like she had seen a ghost.

He bowed, no longer certain of the words he had planned. He couldn't be certain of anything. His throat was dry, his pulse racing. "You look...surprised to see me." He searched for clues in her expression.

Her dark lashes shielded her eyes from his view. Her lips parted, her throat shifting with a swallow. "I—I didn't know you received an invitation."

"I'm as surprised as you are." Isaac smiled, but Sophia's expression was cold. Panicked.

Something was wrong. Sophia's gaze darted to the right, then back to Isaac's face. Her hands twisted together.

Lord Finchley came into view, a vision of bright orange. His stiff curls shone like brass. "Ah, Mr. Ellington, I'm pleased that you accepted my invitation." His eyes were colder than a sheet of ice as he took Isaac in, an arrogant smile plastered on his face. "I apologize for the late notice, but I thought you might like to be present to celebrate the engagement of one of your dearest friends." He took Sophia's hand, pressing a kiss to the back of her glove.

Her face was still pale.

Isaac's entire body felt numb. He didn't speak. He couldn't.

"My congratulations." Isaac's voice came from the depths of his chest, nothing more than a weak mumble. He cleared his throat. His heart was on fire, burning into a pile of ash. Sophia's eyes came into view. Were they sad? He couldn't tell. But in that moment, they were the color of the sea, her cheeks were dotted with freckles, and her hair was bleached by the sun. Isaac was twenty-two, and she was nineteen. His heart was in pieces as he ran home on the back of his horse, back to an empty house with no grandfather. And no hope for Sophia Hale.

He had lost her. He had lost her a second time.

The walls seemed to close in around him, and the voice from his nightmare whispered in his ear: *"I have everything I have always wanted. Are you not happy for me?"*

What he felt now was not happiness, not even close. A storm raged inside him, a bitter rain that drowned him from the inside out. He took one step back, then another. He had known that Lord Finchley's reasons for calling him there couldn't have been cordial. No doubt the earl had planned this moment with great pleasure. Isaac had won the painting, but Finchley had laid his claim on Sophia's hand.

But did he have any claim on her heart?

Sophia was stiff beside him, her neck straight and her eyes averted. Isaac's arrival had rattled her, just as the announcement of her engagement had rattled him. He *knew* she didn't love Finchley. But that didn't matter. She had still chosen him. The fight was over.

There was no need for more false pleasantries. Isaac couldn't bear to look at the two of them a moment longer. He would endure the evening with as much civility as he could muster, and then he would leave. And he would never come back.

With a bow, he turned, searching the crowd for someone else to speak with. He felt Sophia's gaze on his back as he crossed the room to a gentleman he recognized from Blackstone's—Mr. Nash Markham. At least that was one stroke of luck.

The sickening sensation in Isaac's stomach remained, weakening his steps as the group made their way to the dining room. Isaac took his place at the long mahogany table. The china and silver cutlery gleamed under the crystal chandelier. How could Isaac eat when he felt so ill? His heart was like a rock in his chest, heavy, cold, and growing harder by the second.

He looked across the table at Sophia. She smiled at the woman beside her, giving a polite reply to something she said. But the moment the exchange was over, the smile faded from her face.

She seemed intent not to look at him.

Throughout the meal, the conversation varied from group debates to smaller discussions. Isaac ate what he could in silence. When the ladies retired to the drawing room, he remained at the table with the other men. He stared into his glass of port, rocking the red liquid from side to side.

"Lord Blackstone has been generous enough to provide me with a few exotic delicacies." Lord Finchley waved a footman forward, who placed a small bowl at the center of the table. "I thought I might share them with you all." His eyes lifted casually in Isaac's direction. Isaac didn't even have to look to know what the 'exotic delicacies' would be.

Lord Blackstone peered into the bowl. And then his eyes snapped toward Isaac with concern. "I should hope that you boiled them, Finchley. They are quite unpredictable in nature. Mr. Ellington can attest to that."

Isaac stared at the bowl of cashews, his jaw tight. The lengths Lord Finchley had taken for his revenge were ridiculous, yet he had to give him credit for the creativity of this particular hit.

"There should be no need to boil them, Blackstone," Lord Finchley said with a laugh. "I have been eating them all week and have experienced nothing out of the ordinary." To prove his point, he popped one in his mouth. His lips twisted into a smirk as he chewed.

Lord Blackstone's brows shot up. "How peculiar. Is your throat burning at all? Itching? Swelling?"

"Not in the slightest. I imagine one would have to be very delicate to experience such effects."

Isaac leaned back in his chair, crossing his arms over his chest. He considered himself to have a temperate disposition, but it was close to cracking. Lord Finchley's desperation to prove his superiority, or masculinity, or whatever dominance he was trying to assert made Isaac's skin crawl. How could Sophia promise herself to *this* man? How did she plan to tolerate spending every day of her life at his side?

Isaac picked up his glass, draining every last drop of his port as the other men at the table sampled the cashews. Lord Blackstone sat in high alert, ears perked, eyes round, clutching the sides of his chair. He had likely been waiting for an experiment like this but had been uncertain of the appropriateness of the endeavor. None of the other gentlemen were affected by the cashews, leaving Isaac the weak outlier.

"How fascinating," Lord Blackstone muttered.

Lord Finchley finished off the bowl, a wide grin

stretching across his face. He could amuse himself all he wanted, but Isaac refused to react. He remained still, rigid, even as his heart ached within him. His frustration boiled close to the surface, but he kept it submerged. Lord Finchley would be far too satisfied to see it.

Isaac was the first to leave the dining room when Lord Finchley's display was over. In the drawing room, Sophia shared the settee with her aunt. Isaac chose a chair straight across from her. He would no longer allow her to avoid meeting his gaze. The moment he sat down, her posture straightened, her eyes flickering over his face and back to Mrs. Liddle. Did she feel guilty that he had been dragged into this trap by Finchley?

Or was she just as amused?

A few ladies played numbers on the pianoforte before Lord Finchley called the room to attention. "I should like to share a verse of poetry with my betrothed." He rose to his feet and moved to stand directly in front of Sophia, blocking her from Isaac's view. It was clearly intentional.

"She walks in beauty, like the night
   Of cloudless climes and starry skies;
   And all that's best of dark and bright
   Meet in her aspect and her eyes;
   Thus mellowed to that tender light
   Which heaven to gaudy day denies."

Lord Finchley pressed a hand to his chest when he finished, hinging into a bow. The room applauded, but Isaac kept his hands in his lap.

"Byron, is it?" Isaac's voice overlapped with the applause but captured the attention of Lord Finchley. As he turned, Isaac caught a glimpse of Sophia's face. He held her gaze for a long moment.

This was the last time he would see her. He wouldn't put himself through the torture of hearing about her wedding plans. For the first time, he understood the sentiment of Byron's verse in the letter she had written him. If he was going to cut her out of his heart properly, their farewell this evening would have to be sudden. And this time, it would have to be forever.

"Indeed," Finchley confirmed with a slow nod. "Are you an admirer of his work?"

"Yes. He is a favorite of mine." Isaac's legs seemed to act of their own accord, lifting him to his feet. "May I share one of my favorite lines of his?"

Lord Finchley hesitated but relented with a step backward. "Of course."

Isaac felt the weight of all the gazes in the room, but Sophia's was the heaviest. It clawed at his heart without mercy. But that was how Sophia was: merciless. He had forgotten. He might have forgotten the cruelty of those words she had written to him, but tonight, he would ensure she never did.

"All farewells should be sudden, when forever." His voice was low, devoid of the pain he was feeling. No one could know, especially not her. He drew a breath. "Lest they make an eternity of moments, and clog the last sad sands of life with tears."

He found Sophia's eyes, hanging there in front of him, waiting to capture his. He could see the emotion now, playing across her features. But he didn't look for long. At the close of his words, he settled back into his chair.

"How...insightful," Lord Finchley broke the silence. "One cannot argue with the wisdom of such a talent as Byron."

Isaac searched for Sophia's gaze again, but she was staring at the floor. Her cheeks had darkened a shade, her brows pinched together. Surely she hadn't expected him to use her own words against her. He could still envision the slant of her writing, the thin strokes of ink and the paper unmarked by even a single teardrop. In her letter, she had dismissed him as suddenly as the quote suggested. He might have lost her again, but at least he had taken the last word.

As Lord Finchley invited his other guests to share their favorite verses and lines, Sophia's eyes finally lifted from the floor. In the candlelight, Isaac caught a sheen of moisture in them. She blinked fast, her lower lashes wet, clinging together. She wiped the corner of her eye. She refused to look at him.

Isaac froze. Was he the only one who had noticed her tears? A gentleman in the corner was reciting a sonnet, distracting the other guests.

Isaac's heart sank, but he quickly banished his sympathy. She had hurt him deeply with those words from Byron, and if they hurt her now, it was her own fault. Perhaps she felt guilty for the way she had abandoned him in Cornwall, and tonight he had struck a chord within her. Since seeing her again, she had been difficult to read, so he might have been mistaking her sadness for guilt. That was the only reasonable explanation.

After the guests had grown weary of poetry, they broke into groups for cards.

But Isaac didn't move from his chair.

His limbs were heavy, his heart even more so. He wanted to leave, but he didn't want to give Lord Finchley the satisfaction of an early departure. In his planning, the earl must have assumed that Isaac would flee from the drawing room after learning of the engagement, or from watching him devour a bowl of cashews. But Isaac would stay until the final moments of the party.

He watched as Sophia declined Lord Finchley's invitation to join his table for cards. Her aunt volunteered in her place. To avoid joining a game, Isaac ventured to the nearest shelf and picked up the first book he saw, bringing it back to his chair.

Was Sophia still upset? He stole a glance at her face. Her eyes were dry, but her mouth was a firm line.

Lord Finchley directed some of the guests to a room across the corridor, where he said more tables had been arranged. Mrs. Liddle and Lord Blackstone followed. Their voices grew distant. Lord Finchley would be sure to return shortly, after seeing his guests settled, but for a brief moment, he was gone.

Sophia was alone.

Their eyes met over his book, and the tears he had seen in her eyes sprung back to life.

"Please excuse me," she breathed, rushing past Isaac and out the drawing room door. She moved in silence, a quick flash of white fabric and golden-brown hair, and she was gone.

Once again, Isaac's legs acted of their own accord. He leaped to his feet and followed Sophia into the corridor.

Chapter Eighteen

A tear rolled down Sophia's cheek, then another. She wiped them frantically with her glove, searching for a place to hide. The dark walls were disorienting, the candlelight flickering in all directions as she made her way past the open door of the parlor where Lord Finchley stood with his back to the doorway. She rushed past it to avoid being seen. She had been holding back her tears for long enough to build up a great deal of pressure, and now they fell freely down her face.

"Drat." She rubbed the heel of her hand over her cheek, a sob rattling her chest. She drew a deep breath. She hadn't meant to lose her composure, but she couldn't help it. Her emotions spun wildly around her heart. Isaac's recitation of Byron's words had felt like a death blow. He had always known the best way to wound her. She hadn't meant to taunt him with the news of her engagement! She hadn't known Finchley would invite him to dinner with such an obvious motive.

She turned a corner, walking as quickly as she could.

"Sophia?"

Her heart all but stopped. Her feet froze on the marble floor. Isaac was the last person she wanted to see in her current state. She dried her eyes one last time before turning around.

He walked toward her with long strides, making up the space between them in seconds. To her surprise, he didn't stop in front of her. Instead, he moved past her to the nearest door, checking the brass knob. He glanced behind them, and before she could protest, he reached for her hand and pulled her forward. Her mind roared with objection, but her legs carried her willingly into the room behind him.

Her heart picked up speed as Isaac tugged the door shut behind her.

A single sconce lit the small space. Sophia's eyes adjusted to the dimness. A desk, shelves, and rows of books came into view. It was a study or small library of sorts, decorated in the same dark tones as the rest of the house.

Isaac's eyes were just as moody and dark as their surroundings. In an instant, she snapped back to her senses, tugging her hand from his grip. "We cannot be in here alone." If anyone from the party saw them, she would be in dire straits. She didn't dare imagine how furious Lord Finchley would be.

Isaac's gaze searched her face. She could still feel the path her tears had torn down her cheeks, the skin dry and tight. Her throat was still raw. Isaac toyed with hearts. That was his way. It was infuriating that she had allowed him to unravel her again, even after she had accepted Lord Finchley's proposal. Her conversation with Miss Baker had driven her to make her final decision—one last attempt to protect her heart from further damage.

Isaac's chest rose and fell with a deep breath. "Did you know Lord Finchley was planning to invite me?"

She shook her head fast. "No. Our engagement hadn't been made public before today. Had I known, I would have discouraged him. I-I'm sorry you heard the news this way."

Isaac's jaw tightened, and he looked down at the floor. "So you will marry him?" The rawness of the question caught her by surprise. She could hear the pain in his voice.

"Yes." Her voice was strong, but she could feel that strength waning.

She reached for the door again. The longer they were missing, the more suspicion would arise. Before she could turn the knob, Isaac stepped closer. She backed away, colliding with the door. It rattled in its frame. Her heart threatened to leap out of her chest.

Isaac found her hand without any effort, and she felt his fingers wrap around hers. Her arm was limp and weak as he lifted her hand and unraveled her fist, his movements slow and careful. He ran his fingertips over her knuckles. Shivers followed his touch all the way up her arm, and then he dipped his head, pressing a slow kiss to the center of her palm.

Her breath caught in her chest, her heart jumping like a wild thing. How many times had he done this very thing? It had been their tradition, a detail that she had schooled herself to forget.

He lifted his gaze to hers again as he wrapped her fingers back into a fist. "A keepsake." His eyes flickered with pain. "Goodbye, Sophia." His voice broke. He didn't let go of her hand for a long moment, and she didn't tug it away either.

A lump formed in her throat. Her lip quivered, but she ducked her head to hide it. She had made her decision. Why then was she still holding on? Her face burned, her pulse thrumming fast in her throat. *Say it*, she commanded herself.

Goodbye, Isaac.

But she couldn't bring the words to her lips. They burned in her throat. There were answers she still needed if she ever hoped to forget him.

"What you did tonight was cruel," she said. A stray tear slipped down her face, but this time she didn't bother to hide it. "Reciting those words from Byron."

"What *I* did was cruel?" Isaac's brows lowered, canopying his eyes in a look of hurt.

"You cannot fault me for accepting Lord Finchley's proposal!" The outburst caused a deep ache to spread through her chest. "You never asked me to marry you, and he did. You found me lacking, but he did not."

He shook his head. "I never found you lacking."

"You cannot take back what you wrote in that letter." She glared up at him. "Especially not when you quoted those words in front of all the guests this evening."

"What letter?" Isaac's eyes searched hers, his grip tightening on her hand. "You're the one who wrote those words to me."

"No." She shook her head. "I didn't write you a letter. I received yours the day my family left Cornwall."

Isaac released her hand, taking a step back. "Sophia. I *didn't* write you a letter." The sincerity in his gaze made her stomach flip. His features were tight with confusion.

The smooth wood of the door was cold against her back, but she leaned into it. Her legs were weak. "You said my dowry was insufficient. You had to make repairs on the house, and you needed money. My father handed me the letter himself." Her voice came quickly, and she didn't pause to breathe. "You said that all farewells should be sudden. You said that you hoped I would forget you." Her throat tightened.

Isaac was shaking his head. "I never took any issue with your dowry! None of that is true." His wide eyes raced over her face. "I spoke with your father and obtained his permission to marry you two days before your family left Lanveneth. By the time I came to your house, it was empty. The butler handed me a letter from *you*."

Sophia's mind raced, her head growing foggy. "What did it say?"

"All farewells should be sudden." Isaac's voice was faint. "And that you had chosen to seek a better match in London. That you desired more than me."

"I didn't write that." Her face flushed with heat. "As soon as my father gave me the letter from you, we made our quick preparations to depart for London. He said you didn't wish to see me."

Isaac scowled, putting a hand to his head in confusion. Silence hung in the air, and Sophia could hear her own pulse in her ears. If it were true—that Isaac hadn't sent her a letter at all, then who had? His eyes found hers, his features flooded with caution. He seemed afraid to speak. "We both received a letter from the other, yet neither of us wrote one?"

She swallowed. "It would seem so."

"And both letters contained the same quote from Byron."

Sophia could hardly believe what she was hearing. Her mind struggled to comprehend the idea. Her stomach was sick with dread, her legs shaking beneath her. She knew what Isaac was implying: That the two letters must have had the same author. Someone who had been intent on separating the two of them.

Someone who had wanted to sabotage their courtship.

Her heart hammered, the reality of the situation finally catching up to her.

"Miss Hale?" A distant voice echoed in the corridor. "Have you seen Miss Hale anywhere?"

"Finchley," Isaac muttered. His voice was weak, still enrobed with disbelief.

Sophia's senses came pouring back to her. "You must hide."

He didn't move, his face still blank, his brow furrowed in confusion. His senses seemed to still be absent.

She lunged forward, pushing against his chest until he backed up a step. "You must hide, now! We mustn't be seen in here." She pushed him toward the desk in the corner. A large armchair rested in front of it.

Isaac blinked, his eyes settling on her face. The candlelight of the nearby sconce caught his features. For a moment, he looked like he might kiss her. But there was no time for that.

"Under the desk," she demanded, her face hot.

Isaac finally obeyed, struggling to fold his tall body into the small space. If Lord Finchley saw them there, he would be swift to do something rash, like challenge Isaac to a duel. Despite all that she had just learned about the letters, this new information didn't change the fact that Lord Finchley was still her betrothed.

Sophia leaned her hip and both hands against the heavy armchair, sliding it a little closer to Isaac. She prayed it would hide him sufficiently from view.

With a deep breath, she crossed the room and opened the door.

Lord Finchley was already halfway down the corridor, a scowl on his brow. He took her hands as he reached her.

"Miss Hale, what were you doing in my study?"

She searched for a reply. Her thoughts were still cloaked in a haze, her heart beating out of her chest. "I was hiding from Lady Sunderland. She was insisting that I play whist, so I told her I was unwell."

Lord Finchley cast her a suspicious look. "Mr. Ellington was not in the drawing room either."

"He must have taken his leave." She held perfectly still, too afraid to even breathe as Lord Finchley stared down the corridor. He took one abrupt step forward, then another, until he reached the study door. He threw it open, casting his sharp gaze into the dim room.

Sophia's cheeks flamed, and she hung back a step. Had Isaac's hiding place been enough? She didn't dare look at Lord Finchley's face.

After a long moment, she heard the door close again. "Hmm. Well, Mr. Ellington did seem out of sorts all evening. I cannot begin to imagine why he was so discomposed." He laughed, as if that would excuse his abrupt search of the study, and the accusations it had implied. Little did he know that Isaac was hiding beneath his desk, likely just as awestruck and mortified as Sophia felt.

Her stomach twisted as Lord Finchley led her back toward the drawing room. She tried to sort through her thoughts, but they spun too violently to grasp.

Isaac's letter had been a forgery.

And he had received one from her.

All of these years, he had been under the impression that *she* had run away from him.

A deep sense of betrayal washed over her as she reclaimed her seat in the drawing room. How could it be true? Who could have forged those letters, and why? She had to find out.

~

The house was silent when Sophia awoke the next morning. A sliver of light leaked through the edges of her drapes, but when she pulled them back, her eyes stung with the brightness. It had taken her hours to fall asleep the night before, but all her fretting had achieved nothing.

She was still shocked by her conversation with Isaac, terrified of marrying Lord Finchley, and completely at a loss over what to do.

She had returned home well after midnight the night before, and she hadn't bothered to wake Prudence. But now, she couldn't wait a moment longer to speak with her sister.

She wrapped a shawl over her nightdress and crept down the corridor. She knocked on her sister's door. "Prudence?"

There was no reply.

She tried again, with a little more force. "Prudence? Are you awake?"

She was met with prolonged silence. Sophia turned the doorknob and peeked inside. The bed was empty, blankets tucked neatly into place. She wrapped her shawl tighter as she crossed the room.

A folded piece of lavender stationary rested between the two pillows. Sophia picked it up, unfolding it quickly. Her eyes raced across the page.

To whom it may concern,

I could not bear to be away from Flora and Thistle a moment longer. Please do not fret, for I have not taken the journey to Cornwall alone. I am in safe and reputable company. I shall return to London with Mama when the time comes for her to make the journey.

Prudence

Chapter Nineteen

Adjusting the corner of the gold frame, Isaac took a step back from the newest addition to the wall in his drawing room.

Sophia's painting of the coast.

He had already been staring at it for several minutes, his heart in his throat. To him, the painting represented hope. Until that day, he had kept the painting in its wrapping, too afraid to make a space for it on the wall. Perhaps there would come a time that he didn't want to be reminded of Sophia, but at the moment, she was all he could think of.

His eyelids were heavy as he finally turned away from the picture of the sea. He hadn't slept more than an hour or two the night before.

For more reasons than one.

A servant had locked the door of Lord Finchley's study, so Isaac had spent the night on the floor. He had only managed to escape early that morning, and he was still shaken from the ordeal. To pass the time through his sleepless night, he had been running possibilities through his head, potential answers to the questions that had been haunting him since his conversation with Sophia. If both letters had been forged, then who had done it? If only Isaac had kept his. In his effort to forget Sophia, he had torn it up and disposed of it. She had likely done the same.

The culprit could have been either of Sophia's parents. It could have been her sister, or a servant, or even Isaac's grandfather. He had considered each and every one of them. He recalled what Percy had said to him at the ball: *There's a great deal you don't know about Grandfather.*

But how could Grandfather have written the letters? He had died the day before they were received.

Still, Percy's words lingered in Isaac's mind with eerie finality. It was one of the last things Percy had said to him before he all but disappeared. Isaac hadn't seen him since the ball. He seemed to be hiding from the consequences of his actions. Lord Blackstone hadn't made a scene over the situation for Prudence's sake, but Percy was wise to avoid a confrontation of any sort. Was he even still in London?

The mystery remained unsolved, and it vexed him. Almost as much as the fact that Sophia was engaged to Lord Finchley. Had their conversation the night before changed her mind? Isaac could hardly dare to hope for such an outcome. He had been betrayed by his hopes too many times. Despite the dangers of doing so, he needed to call upon her that day.

He didn't have a moment to lose. Blackstone could drive him out of the house if he wished, but Isaac had to finish his conversation with Sophia. He had to know if his hope was in vain.

The sky was clear for the first time all week as Isaac made his way to her house. At the front door, he raised the knocker and struck it three times, and the butler welcomed him inside. Before Isaac could be directed to the drawing room, he was nearly knocked over by Mrs. Liddle as she rushed around the corner of the entrance hall.

He managed to dodge her, but only just. The woman pressed a hand to her chest, gasping for air. "Mr. Ellington!"

"Mrs. Liddle." He read the signs of distress on her features. "Is something amiss?"

No sooner had the question left his lips that Sophia appeared from around the same corner. Her steps halted when she saw Isaac. Her cheeks were ruddy, her hair hanging loose about her shoulders. She wore a thin white chemise, a brown shawl wrapped around the upper half of her body. She appeared to have just stumbled out of bed and followed her aunt on a rampage through the house.

Her cheeks darkened a shade as she seemed to realize how she appeared. Isaac could never properly tell her how attractive she looked, so he simply stood there, admiring her at his own discretion. He hadn't seen her hair loose since their days in Cornwall, but it suited her. It made his heart ache to realize that all these years, she thought he had cast her aside because her dowry wasn't enough. He wanted to tell her over and over again how false that was.

"Isaac." Her eyes flickered down to her shawl, and she wrapped it tighter around herself. Her aunt seemed too distracted at the moment to notice Sophia's use of his Christian name. But it didn't escape his notice. His heart lifted at the familiarity of it, that flicker of hope growing stronger inside him. He stamped it down before he could become carried away. Breaking off an engagement to an earl was no small feat, and the consequences to Sophia's reputation and family would be severe.

"Yes, something is very much amiss." Mrs. Liddle stepped between them. Isaac had forgotten that he had asked her the question at all. "Prudence has run away."

He reared back in surprise. "Where has she gone?"

"Cornwall."

He frowned. "Surely she hasn't traveled there alone?"

Sophia sighed, and the worry in her features became apparent as she walked closer. "She claims not to be alone, but in safe, reputable company. I don't dare imagine what her definition of reputable company could be." Her eyes glistened with suppressed tears. "She said she missed her dogs, but she has never taken such drastic measures before." Her lower lip quivered, and were it not for Mrs. Liddle standing a few paces away, Isaac would have wrapped her in his arms. "I worry that she didn't leave of her own accord."

A chill ran across Isaac's shoulders. Was Percy capable of kidnapping a young woman and forcing a marriage? Isaac's original assessment of his cousin's character had already proven to be far milder than it actually was. Could Percy have had more up his sleeve? The idea made Isaac's stomach sink with dread.

"I don't know what to do." Sophia drew a shaky breath. "I just found her letter this morning. None of our carriages are gone, so that means she must have traveled with a private coach, or by mail coach. If she traveled through the night, we have little chance of catching her before she reaches her destination."

"Did you not see her when you returned home last night?"

"No. I went straight to bed." Sophia's blue eyes spilled over, and she wiped at the tears. "After all we did to keep them apart, I cannot bear to think of her being taken like this. She didn't want to attend the party yesterday, but I should have made her. I shouldn't have let her out of my sight."

Isaac couldn't take it a moment longer. He would have to test his luck with Mrs. Liddle's eyesight. Stepping forward, he wiped a tear from Sophia's cheek. His touch seemed to take her by surprise, but she didn't pull away from it. She stared up at him, and it was confirmed once again that there was nothing he wouldn't do for her. His heart flopped as her gaze moved gently across his features. He struggled to speak. "We will find her," he promised. "Have you told your stepfather?"

"Not yet. He left for Hampshire early this morning. He'll be back tomorrow, but by then we would be too late."

Isaac gave a swift nod. "I'll prepare my carriage now. If we can't catch her before she reaches Cornwall, we can at least be there shortly after she arrives."

Sophia's brow furrowed. "No, I should not have burdened you with this. My stepfather will be on the road as soon as he hears of it."

"And by then, I will already be several hours ahead of him."

"As will I," Mrs. Liddle blurted. She marched forward, her liquid eyes magnified through the lenses of her spectacles. "My nerves cannot tolerate being left here to wonder what has become of our dear Prudence. Sophia and I will take our own carriage behind you. The journey should only take four to five days if we travel through the night, and should we encounter any highwaymen or other dangers, Mr. Ellington will be nearby to protect us. We might even enlist Lord Finchley's help."

"No," Sophia blurted. "I mean—" her cheeks flushed.

"Lord Finchley is not accustomed to the discomfort of a long journey. I wouldn't wish to trouble him."

A wave of satisfaction crossed Isaac's stomach. Eating cashews was one thing, but being trusted by Sophia was a far greater victory. He tore himself away from her side, despite how badly he wanted to remain close to her. This was his moment to prove his devotion to her and her family—Lord Blackstone in particular. He needed to act. Prudence's safety was the top priority at the moment—not how lovely Sophia looked with her hair down.

"I don't think Percy's involvement is likely," Isaac reassured her. "Let us hope for the best…that she simply missed her dogs."

Sophia nodded, but her eyes still glinted with worry.

He hadn't planned to travel back to Cornwall until it was absolutely necessary. This was that moment. He pushed aside the dread he felt at the prospect of seeing Morvoren House again and what he had caused to become of it through his neglect. The land prospered, the tenants and mines were thriving, but the house itself was likely in disrepair. Percy was right.

Grandfather would be disappointed in him.

Isaac had avoided confronting that truth, but now there was no escaping it. Within a week, he would be forced to face the house that he had abandoned, and the memories of his grandfather's final days he had spent years burying. A chill washed over him. He never could have imagined that he would be traveling to Cornwall with Sophia. They had faced a few parts of their past together in Lord Finchley's study, but now they would be forced to face the rest. There were secrets there that needed uncovering, answers that needed to be found.

Perhaps Prudence was leading him straight to them.

∽

The carriage rocked gently as it traveled across the Great West Road. Isaac hadn't forgotten how rough the road conditions would become in the final days of the journey, so he tried to appreciate the smoothness of the ride. It had been hours since he had escaped the crowded roads of London, and now his window greeted him only with an open landscape of green.

He had packed his trunk hastily, completely forgoing the comforts he would have usually packed for a journey of several days. He didn't have a book, a journal, or even a paper to sketch on. All he had to entertain himself were his own thoughts, and the ongoing mystery he had been trying to solve about the forged letters.

Mrs. Liddle and Sophia were in the carriage behind his, and each time they stopped to change horses, Sophia looked more worried. The end of their first day was drawing to a close, and what hope she had that they might catch Prudence on the road was fading. The only hope they had was that Prudence might have stopped at an inn that evening, and if they persevered without resting, they might be able to make up the time.

The sun hung low in the sky, disappearing behind the hills. Isaac watched with misgiving as dark clouds crowded in, stirring a storm above the road. As the sun disappeared, large raindrops began spiraling down, striking hard against his carriage window. The downfall intensified, until the raindrops merged into sheets.

The carriage slowed, slogging through the mud.

"Devil take it." Isaac squinted through the window, struggling to see behind him. Between the darkness of the night and the constant rain, it was impossible. The moon and stars were covered in clouds, leaving Isaac with no question that his driver's vision was impaired. The horses would need to be changed soon, but taking the carriages back out in the storm would be dangerous.

He needed to ensure Mrs. Liddle and Sophia were still close by.

He rapped on the rooftop, alerting the driver to bring the horses to a stop, and then opened the door to lean out into the rain.

The road behind him was empty. At least as far as his vision could reach.

The water attacked him, soaking through the top half of his jacket. Thunder rattled the sky. He waited, searching for any sign of Sophia's carriage, but it was nowhere to be seen.

Chapter Twenty

Equanimity was not one of Aunt Hester's virtues. She let out a shriek that was shrill enough to shatter the windows of their carriage, clutching her chest as if her heart might fly straight out of it. The carriage tilted to one side, then rocked back with a loud crash. The sound of splintered wood mingled with the rain, and then everything went still.

Aunt Hester searched for her spectacles from where they had fallen onto the carriage floor. Sophia fetched them for her, taking a deep breath to calm her racing heart.

"Have the highwaymen found us?" Aunt Hester lunged for the window, nearly pressing her nose against it. Her breath left a circle of fog on the glass. "Was that a shot I just heard?"

"No." Sophia's shoulder ached from where it had collided with the side of the carriage. She adjusted on her seat, following her aunt's gaze out the window. "But I think our wheel may be broken." The rain seemed to have created trenches in the road, leaving it uneven and thick with mud. Had they slid off completely?

Sophia opened the door, peering out into the rain. The coachman had already stepped down from the box, his hair and clothing drenched as he stooped over one of the front wheels. Sophia wasn't experienced in repairing wheels, or anything really, but she couldn't wait helplessly in the carriage. Traveling at night was not safe, especially for two women. The more distance Isaac traveled without them, the more danger they were in from being robbed by highwaymen and actually hearing a shot, just as Aunt Hester had imagined.

And the longer they were delayed, the farther they were from Prudence.

Before she could lose her nerve, Sophia jumped down from the carriage. Her boots squelched in the mud as she landed, splashing the lower half of her skirts. The rain was blinding as she trudged over to the coachman, Giles. He had been reliable on their journey thus far, safely transporting them from one stop to the next. But now, as he stared at the wheel, he looked perplexed.

"Can it be repaired?" Sophia asked. Water dripped into her eyes as she leaned over.

"Not in the dark, I'm 'fraid." Giles wiped his forehead, a deep line in his brow as he stared down the road in the direction from which they had come. "Nearest inn is two miles that way."

Sophia remembered passing it, wishing she could escape the confines of the carriage for the night. Now, they would have to walk two miles in the mud if they wished to reach it, and Isaac was far ahead of them now, possibly unaware of their mishap. The four horses at the front of the carriage shifted uneasily without the driver commanding their movements. The poor creatures had already been drawing the carriage for the last ten miles. Surely they were craving shelter and food as much as Sophia and Aunt Hester were. But she didn't have time to waste. Prudence could be in danger. Traveling backward two miles and sleeping at an inn would set them back greatly.

"Is there anything up ahead?" Sophia shivered. Her spencer jacket was completely soaked through now.

"A posting house, ma'am, nothin' more. Still another two miles."

Giles stood up straighter, assessing their surroundings again. She could barely see the details of his face in the dark. She froze in her uncertainty. What were they to do? A posting house wouldn't provide lodging for anyone but the horses, and continuing on their journey that night was now impossible. Until the wheel could be repaired, it seemed they had no choice but to walk to the inn.

Aunt Hester hovered inside the carriage but still observed the conversation. It was unlikely that she could hear a word of it over the rain. Sophia took a step to rejoin her aunt inside but stopped when she saw movement on the road ahead.

Was it Isaac? She imagined a highwayman would ride a horse, not be walking on foot through the mud. The man's features were impossible to decipher from a distance, but she could identify him by his height and the width of his shoulders. It was certainly Isaac. As he grew closer, his face came into view. He held his jacket partially over his head, but his hair was still soaked as he jogged toward them. His shirtsleeves clung to his arms, droplets of rain racing down his forehead.

Sophia sighed in relief, picking up her skirts in one large handful and starting toward him.

He eyed her with disbelief. "What are you doing out here?" He took the jacket he was holding and draped it behind her, creating a canopy above her head.

"Our wheel broke."

"That isn't a reason for you to be wandering in the mud and rain." The raw concern on his brow released a flutter in her chest.

"Where is your carriage?" she asked.

"The coachman is currently digging the wheel out of the mud."

Sophia laughed. The tension and fear she had been holding released slowly from her shoulders. Isaac's eyes gleamed with amusement, and then he laughed too. They were both soaked. From under the jacket, she stared up at his face. He looked as exhausted as she felt, and at least equally delirious.

The caution she had been feeling toward him for years had been torn out from under her with their conversation at the party. Now, she had nothing to grasp but her feelings for him—and they were far stronger than she was comfortable with. She had seen him soaked through like this before, when he had gone for a swim in his clothes in one of the coves by Morvoren. She hadn't even reached Cornwall yet and she was already repeating all those memories in her mind, like rereading a favorite book. She thought she had glued the pages closed, but now they ruffled open in front of her, begging her to read the story again. To *live* the story again.

But with a new ending this time.

Sophia felt the warmth of Isaac's body radiating toward

her, trapped beneath the canopy of his jacket. His arms must have been tired from holding the jacket above her head for so long.

Her laughter subsided, and she smiled up at him. "I suppose we shall have to wait, then."

Isaac's lips twitched with a curious smile. "In the rain, or in the carriage?"

"Which would you prefer?"

A trickle of rain fell from his hairline, and she had to hold herself back from wiping it away. He leaned an inch closer. "Well, I know you have always dreamed of being trapped alone with me in a carriage during a rainstorm."

How had she known he would say that? Her heart pounded, but she laughed. "We wouldn't be alone. My aunt is there."

He grinned. "But you don't deny that you dream of it?"

"Of course I don't!"

He laughed, his wide smile creating creases around his mouth and eyes—quiet, soft signs of the years that had separated them. She couldn't believe that all this time, someone else had been responsible. Where would her life have taken her if she and Isaac hadn't been given those forged letters? They could have been married years ago. They could have built a life in Cornwall, surrounded by the sea and mines and small children to care for.

Was it too late for that future?

The very idea of it made her heart ache with longing. How could she break off her engagement to Lord Finchley now? Her stepfather would be astonished—and his relationship with the earl would be sure to suffer. But wasn't her future happiness worth it?

Isaac spoke again, tugging her from her thoughts. "If you

had been honest that day at the picnic, would I have won the game?" Had he leaned closer? His light tone encouraged an honest reply, but his closeness made her words lodge in her throat.

"Yes." She could barely hear her own voice above the rain. "I was surprised by how much you remembered."

"You've proven yourself quite impossible to forget." His eyes matched the night, his mouth just a whisper away from hers. He was smiling, but his gaze was serious as it roamed over her face, as if he were searching for an answer to that question he had posed during their dance. He must have still been wondering if he had a chance against Lord Finchley.

Her heart pounded hard against her chest.

Isaac was the only one who had ever had a chance.

He stared down at her, his lips just inches from hers. Her honor conflicted with her desire, her head with her heart. She had left Lord Finchley in London without a word. It wasn't fair to engage herself to him and yet be standing this close to Isaac, wanting him more than she could ever want anyone else. She had embarked on this journey to save Prudence's reputation, not to ruin her own in the process.

She looked down at her feet, half buried in a puddle of mud. "Perhaps we should go to the carriage."

Isaac glanced up at the sky. The rainfall had subsided, but only a little. If his coachman succeeded in freeing Isaac's carriage, then they could at least ride to the posting house rather than walk. Isaac had always been a gentleman. He didn't object to her request, but kept his jacket positioned over her head as he led her to the carriage where Aunt Hester awaited them.

Sophia took the seat beside her aunt, but Isaac stayed outside, closing the door behind her.

She cast him a curious look from the window, but he jogged in the opposite direction. He must have been going back to help his coachman free the wheel from the mud. Lord Finchley, on the other hand, would have been the first inside the carriage. And he certainly wouldn't have sacrificed one of his finest jackets to the downpour in order to keep her head dry.

Aunt Hester was bundled in a carriage blanket, only her face visible above it. "Perhaps Mr. Ellington's constitution is not strong when it comes to exotic foods, but he does seem quite capable of enduring the weather this evening." She offered half the blanket to Sophia. "You haven't fooled me, my dear."

Sophia turned, finding her aunt's lips pursed in a knowing smile. "What do you mean?"

"You are in love with Mr. Ellington. And he is very much in love with you."

Sophia felt her face growing warmer. She was grateful for the darkness to hide behind. She considered denying it, but how could she? Even her aunt, who was half-blind had seen it. There was a reason Lord Finchley had felt so threatened by Isaac. Perhaps he had seen it too.

"If you marry Lord Finchley, you will regret it for the rest of your life." Aunt Hester gave Sophia a stern look. "You may have thought that an earl was a better choice, but I assure you, no amount of wealth or status can create happiness."

"I didn't know you weren't in favor of the match." Sophia had never heard Aunt Hester's true opinion on the subject before. Why had she withheld it?

"I thought it was what you wanted. But I have seen the way you look at Mr. Ellington."

Sophia fell silent. Lord Finchley had never been what she

wanted. She had only chosen him because she had believed that Isaac didn't truly want her. She recalled her conversation with Miss Baker on her garden walk with Prudence. Was that what Isaac had been trying to do by courting Miss Baker? She had never considered it that way before, but then again, she hadn't had a reason to until she learned the truth about the letters.

But who had written them? The question still bothered her. Who would be so cruel?

An answer flickered through her mind. She hadn't dared to consider the most obvious possibility. Even now, her mind shushed the idea. Her stomach sank with dread, but she refused to acknowledge the thought again.

A few minutes later, a carriage appeared in the distance, and Sophia followed Aunt Hester down to the muddy road. Isaac's carriage was smaller than theirs, but the three of them managed to fit, despite Isaac's long legs.

His knees brushed against Sophia's as the carriage rolled forward. She met his gaze in the dark, her heart skipping all over again. How did he manage to do that? She had so many questions she wanted to ask him, but she could already feel Aunt Hester's gaze on the side of her face. Apparently, there was a 'certain manner' in which Sophia looked at Isaac, and it had already been exposed. She didn't want to give her aunt any further evidence.

At the posting house, the horses were changed, but the road was still soaked with rain. Continuing the journey in such conditions was inadvisable, but fortunately Isaac's coachman couldn't refuse a hearty bit of oil in his palm. He pocketed Isaac's coins and set off on the road toward Cornwall. With hers and Aunt Hester's carriage left to be repaired, they barely managed to fit their trunks on the back of Isaac's.

What remained of their journey would be taken together. Day in and day out.

Sophia was in deep trouble. She had engaged herself to the wrong man, and now the right one—or who she hoped was the right one—would be sitting across from her for the next several days. There was no escaping him, nor her feelings.

It only took a few minutes for Aunt Hester to fall asleep. Her light snores were the only sound besides the light patter of rain that still continued on the windows. Finally, Isaac's voice broke the silence.

"I've been thinking about the other night. In Finchley's study."

Sophia's heart pattered quicker than the rain. "As have I. It's difficult to comprehend." Now that the door was open, her questions came pouring out. "Who could have written the letters? Who could have wanted to keep us apart so badly?" Her voice cracked in her effort to keep it quiet. Aunt Hester stirred, but another snore confirmed that she was still asleep.

Isaac's features were nearly invisible in the darkness. He seemed afraid to answer.

Afraid to accuse.

"Was your grandfather opposed to me?" Sophia asked in a quiet voice.

Isaac shook his head. "My grandfather suffered a fall the night I last saw you. His injuries caused him to die two days later. That was what delayed my proposal. When I came to Lanveneth, I was clearly too late."

Sophia pulled her blanket up closer to her chin. The dread she felt was growing more intense. She couldn't hold still. She hadn't known that Isaac's grandfather's death had occurred while she was still in Cornwall.

He had suffered that loss all alone.

She hadn't questioned Papa's counsel when he had told her to take Isaac's letter and leave. Papa had convinced her that speaking to him would be improper. She had been told to accept Isaac's rejection with grace.

She recalled the panic in Papa's eyes when she had tried to flee his study to find Isaac at Morvoren.

She could still feel his grip on her arm.

"My father?" she whispered.

Isaac was silent for a long moment. "He is the only one who knew that we planned to marry. He must have had a reason, but I don't know what it could have been. When I spoke to him the day before, he gave me permission to marry you."

It didn't make sense. Papa had known how much Sophia loved Isaac. He had given his permission. Then what had changed his mind?

She had felt him grow distant from her after their family had left Cornwall. After seeing how devastated Sophia was, had his guilt driven him away? Or was she placing false blame on him?

Her heart ached. How could she ever know? He had been gone for two years.

She could not ask him.

Would Mama know? Prudence had obviously been kept in the dark, but had her mother? How many secrets were living within the walls of Lanveneth? How many secrets had her father taken to his grave?

Sophia leaned her head back against her seat, her eyelids growing heavy. She knew none of the answers. But if they made it to Cornwall, she was determined to uncover each and every one of them.

∽

The carriage creaked as it topped the crest of a hill on the narrow road, jostling Sophia awake. Early morning light peeked through the windows, but Aunt Hester and Isaac were still asleep.

She leaned close to the window, catching her breath. The Cornish coastline stretched into the distance, the jagged cliffs meeting the restless churn of the sea. Patches of sea thrift nodded in the breeze, their pink blooms scattered across the landscape like freckles. In the other direction, fields rolled in vibrant green and gold, with dry stone walls marking the borders.

And nestled in a grove of trees in the distance, was Lanveneth.

The estate loomed far beyond the cliffs, the weathered cream stone defiantly out of reach of the sea spray. Sea birds circled the crest of the roof, the sides sloping like a pair of shoulders hunched away from the wind.

Sophia's heart picked up speed. After five days of near constant travel, they had finally reached Lanveneth. She could already feel the wildness of the landscape—the way it tugged at the threads of her propriety. Cornwall was far from London. It was a rugged place, steeped in secrets and more memories than she could count. The sea, the caves, the hidden coves and pink flowers had stolen her heart, and even now, they took her breath away. Isaac had been her first love, but Cornwall had been her second. The two were forever tied together in her mind. That was why she had never returned; she had known how incomplete Cornwall would be without its other half.

Her gaze shifted to Isaac. She studied the dark crescents of his lashes as he closed his eyes, his mussed hair, the slow rise and fall of his chest as he breathed. Seeing him in Cornwall was as satisfying as completing a puzzle. They fit together perfectly.

His eyes fluttered open. Her heart leaped, and she looked away just in time, turning her attention back to the passing coastline. She heard him stir and shift on his seat for a better view out his window.

As Lanveneth grew closer, Sophia's dread intensified. They had stopped at a few inns along the journey, searching for any sign of Prudence, but hadn't found her. If she wasn't at Lanveneth, Sophia would have no choice but to assume something had gone amiss on her journey—or that Percy had abducted her. The very thought made Sophia's heart race. She had been fighting an ill sensation in her stomach for almost the entire journey, and now that their destination was in sight, she had never felt more nervous.

The moment the carriage stopped on the drive, Isaac pushed the door open, helping Sophia and Aunt Hester to solid ground. Sophia swayed on her feet for a moment, her head spinning. The air smelled of salt and fish, with a hint of wild garlic and flowers. She remembered that smell, and for a moment, she could think of nothing else. Her bonnet ribbons and skirts tossed in the breeze, and soon Isaac was standing beside her. She felt his fingers hook around hers, squeezing tight. The gentle reassurance gave her a little more confidence.

She was afraid to approach the door, even knowing that Mama was sure to be inside. But Prudence might not be.

Aunt Hester led the way to the front door with surprising speed, especially considering that she had been in a deep sleep only moments before. She struck her knuckles against the door, and Sophia held her breath as the butler opened it. Her heart raced as they stepped into the entrance hall. The walnut furnishings and blue walls were all familiar...but so was the sound drifting from the drawing room.

A melancholy tune on the pianoforte.

Chapter Twenty-One

The first thing Sophia wanted to do when she saw Prudence's dark hair cascading down her back, was tug hard enough on it to make her topple backward off the pianoforte bench. The second thing she wanted to do was burst into tears of relief.

"Prudence Hale!" Sophia marched forward.

Her sister apparently hadn't heard her approach. She jumped, whirling around in her seat.

"What on earth were you thinking?" Sophia stopped a few feet away as Prudence jumped to her feet.

She backed away a step at the sight of Sophia's expression. "What are you doing here?"

Sophia's eyes widened. "What am *I* doing here? I thought Percy Ellington had abducted you! I thought you would have been forced to marry him by now. I had no idea if I would actually find you here or not." Tears wobbled on the edges of her vision. Five days of hardly any sleep, unpleasant food, close proximity to Isaac, and not nearly enough baths had led her to a highly emotional state.

"You didn't have to follow me," Prudence muttered. Her cheeks darkened when she noticed Isaac and Aunt Hester in the doorway. "I'm sorry to have worried you. I missed Mama and the dogs."

"You could have asked Aunt Hester to accompany you!" Sophia's anger slipped through. She couldn't help it.

"Aunt Hester is your chaperone too! I couldn't take her away when you were at such a vital point in your courtship with Lord Finchley."

Sophia sighed. Shouting at her sister would accomplish nothing. She took two long strides toward her and pulled her into a tight hug. "I'm glad you're safe."

Prudence leaned back with a grimace. "You smell like horses and mildew."

Sophia had to restrain herself again from tugging on her sister's hair. After all Sophia had endured, Prudence only seemed faintly apologetic. She steadied herself with a deep breath, ignoring the mildew comment. "Who did you travel with?"

Prudence shifted on her feet. "My maid."

"Only your maid?" Sophia's brows shot up.

Prudence bit her lip.

"'Safe and reputable company?'"

"She knows how to use a pistol!"

"Well, then, that is comforting." Sophia put her face in her hands.

"There wasn't anyone else who would take the journey with me. I know how much you hate Cornwall." She twisted a loose thread on her gown. "Almost as much as I hate London."

Sophia tried to feel compassion for her sister, but it was

difficult at the moment. Sophia *did* know how it felt to be heartbroken. She knew that urge to run away from the place where the pain had occurred and to never return. Being within the walls of Lanveneth again was already awakening a mixture of wonder and dread inside her. The wallpaper in the drawing room was the same as it had always been—white with dark green stripes. The gold velvet drapes of the window flanked a view of the sea. A portrait of Mama and Papa rested on the wall near it, and Sophia's heart lurched at the sight of her father's face.

Those downturned eyes, never revealing if he was troubled or content, and the stern mouth that rarely smiled. Perhaps he had always been troubled, after all. An abundance of secrets could do such a thing to a person.

A rustling sound near the doorway caught Sophia's attention. She turned to find Mama standing there, just a few paces behind Isaac and Aunt Hester. Dressed in blue, with her greying hair pulled into a tight chignon, she looked even more beautiful than Sophia remembered. They had only been apart for a few months, but it had felt much longer than that. So much had happened in London.

Sophia hadn't expected to feel the surge of emotion in her chest, but at the sight of her mother's face, a lump formed in her throat. "Mama."

She rushed forward, falling into her mother's arms. Lady Blackstone was much like Prudence: dark haired, stubborn, free-spirited, and a bit naive. She adored animals just as much as Prudence, which was the only reason Sophia could think of that might have caused her to bond so deeply with Lord Blackstone.

Mama's eyes, wild with surprise, took Sophia in as she

pulled away. "Sophia! What are you doing here? I didn't expect to receive one of my daughters, much less both."

She seemed to notice Isaac standing nearby, and her face fell.

Sophia studied her mother's features closely. She had known about Sophia's attachment to Isaac, but what did she know about the circumstances that had separated them? Had she been just as involved as Papa had been? The idea made her ill.

Mama's gaze shifted slowly back to Sophia's face, but it was clear that Isaac's presence had rattled her. She took a step back, her brow pinching with confusion. Stepfather had written to Mama to announce Sophia's engagement to Lord Finchley, and Prudence would have likely announced the news to her as well.

Knowing that news must have made Isaac's presence even more alarming.

"Mr. Ellington." Mama returned his bow. "It has been years. Forgive me for not recognizing you immediately. Did you…accompany Sophia on the journey?"

Isaac's nod seemed hesitant. "When I learned that Miss Prudence had fled and that Miss Hale planned to follow, I insisted on taking the journey alongside them. The roads are not safe at night."

"No, indeed, they are not." Mama's eyes were blank. "Yes, that is very kind of you. Thank you, Mr. Ellington, for watching over my daughters and sister." She extended an arm to pull Aunt Hester into an embrace.

Isaac seemed to sense the awkwardness surrounding his presence in the room. There was only so much that could be said with him standing nearby, and it was clear that Mama had questions. Many. So Isaac offered a quick bow before excusing himself to the corridor.

Sophia listened to his footfalls as he made his way out of the house. She didn't know whether he would remain close or take the carriage back to Morvoren. She hadn't given a great deal of thought to what they would all do once they found Prudence, only that she needed to be found.

Mama gripped Sophia by the arms so tightly it hurt. "Please do explain why it is *Mr. Ellington* who took this journey with you." Her thin brows arched in dismay. "I heard about his cousin's designs on Prudence and her narrow escape. I never should have sent the two of you to London without me."

"Prudence's escape from Percy Ellington was due to Isaac's interference." Sophia lifted her chin. "As well as my own. I assure you, we had the matter well in hand."

"Interference?" Prudence flew across the room with a scowl. "What interference?"

Sophia sighed. "All we did was provide you with opportunities to see his true nature."

Mama shook her head in confusion. "Knowing your history with Isaac Ellington, I confess I am astonished that you would allow him so close to your personal affairs. I never thought to see him again myself. He wounded you deeply, did he not?" Mama's blue eyes flashed with concern. "And you are engaged to Lord Finchley. Congratulations, my dear. I just heard the news."

Sophia studied Mama's face for any signs of mistruth. "I did think it was Isaac who wounded me, but as it turns out, it was someone else."

Mama's face paled. "What on earth do you mean?"

"He did not find my dowry insufficient. He never wrote me a letter. His grandfather's death delayed his proposal, but by the time he tried to call upon me, we had already left for London. I think Papa wrote the letter. I think he lied to me."

Mama's grip loosened on Sophia's arms, and she looked down at the floor. The tendons in her neck tightened.

"Mama." Sophia called her gaze back to her face. "Did you know about this?" A sinking feeling entered her stomach.

"No." The answer came too quickly. "But I'm certain that your father would not have done such a thing unless there was a very good reason, much like the reason you had for interfering with Prudence's courtship."

Sophia's heart beat faster than usual. Mama seemed to be hiding something.

"I think Percy Ellington has proven that Ellington men cannot be trusted," she continued in that quick voice. "At any rate, you are engaged to Lord Finchley. I would much rather speak of him and your upcoming wedding plans." Mama smiled, taking a few steps away to sit on the settee. She patted the cushion beside her.

Sophia's feet remained rooted in the floor. "There will be no wedding plans."

Mama's brows shot up.

"I am going to break off my engagement to Lord Finchley." The moment the words escaped her, a sense of relief banished the weight that had been resting on her shoulders. Lord Finchley would not have any trouble finding another wife, so long as he was still determined enough. He had implied that she was lacking in some areas, so perhaps he could find someone far better suited to him. Sophia was tired of pretending. She could no longer fathom the idea of settling for a man she didn't love, no matter who in her life encouraged her to do so.

Mama had only been sitting for a short moment, but she sprung to her feet. "Come now, Sophia. You mustn't do that. You have already bound yourself to him in word. It cannot honorably be undone, unless you wish to cause a scandal."

"If that is what it takes, then a scandal I will cause. I do not care." To make her point, Sophia crossed the room to the writing desk and prepared a fresh sheet of foolscap. Prudence and Aunt Hester watched in stunned silence as Sophia picked up her quill. "I shall write him a letter now with my regrets."

Mama marched forward, stopping Sophia's arm with a firm grasp. "Think for a moment about what you are doing. You are rejecting the opportunity to be a countess. You are rejecting a very coveted place in society. Your stepfather has worked very hard to introduce you to his connections, and this would be a great success for our entire family."

Sophia pulled her arm away, her heart in her throat. She knew, deep in her bones, that Mama was hiding something. It could very well be that she was involved in Papa's scheme to keep Sophia away from Isaac. Both her parents might have thought they knew what was best for her, but they had been wrong. A sense of betrayal gnawed at her heart. "I am writing this letter." Sophia dipped her quill, a wave of heat washing over her face. "You shall not be permitted to interfere this time."

Mama fell back a step, and Sophia scrawled her words carefully on the page. The silence was deafening, but also quite telling.

Mama had secrets, too.

She hadn't denied her involvement. At the very least, she had some knowledge of Papa's scheme.

As she wrote, Sophia spoke again. "If you wish to tell me why Papa chose to turn me against Isaac, then I might more easily forgive you."

Sophia waited, her heart pounding fast as she signed the letter to Lord Finchley. She felt a twinge of guilt, but mostly relief. The man's pride would be wounded more than anything else. To avoid the repercussions, she might have to stay in Cornwall a bit longer than planned. But that was fine. It would give her more time to discover Mama's secret.

Her mouth was firm, her eyes heavy as she stared down at Sophia and her letter. "I cannot tell you." Mama's voice was quiet, wavering slightly with emotion. "Before your father's death, I gave him my word." She put a hand to her head, and Aunt Hester bustled forward to steady her. Mama's eyes flickered closed, then opened again. "I must advise you to stay away from Mr. Ellington and Morvoren House."

Sophia's brow furrowed. Her quill clattered on the desk as she stood. "Why?"

Mama shook her head, leaning into Aunt Hester as she led her to the settee. Sophia shot a glance at Prudence, who looked just as confused as she was. Mama did have a flair for the dramatic—much like her new husband—but at the moment she seemed genuinely distressed.

A deep bark came from around the corner. A chestnut brown spaniel followed the sound. Thistle. A second dog quickly appeared behind her, moving a little slower. Flora's tail wagged, but her face was rather squished on one side, as if she had just been sleeping in the parlor.

Both dogs greeted Sophia, sniffing her skirts and boots, and then moved on to Aunt Hester. Thistle jumped onto the settee beside Mama, investigating the signs of her distress with lowered ears.

Now was obviously not the time to press Mama for more information. Sophia had arrived unexpectedly, which had already shocked her. Besides that, Sophia smelled of horses and mildew. She needed a bath, a clean gown, and a moment to gather her thoughts.

And then she was going straight to Morvoren House.

Chapter Twenty-Two

White sheets hung like ghosts over the furniture and portraits inside Morvoren. Curtains blocked every last shred of daylight from penetrating the glass, leaving the air inside eerie and cold. Isaac's steward, Mr. Fenwick, had access to the estate, but he conducted most of the estate business from his own house near the property. Besides Mr. Fenwick's rare visits, the house had remained empty since the day Isaac had left it behind.

A pair of servants, Mr. and Mrs. Nance, kept the house and land in decent condition, though without supervision, it appeared that their efforts weren't at their full capacity. Isaac had arranged for all of it to function like clockwork—all so he wouldn't be expected to return to the house himself.

After a few minutes of searching, he found Mr. and Mrs. Nance in the courtyard. Mr. Nance was a squat man with greying hair and a missing front tooth, but to Isaac's relief, he knew how to draw a bath. His wife, Mrs. Nance, was surprised to see Isaac—a bit alarmed, in fact—but set to work making a pie for dinner. The couple had surely grown accustomed to having the house to themselves, and neither seemed at all pleased at Isaac's arrival.

Mr. Nance had the sheets removed from the furniture in Isaac's old bedchamber. Isaac didn't want to use the room his grandfather had spent decades in; it felt wrong to claim it now when he had been absent for so long. After scrubbing himself clean and dressing in fresh clothes, Isaac made his way through the house, inspecting each room.

Besides a bit of peeling paint and wallpaper, there were few visible signs of disrepair. But on the upper floors, buckets had been placed sporadically to catch the rain that leaked through the roof. The windows were filthy, sealed shut with grime and edged in cobwebs. On the ground floor, a few traps had been set for rats...and had not yet been emptied.

Isaac's stomach sank as he finished his tour, opening the drapes in each room as he passed through, but the light did little to ease the growing guilt in his heart.

This was not what Grandfather would have wished to become of his house.

It wasn't too late to restore it. With a bit of work, it could become everything it had once been. Surely all the house needed was a woman's touch. Isaac pushed away the dream before his heart could swell to an unpardonable size. His hopes of sharing Morvoren with Sophia had died long ago. It was dangerous to bring them to life again without more certainty. She could still choose Finchley. The battle wasn't won—but it also wasn't over.

Mr. Nance walked by with Isaac's tray. The pie looked appetizing at least, with not a fish head in sight.

"Shall I leave it in yer chambers?" he asked.

Isaac nodded, his mind still distant. Mr. Nance tried to slink away, but Isaac stopped him. "Is there wine in the cellars? Brandy?"

Mr. Nance's face fell. His eyes shifted one way, then the other. "Aye, master. Er—you stay here, and I'll be sure to fetch it." He took another step, the tray clattering as he stumbled over a loose floorboard.

"I'll go," Isaac said dismissively. "I'd like to see the selection myself."

Mr. Nance's bloodshot eyes widened. His nose twitched. "'tisn't necessary, sir. There's nothin' to see there. I'll retrieve it shortly." He tucked his chin, picking up his pace as he hurried to Isaac's bedchamber with the pie.

Isaac's brow furrowed. Mr. Nance was the picture of suspicion with those shifty eyes, and suddenly Isaac was quite eager to pay a visit to the cellar.

Isaac listened to Mr. Nance's creaking footfalls moving overhead. Before he could return, Isaac made his way to the servants' stairs and down the cold, spiral steps. The stone walls flanked a bare, dark corridor. More rat traps lined the corners as Isaac made his way through the maze of rooms. He had never set foot below stairs at Morvoren before. It hadn't been his place to do so, and his grandfather had discouraged it.

That memory only added to Isaac's suspicion.

He passed the kitchen, freezing when he saw that Mrs. Nance was still inside. He didn't want to alert her, so he rushed past the open doorway. The scullery was next, and then the still room, the shelves lined with canisters of tea, jars of pickles, jams, and herbs. A candle rested on the nearest table, so he picked it up to light his way as he walked down the corridor.

The pantry smelled of something rotten, so Isaac didn't linger long in the doorway. Finally, he reached what could only be the wine cellar. It was smaller than the other rooms, with far less depth. The air was damp and earthy, flooding Isaac's nose with the scent of aging wood.

He stepped inside, examining the shelves filled with bottles. Why had Mr. Nance been so nervous about Isaac exploring below stairs? Did it have anything to do with the wine cellar at all, or more to do with the rats and that rotten smell in the pantry?

Isaac turned to leave, but stopped when he noticed a section of the wall that looked...different. It was too neat, the stones slightly paler and less weathered than the rows of masonry on the upper half of the wall. The mortar was smeared unevenly across the surface, as if it had been applied in haste. Isaac ran his hand across the stones, holding his candle close to the surface to light every inch of the wall. He stopped when he noticed an iron ring between two stones.

He tugged on it, and a rectangular section of the wall swung outward, revealing a latch. Isaac's heart pounded as he jostled the mechanism, pressing against the wall at the same time. The concealed door swung inward, causing a few flecks of stone to crumble to the ground.

He held up the candle, the light casting shadows over the other half of the cellar. Besides a few wooden crates, the room was empty. Puddles of water gathered on the floor, along with a strand of seaweed. Isaac bent down to examine the crates, which were marked with symbols and foreign words he didn't recognize. None of the crates were marked with a tax stamp.

Was this what Grandfather had been hiding? A smuggling operation?

There was no mistaking the suspicious nature of a false wall. One did not have such a thing built unless there was something they wished to hide.

Isaac set his candle on a crate near the back of the room, catching sight of yet another latch, this one far less concealed. He opened it, and the door opened to a dirt floor. Coils of rope, lanterns, and two pairs of sand-coated boots rested at the base of a ladder. Isaac moved his gaze up the rungs, which led to the open air.

It was a secret entrance.

He whirled around at the sound of footsteps in the corridor. Mr. Nance must have known about this. Who else did?

Isaac's heart thudded as he stared at the piles of emptied crates. Late at night, by firelight, his grandfather had told him wild tales of smuggling and other elicit activities Cornwall was known for. He had entwined the stories with legends about mermaids pulling fishermen out to sea, so naturally, Isaac hadn't given credit to any of it.

He never would have guessed that his own grandfather had been managing one of those legendary operations he spoke of.

Isaac's mind raced. The punishment for such a crime would be imprisonment, sometimes for years. Exile was reserved for extreme cases. Execution was also possible, but social ruin was *certain*.

Even if Grandfather had simply been pocketing a portion of the profits in exchange for a place to store the goods, he still could have lost all his political influence as well as his property. Even being aware of smuggling made one vulnerable if they did not report it.

But these crates were not coated in dust and abandoned

like the rest of the house. They were fresh. The seaweed wasn't even dry yet.

Isaac picked up his candle and walked back to the corridor. "Nance!" He cast his light in both directions until the shadows flickered over the man's stooped frame.

Mr. Nance immediately raised both hands in front of him. "I've turned a blind eye, that's all, sir. I tell ye, I've ne'er touched any of it."

Isaac strode forward, casting the candlelight closer to the man's face. His eyes were wide, his other features slack. He didn't seem capable of executing a believable lie, so Isaac willed himself to relax. If he wanted Mr. Nance to tell him the truth, he would have to approach him calmly. "How long has this been happening?"

"Only since the taxes became worse than sense, sir. Long 'fore you came to Cornwall."

"My grandfather knew?"

Mr. Nance nodded. "Oh, 'e knew. 'Twas his operation. Being that it's so close to the coast, Morvoren is the ideal location. 'Twould never be suspect considering Master's reputation, but he reaped the profits to help the estate."

Isaac scowled. "And you're telling me that you've simply 'turned a blind eye?'"

Mr. Nance blinked. "Don't be blamin' me, sir."

"Who else is there to blame?"

His eyes shifted again, left and right. "I helped this house. When the fields wouldn't yield and the rents came late, it weren't silk or spirits—it were jobs. Your grandfather sold the goods so the kitchen fires could stay lit and no one 'ere would go to bed hungry."

Isaac's mind reeled. So Grandfather had justified the crimes to keep the estate afloat during its most difficult years. But at a great risk. "That explains my grandfather's involvement, but after his death, it should have ended. The land has been profitable without smuggling. It's obviously still in operation." Dread sank deeper into his stomach. How had he allowed this to continue under his own roof? He shouldn't have abandoned the place.

Mr. Nance looked down at the stone floor. "Profits are still to be had, sir."

"You're being given a piece of them for your silence?"

His eyes shifted again.

Isaac sighed, raking a hand over his hair. "Tell me, Nance. I won't expose your involvement if you tell me who is operating it. You do realize the punishment you could face."

He gulped. "When Mr. Fenwick recognized your intentions to leave the estate entirely to his care, he took the opportunity to continue the operation with the help of…" his voice trailed off. "With the help of Mr. Percy Ellington, sir."

"Percy?" Isaac's skin grew cold. Had he known this secret about their grandfather all along? He had spent many summers at the estate with Grandfather, while Isaac had remained with his family. Percy must have discovered their grandfather's secret during that time. Perhaps that was why he wanted Lanveneth so badly. More storage, more secret routes, more hidden doors. He could live nearby in grandeur while operating his high profit illegal business with the help of Isaac's steward.

Percy gambled often, but Isaac wouldn't have guessed he was capable of taking such a risk with the law.

"Thank you, Nance." Isaac's head spun. If he wasn't careful, he could be framed for the crimes. He would need to find proof of Percy's involvement.

But how?

Chapter Twenty-Three

The sun was already setting by the time Sophia managed to escape Lanveneth. Mama had been keeping to her room, most likely to avoid another confrontation from Sophia. Aunt Hester had retired early, allowing Sophia the opportunity to sneak out of the house unseen.

With her cloak wrapped tightly around her shoulders, she made her away through the coastal trail that led to Morvoren. The sea reflected the sun, the soft glow illuminating the patches of wildflowers that cascaded down the cliffside and spilled over the edges of the path. Pink sea thrift, oxeye daisies, and bright yellow Alexanders. Sophia had forgotten how beautiful it all was. She had forgotten how calming the swell of the sea was to her heart, how invigorating the salty air felt against her skin and hair. She felt like she could breathe more easily here, as if some piece of life had been restored to her soul.

Lanveneth was positioned more inland than Morvoren, so the closer she drew to the house, the closer she came to the cliffs. Dark rocks peeked above the surface of the sea below, the waves cresting in foamy white as they crashed against them. She moved quickly toward the grey stone facade of Morvoren, knocking hard against the front door. She didn't know how close Isaac would be to hear it. The staff was sure to be scarce.

After waiting for a long moment, she knocked again. The moment her fist left the door, it flew open.

Isaac stood behind it with a look of surprise. His expression softened. "Sophia."

He wore shirtsleeves and a waistcoat, the top three buttons undone. His neck lacked its usual cravat, leaving her with no question as to the sharpness of his jaw. On their journey, the stubble on his face had grown away from his skin, leaving a shadow that she was fairly certain he wouldn't have grown so quickly the first time she had met him in Cornwall.

She realized how long she had been staring at him without saying a word. She cleared her throat. "I'm sorry to have visited without warning, but I have much to tell you."

He stepped aside, motioning for her to enter the house. "You are always welcome to visit me without warning."

She caught a glimpse of his smile as she passed.

She turned to face him as he closed the door behind her. From the corner of her eye, she saw the white sheets that shrouded every piece of furniture, and the flicker of a few candles on the walls. But she could hardly focus on her surroundings. Only on Isaac.

"I have much to tell you, too," he said.

"Would you like to speak first?" she offered.

Isaac's soft brown eyes traced over her face, and that one look was enough to elevate her pulse. Perhaps it hadn't been wise to walk here alone. The atmosphere was clawing at her sense of propriety, stirring up the emotions she had been fighting to keep in a cage.

He shook his head. "I'd like to hear what you have to say first."

"Very well." Sophia interlocked her cold fingers, taking a deep breath. She wanted to tell him about the letter she had written to Lord Finchley, but she was suddenly struck with a pang of fear. What if Isaac didn't react as she hoped? What if her mother was right…and there was a very good reason she should stay away from him? She still didn't know why her father had kept her away from him, and she still didn't know why he had falsely led Miss Baker to believe he would marry her. Perhaps the Lord Finchley news should stay a secret for a little longer.

"I told my mother how we suspected my father forged the letters," she began. "When I asked her why he did it, she refused to answer. She claimed that she was bound to secrecy before his death. She was still insistent that I avoid you *and* Morvoren house." Sophia's heart pounded as she looked up at Isaac and his open, kind features. What could possibly be so dangerous about him?

"I think I know why," he said in a grim voice.

Sophia froze. "What?"

Isaac glanced down the corridor before reaching down to take her hand. "Come with me." He led her past the drawing room to another door with light flickering behind it. He released her hand as they stepped into a room that must have been the study. A long desk was at the center, with papers and books lining the shelves behind it. "I found a false wall in the wine cellar this afternoon," Isaac said. "Behind it was a cellar full of smuggled crates from Spain and France."

Sophia's jaw dropped.

"My servant enlightened me about the history of the operation, and how my grandfather conducted the business out of desperation. But I also learned that Percy, with the help of my steward, has been carrying on our grandfather's legacy."

Sophia's mind spun. "Percy has been smuggling goods into Morvoren? How?"

"Besides working with my steward, he could also be coordinating his efforts with dozens of my tenants, local miners, or other tradesmen looking for additional profit, and taking the bulk of it for himself."

"And that's why he wanted Lanveneth so badly." Sophia covered her mouth as the realization dawned on her. "He could double his efforts and his profit with the use of another route." Her heart sank. "But how will you prove you weren't involved?"

Isaac rifled through the papers on the desk, withdrawing one that looked like a letter. "My steward wouldn't have expected my sudden arrival, so it seems he neglected to burn this correspondence between himself and Percy." Isaac met her gaze. "It details their upcoming shipments and the plans to secure them. It's all the evidence I need to put a stop to it all."

Sophia took a step back as she connected the pieces in her mind. "My father must have discovered evidence of your grandfather's smuggling. That must have been why he drove us apart."

"That was my conclusion as well." Isaac folded the letter and tucked it into his waistcoat.

Sophia swallowed, gripping the sides of her skirts. Her father must have known something and feared that connecting herself to Isaac could put her in danger. Any association with smuggling could taint even the most pristine reputation.

But why hadn't her father told her the truth?

Why go to the effort of fabricating those letters? Perhaps he thought it was the only way to keep them apart forever. He had wanted their farewell to last that long, after all. He had likely expected that Sophia would marry sooner, and that Isaac would not have had a chance to cross paths with her again.

"He was trying to protect you." Isaac's voice broke through her thoughts, and his face came into view again. "From me."

"From your grandfather's secrets, not from you." Sophia took a deep, quaking breath. "My father liked you very much."

Isaac's lips curved upward. "Very much?" He looked down at his desk. "More or less than *you* liked me?"

Sophia's face burned, but she laughed. "Much more."

When Isaac looked up, he was smiling. At least he had understood her joke. Why could she not tell him how she truly felt? Why was she continuing to avoid the subject? Her heart raced, as if urging her to run away. It was still afraid of being hurt.

Was Aunt Hester right? Did he still love her?

His actions seemed to have made it obvious, yet she was still terrified to know the answer. For years she had forbidden herself to trust him again. She was still learning how to lower her defenses. Isaac was tearing them down one by one, and she shivered in the vulnerability of it all.

She remembered what he had told her about his grandfather's death that night in Lord Finchley's study. She had still been in Cornwall when it happened, and yet she hadn't been there to support him. She hadn't known the pain he was going through. When she had received her forged letter from Isaac, that had been the only pain she was forced to endure, but Isaac had been struck with two blows at once. She couldn't imagine how he must have suffered, all alone in his grief. It was no wonder why he left Cornwall and all its sorrows behind.

She searched for a change of subject. He was standing far too close to her in that dim room, and it reminded her once again of that night in Lord Finchley's study when he had kissed her hand. "How did you escape Lord Finchley's study the night of his party?" she asked. She had been wondering about the answer.

Isaac's eyebrow lifted, and a smile tugged on the corners of his mouth. "I didn't."

Her eyes widened. "What do you mean?"

"I didn't manage to escape until morning."

She leaned forward with a jolt of surprise. "You cannot be serious."

Isaac's smile spread across his entire face now. "A servant locked the door. The height of the window was too great to escape through, so I slept under the desk."

A laugh escaped her. "You're lying."

"I wish I was," he said amid a chuckle. "I hoped a servant would unlock the door the next morning, but it was Finchley himself. Thankfully, I was still hidden, but I was trapped in my hiding place until he finished his morning additions to his ledger."

Sophia covered her mouth. "And he didn't see you?"

Isaac shook his head. "He was preoccupied. Did you know he sings while he manages his finances?"

She snorted as she burst into laughter. "You were on the floor at his feet while he…sang to his ledger?"

"I rather liked to think he was singing to *me*, but yes."

She wiped at the corner of her eye as she laughed, and Isaac's quiet laughter sank through her, settling somewhere deep in her chest. She never wanted to forget the sound again. She never wanted to be parted from it.

She felt the softness of his gaze on her face. A spiral of nerves erupted in her stomach, and she looked down at the floor. Why was she so blasted nervous? It was because she knew, without a doubt, that if she told him what she had written to Lord Finchley that day, he would kiss her senseless. And nothing could prepare her for that.

Her heart leaped violently, and she jolted toward the door. "Well. I should take my leave. My mother will wonder where I have gone."

"I'll walk with you. I have to ensure you don't stand too close to the cliffs." She could hear the smile in his voice from behind her.

He had always accused her of doing that.

She relented, allowing him to lead her out the front door and into the fresh sea air. The sun had faded completely below the horizon now, leaving just a few streaks of light behind. The sky was pink and peach where it touched the water, but the rest of it was dark. There was just enough light to see the path in front of them, but the vibrancy of the wildflowers was shadowed by the night.

They walked in silence for a moment. Sophia listened to the sounds of the dirt under their feet, the rustling wind and crashing of the waves below. She had never imagined she would ever walk that path again with Isaac, yet here they were, walking side by side, but not hand in hand as they once did. Propriety did not thrive here like it did in London. It was beaten down and weathered, just like the rocks, the old mines, and the miners themselves. Sophia was a different person in the unkempt wilderness of Cornwall than she was in a London ballroom. Perhaps this version of herself was braver.

"What did you do with my painting?" she asked. She had been curious ever since the auction but had been too afraid to bring up the subject. She dared to look up at Isaac's face as they walked. She could barely see his face above the brim of her bonnet.

"I hung it on the wall in my drawing room in London. Temporarily, of course. I plan to take it with me wherever I live." He cast a soft smile in her direction. "Perhaps I'll even remain here. At least until the smuggling is under control. Maybe longer."

"You would stay in Cornwall?"

He hesitated but nodded. "Spending the day at Morvoren made me realize that it wasn't the house that kept me away, or even the memory of my grandfather's death." His eyes met hers. "It was always you. But now that I know you didn't write me that letter…" he exhaled slowly, a pinch on his forehead. "My thoughts haven't shifted from the subject since we made the discovery. I only wish the discovery hadn't come too late."

Sophia's heart pounded. The path became smoother as they approached Lanveneth. Only a few of the windows glowed with candlelight as the final tendrils of daylight faded. She couldn't think clearly with Isaac standing so close. She was only a few feet away from the house now—she could still escape if she wanted to and save her confessions for another time when she felt more prepared.

Her heart beat wildly, but she forced herself to speak. "I only accepted Lord Finchley's proposal because I was certain you would hurt me again." Her voice shook. "My stepfather warned me of your reputation, and then I met Miss Baker on a walk with Prudence. She—she told me everything that happened between you."

Isaac stopped walking.

His features tightened as he stepped closer, until his hands found both of hers. His fingers were soft and warm, familiar and safe. A shiver raced across the length of both her arms, meeting in the middle of her shoulder blades. "I came to London determined to marry," he said. "I thought if I tried dearly enough, I could fall in love. The only reason I couldn't marry Miss Baker was because she was not *you*."

Sophia listened, her heart thudding in her chest.

"I regret my treatment of her, but she deserves to be married to someone who loves her—who treasures her and thinks of no one but her. I could not give her that." He lifted one of Sophia's hands, placing it against his chest. She felt his heart beating beneath his shirt. "You consume my thoughts, Sophia. You consume my heart. You are the only woman I have ever loved. That is why I couldn't bring myself to propose to Miss Baker. That is why I fought Lord Finchley for you. And I *will* continue to, if you tell me that I have any hope."

She stared at her fingers against his shirt. Her breath caught in her lungs, and a reckless idea stole through her mind. She didn't want to tell him anything. She wanted to show him in a way that would leave him with little doubt.

Before she could question the wisdom of her idea, she rose on her toes and pulled his head down to hers. She pressed her lips to his, briskly and without thought—her lack of practice quite evident. She pulled away fast, her heart racing.

What had she been thinking? Isaac's eyes were heavy with shock, and for a moment, she was frozen, staring up at him.

But then his hands took her waist firmly, tugging her back toward him.

His mouth found hers again, deliberate and insistent. His kiss was just as she had remembered it: devastating. Her eyelids collapsed, her legs melting as his arms surrounded her. Every thought fled her mind besides the one that told her that Isaac was kissing her, and how very unfair it was that she had been robbed of so many years of this. Isaac seemed determined to make up the lost time, though. His lips parted hers again and again, his hands surrounding her face now, his fingers buried in her hair. A sigh escaped the back of her throat.

She wanted to continue kissing him, but there was still more she wanted to say. She pulled away just enough to look in his eyes. His hands were warm against her face, cradling her jaw as he gazed down at her.

She held tight to the front of his waistcoat, her heart beating so hard it hurt. "I wrote a letter to Lord Finchley today." Her lips still tingled from Isaac's kiss. "I am breaking off the engagement. I don't care what the consequences are." She swallowed, shaking her head fast. "I don't love him."

Isaac's fingers caressed her face. "I knew you didn't."

Her laugh was breathless. "How did you know?" Her head was light as he traced the crest of her upper lip with his thumb. The pure adoration in his gaze spread warmth though her entire body. He leaned down to press another kiss to her lips, then another in quick succession. She laughed, and she felt his mouth curve into a smile.

He pulled away an inch and said in a low voice, "I knew you could never love a man with such a strong constitution."

She threw her head back with a laugh. Isaac pulled her against him and feathered a kiss against the corner of her jaw, marking a trail down her neck to her collarbone. One uniform shiver captured her entire body, every last inch. Her heart was on fire. He had never kissed her like *this* before. Each soft touch of his lips against her skin unraveled another thread of doubt, unfolding a bloom of joy so potent she hardly knew how to respond. She was utterly, blissfully overwhelmed. Tears sprung to her eyes. But they fluttered closed as his mouth found hers again.

He kissed her, deeply and slowly, until her head spun in circles. She had never felt more wanted. Isaac's fingers curled around hers, anchoring her hand in his.

A deep bark came from behind them, and then a prolonged growl. Isaac pulled away just as Flora and Thistle nearly collided with his legs. Both dogs barked again, but relaxed when they recognized Sophia's scent.

Her vision was hazy, her head light with exhilaration. Somewhere along the way, her bonnet had slipped from her hair. Flora picked it up from the grass with her teeth, tail wagging.

Isaac laughed, his arms still wrapped around Sophia's waist. The amusement in his eyes knocked against her heart, and she smiled so widely her cheeks ached. Slowly, he released his hold on her, stooping down to fetch her bonnet from Flora.

"What a good dog," he said through a chuckle. He scratched the top of her head.

With the bonnet in hand, Isaac faced Sophia again. His chest rose and fell quickly, just as quickly as hers. She was still reeling from their kiss—from his words about loving her—from all of it. Isaac placed the bonnet over her hair, his movements slow and methodical as he tied the ribbons beneath her chin.

"Perhaps I should leave," he said in a quiet voice, a smile curving his lips. He picked up her hand, leaving a kiss at the center of her palm, then the inside of her wrist. "I'll set to work dismissing my steward and contacting Percy. Soon it will all be behind us." He squeezed her fingers before letting go. "Goodnight, Sophia." He smiled as he backed away.

Her heart soared. "Goodnight, Isaac."

She had never been so happy to do away with formalities. There would be no more Miss Hales and Mr. Ellingtons.

But she certainly wouldn't object to any *Mrs. Ellingtons.*

Chapter Twenty-Four

Sophia watched Isaac's form retreating in the dark for a long moment before she reached down to pat Thistle atop the head. Her cheeks ached from smiling as she crept toward the front door, ensuring her bonnet covered the mess Isaac had made of her hair. She could hardly comprehend all that had just occurred. It felt like a dream. It felt far too perfect to be true.

She expected to hear the pianoforte when she walked through the front door of Lanveneth, but instead she was greeted by silence. She would be an atrocious daughter if she didn't stop by Mama's room to ensure she wasn't still as distraught as Sophia had left her earlier that day. She didn't want to fight with Mama. Now that Sophia knew the truth about the smuggling, she could put her mother's mind at ease that Isaac was going to quietly put a stop to it. There was no longer anything to fret about. Perhaps Sophia was too optimistic, but she hurried up the stairs with a lingering smile.

"Mama?" Sophia started in the direction of her room, but stopped when she heard a voice from the open library door.

"Where have you been?" Mama stood with a candle in one hand, a scowl creasing her brow. Her hunched shoulders were draped with a shawl, her eyes wary as they took Sophia in. "I have been worried enough over Prudence, and then I realized that you had left the house unchaperoned."

"I'm sorry to have worried you, Mama." Sophia chose her words carefully. "But I was just at Morvoren to call upon Isaa—er—Mr. Ellington. I have no wish to keep secrets from you."

Mama's dismay deepened, but Sophia strode quickly into the room, taking her by the arms gently. "I know why you advised me to keep away from him and Morvoren House. I understand that you and Papa were concerned about my reputation. But it will not be a problem any longer."

Mama listened in silence, but the concern did not vanish from her brow as Sophia continued her explanation.

"Isaac had no knowledge of his grandfather's smuggling ventures until this evening. Percy Ellington, with the help of Isaac's steward, has been continually smuggling goods into the house through a secret entrance. Isaac found a letter between Percy and the steward that proves his own innocence."

Mama's eyes rounded. "Percy Ellington was involved?"

"And that is why he wanted Lanveneth."

Mama seemed to put the pieces together in her mind, her face growing paler. "Thank heavens Prudence managed to escape him."

"All with the help of Isaac." Sophia gave Mama's arms a squeeze. "Isaac is innocent. He is going to rid his house of the crimes once and for all. Percy and the steward will not be permitted to set foot on the property again at the risk of being exposed and possibly hanged." Sophia took a deep breath. She wasn't entirely certain what their punishments would be, but she hoped the threats would be enough to stop them. Trespassing on Isaac's property was already a great enough crime on its own.

She searched Mama's face expectantly. "Are you not pleased with the news? As soon as the ordeal is put to rest, Isaac and I should be free to marry." Her heart lifted at the thought, but Mama continued to scowl as she stared at Sophia. Her eyes welled with tears.

"What is it?" Sophia took a step back. "Do you still not approve?"

Mama released a slow breath, wrapping her arms around herself. Sophia had never seen her so troubled. It was unsettling. Mama turned toward the fireplace, inviting Sophia to join her on the sofa in front of it. The flames crackled, emitting far too much warmth to the room. Sophia's face burned as she awaited Mama's reply.

"I wish for you to be happy. I wish for that more than anything." Mama wiped at the corner of her eye. "I can see how dearly you love him. I have been burdened with guilt all these years for what your father did. Not even Lord Blackstone knows the extent of it, but I hoped that he could help find you a match in London so you might forget about Isaac. So you might one day forgive me."

Sophia clutched Mama's hand. "I do forgive you. I understand that what Papa did was only meant to protect me."

Mama drew a deep breath, the flames reflecting in her eyes. Her lips quivered. She was silent for a long moment. "There is something you must know."

Sophia waited, her heart in her throat.

"Your father did not flee Lanveneth that day only to protect you. He was also protecting himself." Mama sighed, closing her eyes. "The fields at Morvoren were not the only ones struggling to yield. Lanveneth was under equal pressure, and the burden was becoming too great. Your father struck a deal with Isaac's grandfather."

Sophia's heart raced. "Papa was involved?"

Mama nodded, her mouth grim. "Your father provided him with additional routes and storage. In return, he was given a piece of the profits."

Sophia scowled in confusion. "If he was involved, then my reputation was already in danger! Why did he care if I connected myself to the Ellingtons?"

Mama took a deep, quaking breath. "One night, there was a disagreement between your father and Mr. Ellington on a matter of payment. Your father visited him at Morvoren to take what he was owed, and...there was an accident." Mama covered her face with one hand. "As they argued, your father drove Mr. Ellington too close to the stairs. He fell, and when your father saw that he would likely die from his injuries, he returned home and urged us all to leave Cornwall immediately." Mama's voice broke. "Your father was responsible for Mr. Ellington's death."

Sophia's heart fell, the room tilting around her. She refused to believe what she had just heard. She stood from the sofa, whirling to face Mama. "And you knew all this time?"

Mama looked so small sinking into the cushions, far too sweet and kind to have kept such a dark secret. "He didn't tell me what had happened until years later," she whispered. "Not about the letters. Not about his part in Mr. Ellington's death." Mama twisted her fingers together in her lap. "He kept it all hidden. He would've taken the secret to his grave, but it weighed too heavily. I was the only one he ever told, and he made me promise not to reveal it. If that piece of his past were ever discovered, our entire family would be ruined. Lord Blackstone would never have married me, and you and Prudence would have no chance at a suitable marriage."

Sophia took a step back, her mind still spinning. Knowing Lord Blackstone's love for outcasts, he might have actually adored her mother even more if he had known. But Isaac...he could never be so forgiving. If he knew that her father had been the cause of his beloved grandfather's death, he would never see Sophia the same. He might come to despise her. Papa had fled Cornwall to cover his own tracks, to hide his secrets instead of taking responsibility for what he had done.

She had been wondering why Papa had given Isaac permission to marry her, but then changed his mind so suddenly.

Now she knew why.

Sophia pressed a hand to her stomach. Her head was faint.

"Sit down, Sophia." Mama was standing beside her now, pulling on her arm.

Sophia fell into the cushions again. All the elation she had been feeling before she entered the house had vanished. All she felt now was dread.

"This must remain a secret," Mama said in a hushed voice. "You cannot tell anyone, not even Mr. Ellington." She brushed a strand of hair from Sophia's forehead. "We cannot risk the past being exposed. This is why I have discouraged you from growing close to him again. Certainly he couldn't marry the daughter of the man who..." her voice faded. "After all that occurred, it would be a disgrace to his grandfather's memory to tie himself to our family."

Sophia's heart felt like it had been cracked open, pain spreading through each of her limbs and out to her fingertips. She was shaking her head. Mama took her face in her hands, turning her neck until Sophia met her gaze. "It is important that you understand this, my dear. I know you love him, but it is time for you to let him go. Come back to London with me, and you might marry Lord Finchley as planned."

Sophia tore her face away from Mama's hands. "No." Tears burned her eyes. How could she have come this close to her happiness only to have it torn away again? It wasn't fair.

She heard Mama calling her name, but she didn't listen. Down the corridor, up the stairs, and toward her room, she ran as fast as her legs could carry her.

She had known she would find secrets in Cornwall, but nothing as dreadful as this.

Chapter Twenty-Five

A plume of dust floated in the air as Isaac dropped the white sheet to the floor, revealing Grandfather's portrait. Light from the window at the end of the gallery illuminated the brush strokes, bringing life to his features.

At the time the likeness was painted, he looked to be similar in age to Lord Blackstone, with the same gleam of confidence in his eyes. Much like the viscount, Grandfather had his own eccentricities, but he was far less public with them. Some people in town had thought him reclusive, or strange, but Isaac had loved him.

Isaac's heart stung as he stared up at the face of the man who had spent hours playing cards with him, shooting, drinking, and laughing. Though Isaac had only spent one year at Morvoren, it had been one of the best of his life. Grandfather had been the one to encourage Isaac to buy Sophia a ring as a symbol of their love. To marry her.

Isaac reached in his pocket, searching for the dainty piece

he had just purchased in the village. The ring was delicate, nothing extravagant—gold with a small pearl at the center. Sophia was not one to seek attention or praise, so he knew she would love the simplicity of it. Isaac's day had been eventful, his morning spent writing letters to Percy, his steward, and beginning his search for a new staff. He would allow Mr. and Mrs. Nance an opportunity to stay at Morvoren—so long as they didn't create any further trouble.

Isaac held the ring in his palm, turning it over to reflect the afternoon sunlight. Four years had led him to this moment. A flock of emotions rustled around his heart, his stomach flopping with nervousness. Why did part of him still doubt his good fortune? After learning that Sophia was breaking off her engagement, holding her in his arms again, kissing her...he shouldn't have doubted that she cared for him. He had seen the affection in her eyes, the hope shining back at him like his own reflection.

He hadn't been able to carry out his proposal the first time, but today he would finally see the end of his torment. He would see that ring on her finger.

A smile split his face as he took a deep breath. Being in Cornwall had awoken a sense of courage inside him, an ability to confront his past without fear. Grandfather had died within the walls of Morvoren, but he had also *lived*. Isaac had always admired him for living the way he saw fit, not the way he was told. *Criminal activities aside, of course.*

If Isaac could turn Morvoren House into a home again, with Sophia at his side, Grandfather might smile down upon him. He might forgive Isaac's neglect and be proud. The idea eased the nerves inside him, giving him the courage to begin his walk to Lanveneth.

But first, he needed to check on Mr. Nance's progress.

Circling around the side of the house, Isaac found him exactly where he had left him earlier that day, shoveling dirt and rocks into the passageway that led to the cellar. It was enough to keep anyone from entering for now, but later Isaac would have it permanently sealed. If he was going to be worthy of Sophia and keep her reputation and family safe, then he couldn't even have the temptation of participating in smuggling in the future. He would continue to earn a respectable living from the land, nothing more.

If the late Mr. Hale had been wary of him, *and* Lord Blackstone, it was all Isaac could do to prove that he wasn't going to put Sophia in danger.

"Fine work, Nance," Isaac said with a nod. The man grunted in reply, dropping another shovel full of dirt into the shrinking hole behind the shrubs. Isaac would have felt guilty for putting him to work for so many hours, but Mr. Nance knew he was earning every penny he had been slipped for aiding the smugglers.

Isaac set off toward the path that led to Lanveneth, passing a few villagers on his way. The landscape was as rugged as the faces that passed, men and women who had spent the day working in the mines, farming, or fishing. Isaac had taken his position in society for granted. He needed to be here, tending to his estate himself, aiding those he could with additional employment and food.

His guilt transformed to determination inside him, growing stronger with each step. He couldn't be certain of his grandfather's motivations for participating in smuggling, but knowing the man, Isaac supposed he had done it for the reasons Mr. Nance had said: to keep his estate thriving, and perhaps even to give parts of the spoils to the fishermen and others who helped him bring the goods ashore. Grandfather wasn't selfish. It was those who carried on his legacy for their own designs who were.

Isaac's steps slowed as he moved inland toward Lanveneth. He froze. Up ahead on the path, was a man dressed in all black, a beaver hat shadowing the upper half of his face. It couldn't be...

Percy?

There was no mistaking his black hair and the nefarious edge to his gait. Even from a distance, Isaac recognized his cousin's saunter, walking stick and all. What the devil was he doing leaving Lanveneth? After his motives had been exposed to Prudence, Isaac hadn't seen him in London anywhere. He had assumed Percy had fled to avoid scandal, but he hadn't guessed that Cornwall would be his destination.

Isaac approached with caution, his jaw tight. He watched Percy's face for any sign of panic, but his features remained smooth, as if he was not surprised in the slightest to see Isaac there.

"I was just on my way to Morvoren," Percy called out. The breeze muffled his words.

Isaac scowled, holding in his response until the gap between them was only a few paces. "Off to collect another shipment?"

Percy's mouth spread into a smile, but his eyes were unamused. "I knew Nance wouldn't be capable of holding his tongue." He dug the end of his walking stick into the dirt before meeting Isaac's gaze. "And that is why I have made my hasty departure from London."

Isaac lifted his eyebrows. "Are you here to beg for mercy?"

Percy gave a dry laugh. "Blackstone revoked my membership in his club, but not before he mentioned that you had fled to Cornwall after Prudence. I thought I ought to come speak with you in person about the possibility of becoming partners."

Isaac scoffed, a deep laugh escaping his throat. "You rushed to Cornwall because you knew your sham was about to be uncovered. You knew that if I wished to turn you over to the law, I very well could." Anger surged beneath his skin. "What were you doing at Lanveneth?"

"I was apologizing to Miss Prudence."

"And trying to win her back?"

"No. I knew that would be impossible. You made certain of that." Percy's voice was bitter.

Isaac couldn't believe a word his cousin said. He may have come to Cornwall to plead his case and try to cover his tracks, but he certainly hadn't gone to Lanveneth just to apologize to Prudence. He had likely made one last grand effort to regain her favor. The poor girl must have been shaken by his visit.

Isaac drew a step closer. "You are to stay away from Lanveneth and Prudence."

"Oh? Do you dictate my decisions now?" Percy's arrogant smile made Isaac's skin prickle with distaste.

"If you wish to keep your head out of the noose, then yes, I do."

Percy's smile faltered. He dug his walking stick deeper into the dirt. He could act arrogant all he wanted, but he knew he had been caught. What did he expect would happen when Isaac finally made his way back to Morvoren? Did he think Isaac would never discover the secret door in the cellar, or eventually catch sight of men sneaking around his property at night with wagons full of crates? Percy must have known his ruse would be up at some point. That must have been why he offered Isaac partnership instead of giving up the profits entirely.

"You don't have any proof," Percy snapped. "A servant's word isn't going to convict a man of my standing."

"What standing? Blackstone could destroy your reputation if he wished." Isaac crossed his arms over his chest. "I have letters between you and my steward. I have plenty of evidence to prove that you not only trespassed on my property on multiple occasions but have been coordinating illegal shipments for the past four years."

A muscle jumped in Percy's jaw as he stared down at the ground. "Obviously grandfather condoned the practice. Would you not have any interest in continuing what he built? We could keep it hidden easily enough. The tradesmen here turn a blind eye when they're given a portion of the spoils."

"Not for my personal gain." Isaac glared at him. "And not at the risk of those I love."

Percy bit the inside of his cheek, releasing a tense breath. He seemed near to bursting with anger, but he was hiding it behind a show of arrogance. "What are your terms?" His voice was barely more than a mutter.

"Leave Cornwall and never return. If you're seen on my land, or Lanveneth's, I won't hesitate to turn my evidence over to the law. Blackstone will expose your reputation to society in London, so you'll have no place there."

Percy's upper lip curled, but he said nothing. His nostrils

flared. "What a way to repay me. I never should have introduced you to Blackstone."

"You're fortunate I haven't demanded reparations of the profits you made from *my* land." Isaac shook his head in disbelief. "Keep the money and leave. Consider it your compensation for the courtesy of introducing me to Blackstone." Isaac couldn't hide the sardonic tone from his voice.

Without warning, Percy lunged forward, thrusting his fist into Isaac's face. Isaac reared back, the side of his nose and cheekbone throbbing in pain. He wiped blindly at a trickle of blood beneath his nostril. He was grateful they weren't closer to the cliffs. From the rage in Percy's eyes in that moment, Isaac would have guessed he was capable of pushing Isaac off the edge. "That was for sabotaging my courtship," Percy seethed.

Isaac found his bearings, but he was still in shock over the pain spreading across his face. Perhaps his terms had been too generous. A man as volatile as Percy could benefit from a few years of imprisonment or exile. He was mad.

Isaac took a swing at Percy's face, making contact with his mouth. His aim had been for his nose, but the result was still sufficient. While Percy reeled from the hit, Isaac reached for his walking stick, wrenching it from his hand.

And then he threw it.

It spun in the air, soaring far off the path and off the edge of the cliff.

"That was for Prudence."

Percy cupped his face in pain, removing his hand to reveal a red and white smile. He spit blood onto the ground, backing away with an unsettling laugh. It grew in volume, until it verged on maniacal. "Touché." He didn't seem inclined to strike Isaac again. Instead, he sauntered past. He declined his head, a smirk lifting his blood-stained upper lip. "Farewell, cousin. Perhaps you might visit me and my mistresses in Spain."

Isaac laughed, surprising himself with the reaction. Even in his disgrace, Percy managed to return to his arrogant ways. Isaac didn't care what Percy did with his life, so long as he stayed far away from Isaac and his family.

Well, who he *hoped* would become his family.

His shoulders remained tense as he watched Percy's retreat. He wiped at his nose again, relieved to see that the bleeding had been minimal. The surface of his cheek was sore to the touch, as well as the bridge of his nose. But at least it wasn't broken.

He turned his attention to the cream facade of Lanveneth, taking a moment to calm his heightened senses. He felt like he was still boiling from his interaction with Percy, his nerves on edge. He took several slow breaths as he finished the walk to the house.

When he reached the front door, his palms began to sweat. *Blast it*, he was still nervous. This moment felt familiar, much like the day he had rushed to Lanveneth the first time to propose to Sophia. He could easily recall the grim expression of the butler as he told Isaac that the Hales had left Cornwall. He could still see the black ink on that letter that had been passed into Isaac's hand. The pain was distant now, but it still poked at him as he stood on the doorstep.

It will be different this time, he reassured himself.

He waited several seconds before the staunch butler opened the door. Isaac's gaze flickered to his gloved hand, half-expecting to see a letter clutched in his fingers. Isaac was ushered inside to the drawing room, where Prudence sat on the settee. She leaped to her feet the moment she saw

Isaac. She was holding a small animal. A rabbit, perhaps? Isaac had only seen a flash of grey fur.

Flora and Thistle bounded across the room, greeting Isaac with no small measure of enthusiasm. He hadn't expected them to be allowed inside the house at all times, but if Prudence had her way, they would be dining with her at the table for each and every meal. She offered a curtsy, her dark brows knit together.

"I just sent Percy away," Isaac assured her. "You will never see him again."

Prudence's eyes were still wet with tears. She looked flustered, but not as unraveled as Isaac had expected. She eyed his face. "Did he hurt you?"

So it was worse than he thought. "It is no matter. I'm sorry that I didn't arrive a few minutes earlier. Are you unharmed?"

"Yes." Prudence released a tense breath. "I was more worried for Flora and Thistle. He was holding that walking stick again. Thankfully the footmen escorted him out."

"You may rest assured that he will never wield the walking stick again. It's currently on its way to the sea floor."

Prudence gasped, a delighted grin taking over her face. She quickly hid it from view behind the head of the creature she held. It was clear now that she was holding a dog, a small, scrappy terrier of some sort. It was thin with matted fur, but its tongue lolled out as it seemed to smile up at Isaac.

"He brought me this little dog in an attempt to win my affections." Prudence rolled her eyes in dismay. "Of course it didn't work, though I am grateful to have another pet. I suspect he found him wandering the kitchen yard or fields somewhere."

Isaac laughed, relieved to find her in good spirits. "Is Sophia in?" His heart picked up speed.

Prudence's gaze flickered to the open door behind him, and she gave a subtle shake of her head. "I haven't seen her for most of the afternoon. I think she went for a walk…or to find a place to paint."

"Hmm. Thank you. I shall have to go looking for her."

Prudence's eyes widened. "Perhaps you shouldn't."

Isaac took another step into the room, throwing her a curious look. "Why?"

She pressed her lips together, a secret burning behind her eyes. Fortunately for Isaac, Prudence didn't seem to be the sort of young woman who could keep one. "She was quite upset this morning. I wanted to accompany her to the ruins, but she wished to be alone."

Upset? Isaac's heart sank. Why would she have been upset? He had been up half the night, unable to sleep because of how eager he was to see her again. What about the night before could have upset her? Had he spoken too freely…or kissed her too thoroughly? She had been the one to kiss him first, so that couldn't be the reason. He would hate himself forever if he had done anything to frighten her. "Trelowen ruins?"

Prudence winced. "Perhaps I should not have said that."

Isaac's skin grew cold with dread. "Is she hiding from me?"

The fact that Prudence didn't answer immediately made Isaac's heart sink further. She crossed her arms, a hesitant wrinkle on her forehead. "Well…I rather think she is hiding from everyone."

Isaac drew a deep breath, steeling himself for the worst

possible news. "What happened?" He eyed her secretive features. "What do you know?"

Prudence sat on the settee, stroking the terrier's head. She sighed. "Last night I overheard Sophia's conversation with my mother in the library. I did not *mean* to eavesdrop, but I was on my way up the stairs when I heard Sophia return home. I wanted to know if she had been sneaking off to Morvoren House." She blinked innocently. "I learned about the smuggling, and that our father was not only aware of it, but he was involved."

Isaac scowled. "Involved, how?"

Prudence shrugged. "Storing items, providing routes, securing profits of his own through our estate. It is no wonder Percy wanted to steal my inheritance for himself." Her eyes darkened with anger. "I listened to every word Sophia told my mother about what he did. Wicked scoundrel. I don't know why I ever liked him." She lifted her chin.

Isaac's head was spinning. If the late Mr. Hale was involved in smuggling, then why would he be so opposed to Sophia marrying into the Ellington family? His *own* behavior could have tainted his daughters' reputation just as harshly.

He needed more answers.

Finally, Prudence seemed to remember the topic of their conversation. She lowered her voice to a whisper. "Sophia thinks you would never marry her because of what our father did."

Isaac shook his head firmly. "My own grandfather was involved in smuggling."

"There is more." Prudence sat up straighter. Her eyes were heavy on the corners, much like how Isaac remembered her father's to be. "Surely I am not supposed to tell you this, so you must promise that you will love my sister no matter what."

Isaac's heart raced. "Nothing could convince me not to love Sophia."

She inspected his face with scrutiny.

"*Nothing*, Prudence."

She sighed, giving a nod of approval. She glanced at the door again before leaning forward and whispering her secret.

Chapter Twenty-Six

Sophia was not entirely insensible. She had brought one of Mama's maids with her to the ruins of Trelowen castle. As a result, she was not quite as alone as she would have liked to be.

Her eyes stung with tears as she tried to focus on the paintbrush in her hand. She had been debating between paining the ruins or the view from the window. It was fascinating to think that the people who had once lived there had seen exactly what she was seeing now, but through a sheet of glass. Now, all that remained of that wall and window was an assortment of stones, a rectangular hole in the ruins of what was once a grand, beautiful place.

Sophia's heart ached as she dragged the bristles of her brush over the canvas. The blue paint would separate the sky from the sea. Now she had to decide which one to paint first, but her mind was soaring from thought to thought aimlessly. Her legs were heavy. Her heart was on the brink of a ruin of its own.

She pulled the brush away from the canvas, casting her

gaze around the desolate pile of stones that barely resembled a castle. After hearing Mama's secret the night before, Sophia had convinced herself that she and Isaac were destined to be much like Trelowen. No matter how grand and beautiful their love had once been, it could not last forever. She had tried to rebuild their ruins, but they continued to crumble in front of her. It would be a pile of rubble once Isaac knew what her father had done.

She could barely see the canvas as she painted, her eyes blurred with tears. She had been trying to decide how to tell Isaac what she had learned. She would not obey all of Mama's requests. Isaac deserved to know what had happened to his grandfather, even if it meant he would see her differently. Even if it meant he would not want her.

Was Mama right? Would Isaac change his mind about marrying her if he knew the truth? How could she live in Morvoren house when her own relation was the one to take the life of the previous master? The very thought made her ill. She imagined the sorrow on Isaac's face when she told him, and it broke her heart to pieces.

She added a dark bird to the sky, blending white paint into the blue to make the clouds. The maid who had accompanied her was walking on the beach down below, enjoying a moment free from the confines of Lanveneth, no doubt. She must have sensed Sophia's desire to be left to herself.

The wind caught Sophia's hair, and she pushed it aside, accidentally smearing the end of her paintbrush across her forehead as she pulled her hand back.

"Drat," she muttered.

A voice from behind made her jump. "Sixty guineas."

She whirled around, nearly knocking over her easel. Isaac stood in the overgrown grass just outside the ruins. He ducked his head to walk through the squat doorway. Sophia's heart pounded fast at the sight of him, his hair wild from the breeze, his soft brown eyes picking up streaks of golden sunlight.

"It's not for sale." She moved to stand in front of the painting. "This one is going to be atrocious."

"I doubt that." Isaac's mouth lifted in a smile, but his eyes were gentle as they traced over her. He would not be smiling once she told him about Papa's secret. Her heart ached.

She scowled when she saw a dark red bruise forming on his cheek. "What happened to your face?"

"I could ask you the same question." His eyes glinted with amusement.

She put a hand to her forehead, pulling her fingers back to find them coated in blue paint. She laughed, but her amusement was quickly swallowed up by dread. How could she laugh at a moment like this? She didn't even know how Isaac had found her, and he looked like he had been struck in the face. Soon, she would deliver another blow that would break his heart.

"Percy followed us to Cornwall," Isaac said. "I saw him on my way to Lanveneth. We…sorted out our disagreements. He knows I have the necessary proof to have him convicted, so he's making plans to leave England."

Sophia set down her brush, eyes wide. "Why was he here?"

"He knew he would be caught when he learned I was coming to Cornwall. He also made one last effort to win Prudence's hand. He brought her a dog."

"You cannot be serious."

"A scrappy terrier from the kitchen yard. She didn't seem upset by his visit after that."

Sophia was tempted to laugh again, but her shock was too immense. "And he…hurt you?" her voice cracked.

Isaac shook his head fast. "It doesn't hurt." He walked closer, and her defenses rose. She instinctively moved back a step.

Isaac's brow furrowed. "But that does."

She met his gaze, but immediately wished she hadn't. His eyes captured hers, far more intense than she had expected.

"Did you truly believe I would blame you for your father's mistakes? Did you really think that it would stop me from wanting you?"

Her heart raced. She didn't know how to answer.

"I will always want you. I have never stopped." He reached out and tucked a strand of hair behind her ear. "I love you, Sophia. Do you understand what that means to me? A day doesn't pass that I don't long for you. I have missed you for four years, even despite thinking that you despised me. I have undertaken battle with an earl and a viscount for the chance to be yours." He nudged her chin up with his fingers, his eyes boring into hers. "Your stepfather cannot stop me, and nor can your father."

Sophia's throat ached with emotion. Her head spun. "I'm sorry, Isaac. I'm so very sorry for what my father did." Tears spilled down her cheeks. "How did you know?"

"Prudence told me." Isaac took her face in both his hands, wiping her tears with his thumb. "It came as a shock, yes, but it doesn't change anything. I still wish to marry you."

Sophia choked on a breath. "But your grandfather—"

"He liked you." Isaac's lips twitched into a smile. "He wanted me to marry you. He encouraged me to buy you a ring, just as he did for his wife." He reached into his jacket, withdrawing a delicate circle of gold with a pearl at the center. It was beautiful.

She closed her eyes. "But surely he wouldn't have liked me if he had known what my father would do to him." Her voice was hushed.

"You are not your father. You have nothing in common with him besides your surname, which I would very much like to change."

She opened her eyes to see the determined look on his face. He leaned down to look in her eyes. "It was their quarrel, not ours. Your father cannot take this away from us. Not again."

Sophia's heart lifted, hope taking root inside her. Tears still fell down her cheeks, but she was no longer certain what they were connected to—joy, fear, relief, and pain, all at once. But Isaac was quickly brushing away the painful parts, leaving her renewed and breathless.

She found herself nodding. She didn't want Papa to take this away.

Isaac's hands, warm and strong, cupped her face. It was the safest feeling in the world. She had never believed that she could be loved so ardently, so unconditionally. But she knew without a doubt that Isaac would treasure her forever.

His words pulsed through her mind.

I still wish to marry you.

Becoming engaged to Isaac would not be a difficult decision at all. Her heart had been his for a very long time. And it would be forever.

"You're wrong," she said in a hoarse voice. "I do have something in common with my father."

"And what is that?"

"We both possess the skill of sabotaging courtships."

Isaac stared at her in surprise, a smile hovering on his lips. "I share that talent, I think."

"Well, it was *my* idea to send the dogs after him."

Isaac leaned closer. "I wasn't referring to Percy. I was referring to your courtship with Finchley." He looked quite proud of himself, but the expression was so endearing that she couldn't help but laugh.

She raised an eyebrow. "You said it was merely a disruption."

"I did keep a few strategies in reserve." He grinned, and she felt a hot blush on her cheeks. Kissing Isaac the night before still felt like a dream, like a distant memory that couldn't possibly be real. All the fear Mama had instilled in her had been for nothing. Papa's secrets could be put to rest, and the consequences were over.

Sophia felt the shackles drop from her wrists and a weight dissipate from her shoulders as Isaac leaned down and kissed her. He pulled back after a brief moment, his lips brushing hers. "Will you marry me?" he murmured.

She clung to his jacket. "Yes." A smile broke across her face, and she dared to say the words that had once frightened her. "I love you."

Isaac's smile grew, and he slipped that perfect pearl ring over her finger.

His arms surrounded her waist, and then he was kissing her again. She buried her fingers in his hair as he lifted her feet off the ground. It occurred to her that they were in clear view of the castle window where the maid walked the trail below. She tore her lips from his just for long enough to pull him away from the window. She had to ensure this moment was theirs, and theirs alone.

Isaac laughed, but the sound was cut short as he captured

her lips again, his mouth exploring hers as he pressed her back against the weathered stone of the old castle. She kissed him with more confidence than she had before, and Isaac responded with all the fervor she would have hoped for. The waves of longing in her stomach were like the swell of the sea, growing stronger with each touch of his lips and hands over her face and neck and hair. She couldn't breathe, but she didn't care. There were far worse ways to drown.

Isaac's kisses became achingly soft, sealing the very last of the wounds on her heart. Behind her eyes, she saw a dream for her future. She saw smiles and laughter and joy. She saw sorrow and hardships, but a hand to hold through it all. She saw wildflowers and waves, cliffside kisses and carriage rainstorms, and farewells that were neither sudden, nor forever.

Isaac leaned his forehead against hers. She pulled back to see the smile on his face.

Most of all, she saw him.

Isaac Ellington—her entire heart wrapped up in a cravat and jacket...with a streak of blue paint on his forehead.

Next in the Bachelors of Blackstone's series

If you've been enjoying the Bachelors of Blackstone's, check out the next book in the series: an enemies to lovers romance by Jess Heileman!

Bachelors of Blackstone's series

A Bachelor's Lessons in Love by Sally Britton
A Trial of His Affections by Mindy Burbidge Strunk
A Gentleman's Reckoning by Jennie Goutet
To Hunt an Heiress by Martha Keyes
Love is for the Birds by Deborah M. Hathaway
Forever Engaged by Ashtyn Newbold
A Match of Misfortune by Jess Heileman

Other books by Ashtyn Newbold

Noble Charades Series

Change of Heart Series

Larkhall Letters Series

Brides of Brighton Series

Standalone novels
To Marry is Madness
In Pursuit of the Painter
The Last Eligible Bachelor
An Unwelcome Suitor
Her Silent Knight
A Heart to Keep

Novellas & Anthologies
The Earl's Mistletoe Match
The Midnight Heiress
At First Sight

About the Author

Ashtyn Newbold grew up with a love of stories. When she discovered Jane Austen books as a teen, she learned she was a sucker for romantic ones. When not indulging in sweet romantic comedies and regency period novels (and cookies), she writes romantic stories of her own. Ashtyn also dearly loves to laugh, bake, sing, and do anything that involves creativity and imagination.

Connect with Ashtyn Newbold on these platforms!
  INSTAGRAM: @ashtyn_newbold_author
  FACEBOOK: Author Ashtyn Newbold
  TIKTOK: @ashtynnewboldauthor
  ashtynnewbold.com

Printed in Dunstable, United Kingdom